SINNER'S CHOICE

Merciless Few MC- KY Chapter
Book 1

Bre Rose

Copyright © 2023 by Bre Rose

All rights reserved.

No portion of this book may be reproduced in any form without written permission from the publisher or author, except as permitted by U.S. copyright law, or for the use of brief quotations in a review. This is a work of fiction. Names, characters, businesses, places and events are either used in a fictitious manner or a product of the author's imagination. Any resemblance to actual persons or actual events is purely coincidental.

Editing by Shayna Turpin

Ebook formatting by Bre Rose

EBook cover and PB Wrap by Shayna Turpin

To all the MC lover's out there!!
GIVE NO QUARTER
SHOW NO MERCY

AUTHOR NOTE

I am so excited to be a part of the Merciless Few MC World. Please note that my stories will only be about those characters who are part of the Kentucky chapter. You may encounter brief references to other chapters, but not in great detail.

Each book in this series will be a stand alone book with the conflict for those characters being resolved over the course of the book. However, with that being said the overall club drama can and will continue over the course of the series. As each book can be read as a standalone I do suggest reading them in order for the optimal reading experience.

Sinner's Choice is a MF romance, but future books will and can include being a polyamorous, menage and RH.

As a final note, we are all human. Even though this book has been through Alpha, Beta, Edited and proof-read several times, errors always seem to slip by. If any are found, please reach out to Bre Rose or Shayna Turpin so that we may correct them quickly and efficiently without hindering anyone from reading and enjoying. You can reach either of us on Facebook or you can email me at breroseauthor@gmail.com

As always, I love hearing from you. If you want to reach out and scream, tell me what you thought, then please feel free to do so.

Happy reading.

TRIGGER WARNINGS

This is a contemporary dark MF romance. This story contains dark content so please be sure to check the content warnings and tropes below. If any of these are something you are not able to read, then please stop now. Your mental health is more important to me.

- Death of a family members in a tragic way
- Suicidal thoughts and reference to it
- Domestic Violence
- Loss of Faith
- Torture/Violence/death- graphic
- Insta attraction- insta love
- Explicit sexual content and physical abuse
- One of MC's is married.

- Second Chance for HEA for both MMC
- Friends to lovers
- Unprotected sex with consent
- Protector romance

BLURB

GIVE NO QUARTER
SHOW NO MERCY

The church was all I knew until my family was murdered in the very place I loved to worship.

I should have died with them.

I was headed on a one way train to the grave until the Merciless Few MC found me.

They brought me back from the brink and gave me a new lease on life.

I was one with God again but in a way that now suited me better.

I had everything I wanted until I saw her.

She was everything I loved in a woman.

Curvy, sweet and brunette.

She was young and married.

Two things I found hard to overcome.

But when danger lurks in the corner ready to drag her down, can I throw everything to the side to be there for her?

SINNER'S CHOICE

Can I choose her?

CLUB MEMBERS- KY CHAPTER

Officers

Hawke – President
Gunner – Vice President
Preacher- (AKA Noah Adler) – Enforcer
Snake- Road Captain
Jenner- Tech Guru
Cyrus- Sgt At Arms

Member

Sundance
Wheels

Prospects

Sam
Dallas
Cole
Alan
Davey
Nixon
Steve

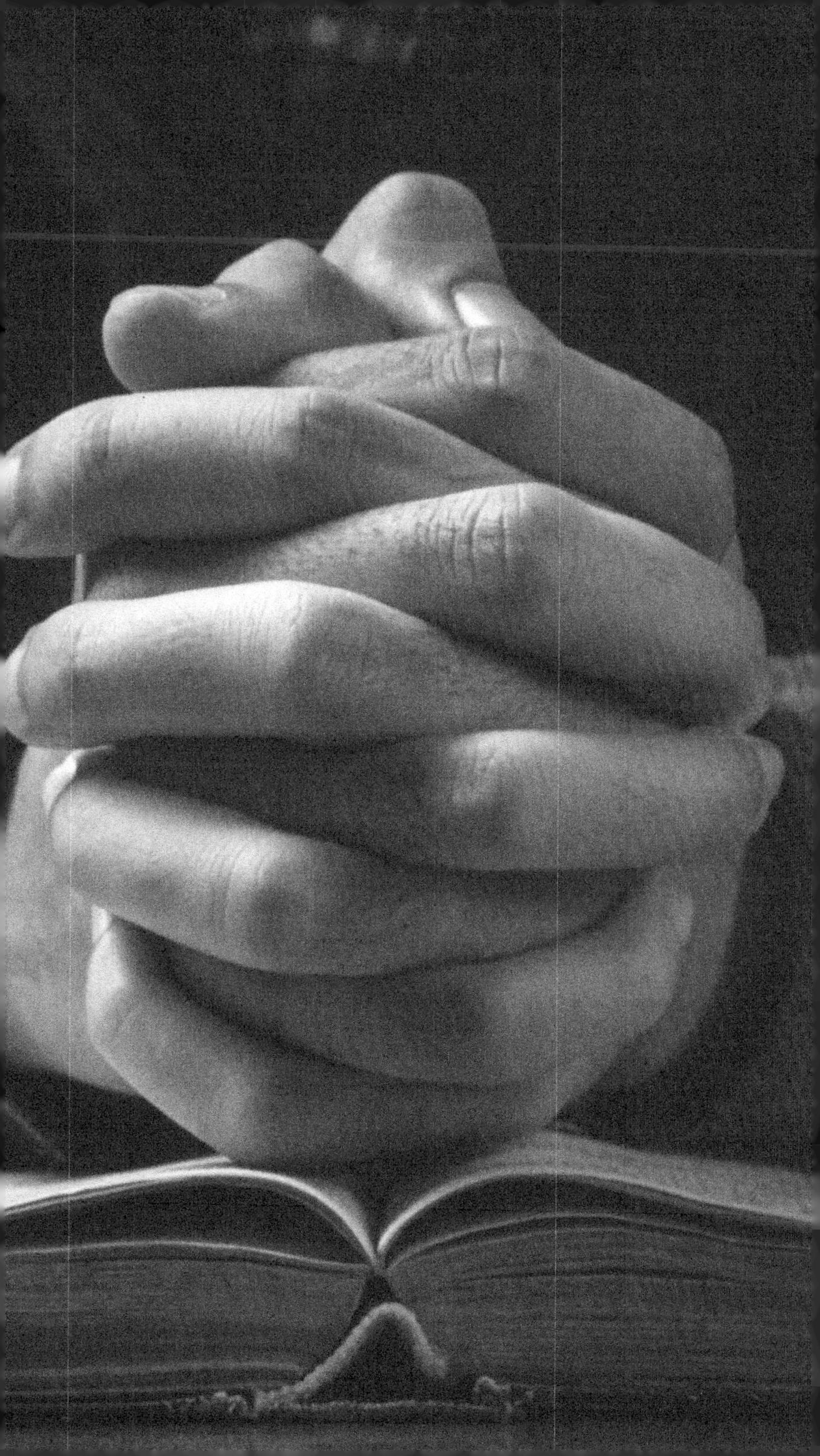

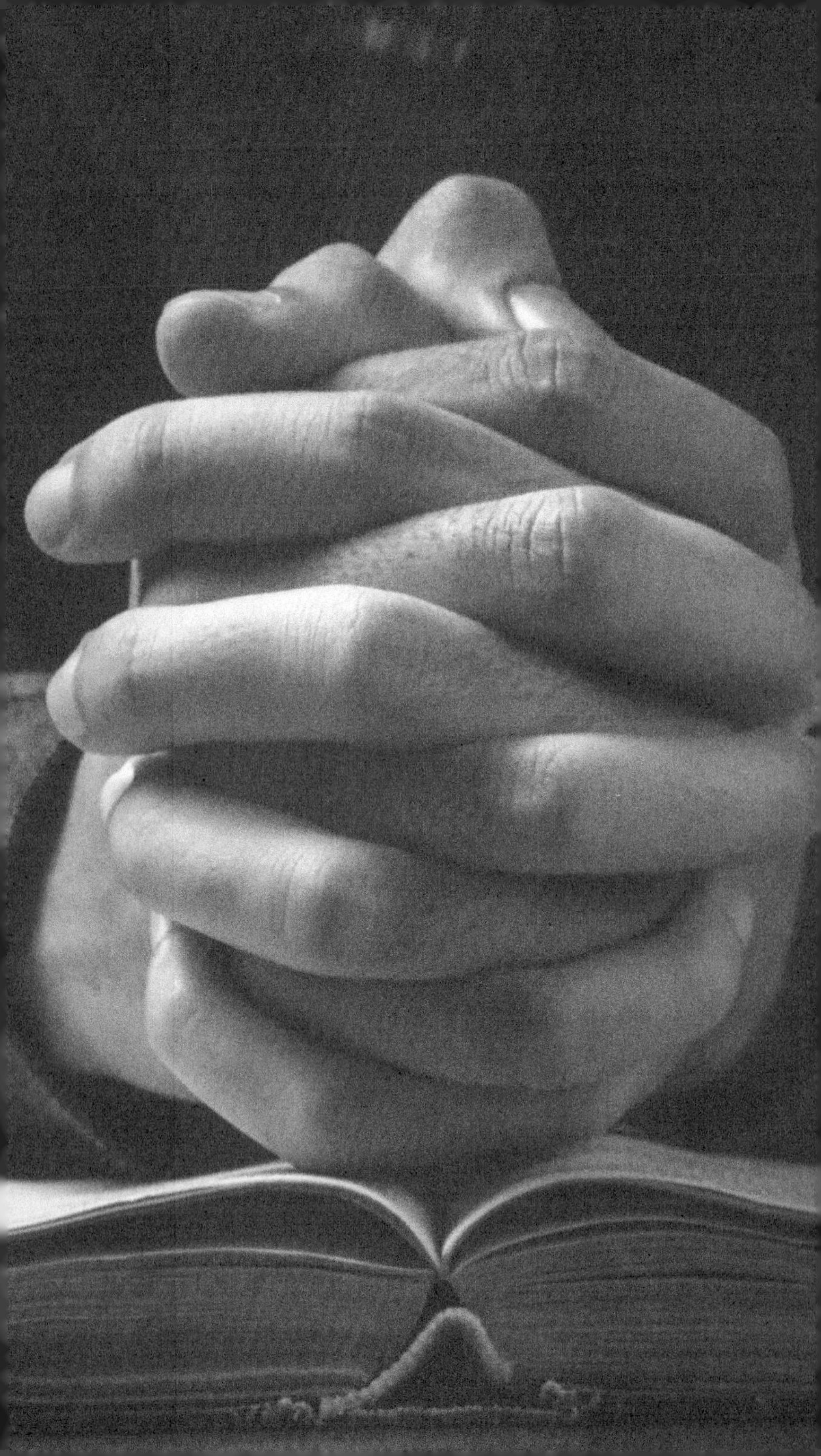

PROLOGUE
NOAH

Five Years Ago, December 18th 2018

"Please Daddy, I want you to go with us," Carmen pleads, which has me both wanting to cave and laugh at the same time. I finish pulling my arm through the sleeve of my jacket before striding across my bedroom and sitting next to her on the edge of my bed. She's lying on her stomach, kicking her feet back and forth in the air. Carmen looks at me with those chocolate puppy dog eyes. Ones that make me want to give her everything. She's our little miracle, born three months early with the umbilical cord wrapped around her tiny neck. I almost lost her and my beautiful wife Bianca that day, but the Lord saw fit to see them through.

"Mija," I say lovingly, using my wife's term of endearment for her. "You know, Deacon Butler is still in the hospital. I need to stop by and see him, as well as do my other rounds at the hospital and then I'll meet you and

Mommy at the church. Youth Pastor Tim will lead the children's service until I can get there."

"Okay, Daddy. I'm just excited for you to hear my solo for Sunday," she says excitedly, jumping up onto her knees. She's so excited about getting to sing *Silent Night*, with Christmas coming soon, the children and youth are going to be leading the choir.

"Mi Amor, she will be fine. Go see Deacon Butler and we'll meet you at church." My beautiful wife steps into the room, wrapping her arms around my waist as she comes up on her toes and places a chaste kiss on my lips. She has always been my little bundle of energy, standing at five-foot-two to my almost six-foot frame. She always thinks it's funny when the older women of my congregation huddle and joke about how my build intimidates new visitors to the church.

"Okay, let me go, so I can be sure to catch our little angel practicing her solo." Releasing her, I pick up my keys and bible from the dresser and head out of the room. Bianca looks at me with a smile, her face full of love.

"See you later," she calls out just as I step out of the room, the smile on my face growing broader. I am truly a lucky man with the most amazing family, church, and faith in my Lord.

Hopping in my car, I head straight to the hospital, needing to make my rounds as the small county hospital chaplain, then to my church. I'm excited about the upcoming Sunday sermon. Not only is my daughter singing a solo, but she's leading the children in their program. They're going to be presenting the story of Moses to the congregation.

It took me twenty minutes to make it to the hospital as I listened to my recording of the sermon I'd been working on. Recording it and then listening back to it gave me a better sense of the impact, as I could hear the same as my congregation. One of the elder deacon's once told me it's what sets me apart from the other pastors who had passed through the church. When I first arrived, I was hit with a lot of pushback from the elders of the congregation, especially with me just being so fresh out of seminary school and being so young. It was unheard of for a twenty-eight-year-old man getting his own church. But I did. I just had to prove myself.

Walking into the hospital, I head straight for the surgical ward. One of our choir members recently had knee surgery, and due to some complications, had to stay longer before being transferred to the outpatient rehabilitation center for her recovery and therapy. Stepping up to room 201, I lift my hand and knock on the door.

"Come in," comes weakly from the other side.

Opening it, I step inside, a smile on my face and bible in hand. "Mrs. Jenkins, you look lovely today."

"Blasphemy, Pastor Alder. You should be ashamed of yourself." She begins to laugh, but it immediately turns into a coughing fit.

Rushing over to her bedside table, I set my bible down, then pick up her cup of water. Placing a straw inside of the cup, I hold it out for her to take a sip.

"There, are you okay now? That's what you get for speaking like that," I joke with her, causing her to blush.

"You're right and yes, that's better. The doctor was by earlier and said he was moving me to the rehab center tomorrow, so don't think I've gone to visit the Lord when you don't see me here next time you come. How is that beautiful daughter of yours? I hate that I'm missing the children's lead service this Sunday."

Reaching out, I take her hand in mine, giving it a small squeeze. "I will make sure to have it recorded for you and bring it so you can watch it."

"Thank you. I would love that." She flashes a sweet smile at me. She was one of my strongest supporters when I first started at First Centennial Baptist, always fighting and lobbying for me, turning into a pseudo grandmother for my little angel.

We sit there talking for the next thirty minutes or so about her surgery, her family, and how much she misses her husband. He passed away and went on to meet our heavenly father three years prior.

"Well, I hate to leave, but I need to get to the church. I promised my family I would make it for practice." I lean over, giving her a kiss on her forehead before standing up.

"Can you do me a favor and turn the television volume up when I turn it on? For some reason, the controller doesn't work the volume and I can't hear a word they're saying, and I need to watch my shows."

"No problem," I tell her as she turns the television on, just as it cuts to a news report.

I focus my eyes on the screen; I can hear Mrs. Jenkins speaking, but I can't make out a word. There on the screen, surrounded by flashing lights, is my church.

If I had only known then what was to come. That my life was getting ready to be ripped out from underneath me and my faith in the Lord to be tested. One moment in time that can cause a ripple effect, altering the course of your life forever.

That day, thirteen men, women, and children were injured and ten killed.

My wife and beautiful daughter were among the ten that died, along with the shooter and the answers to why he did it.

It was at that moment I lost my faith, and started drowning myself in alcohol.

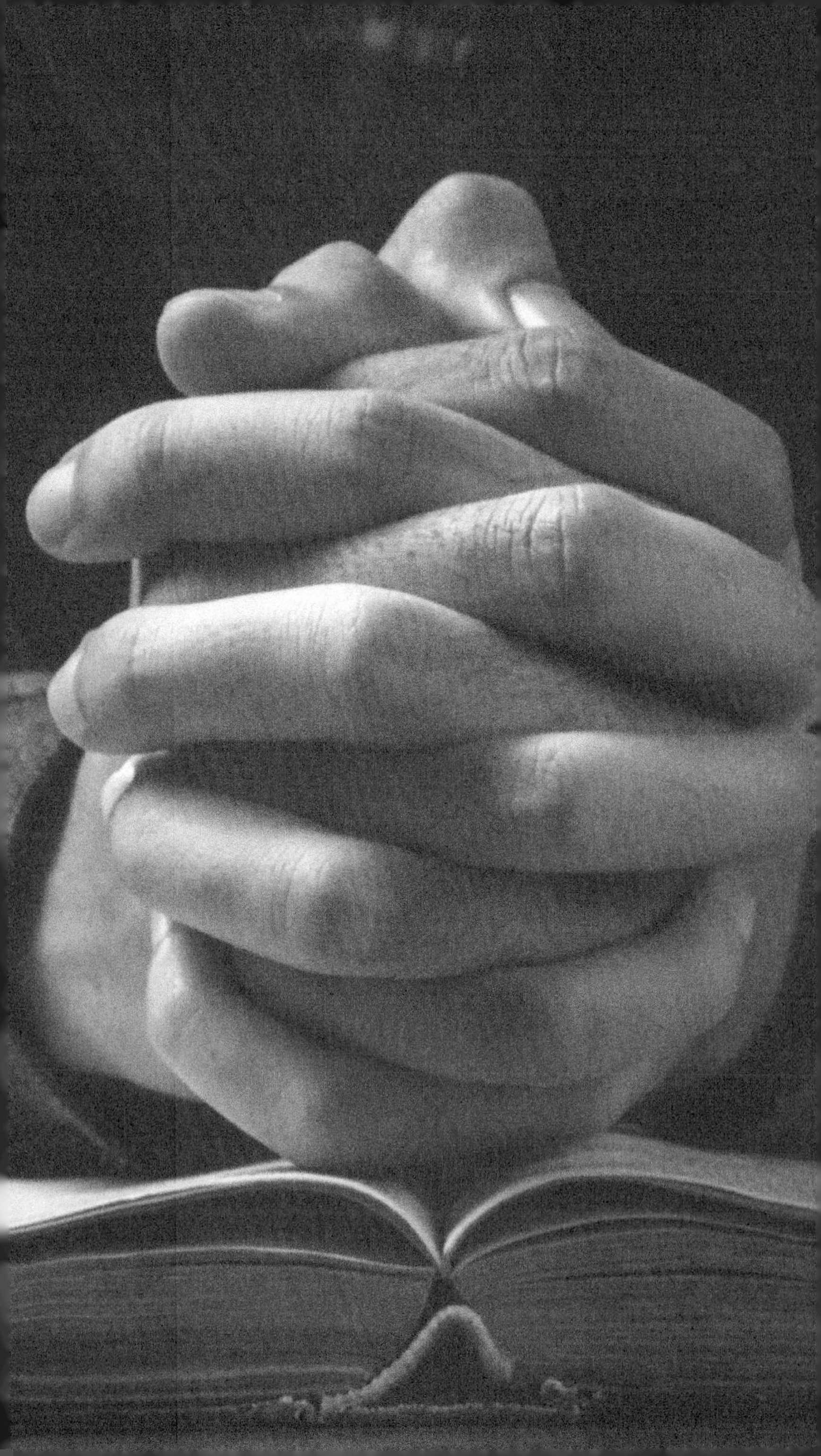

CHAPTER 1

Noah

Four years ago

I want to die.

To be with my wife and child. It should have been me.

If I wasn't making my fucking hospital visits, I would have been there. Maybe I could've saved my family, and if not, I could've died with them. Instead, I'm here, forced to live a life without them.

"Give me another," I tell the bartender as he steps up, a frown on his face as he pours another shot of Jack.

Alcohol has become my new friend, the only thing that's able to dull the pain in my heart for a moment. I did okay for a while. No one suspected how much I was drinking until I showed up at church on Sunday, still drunk from the previous night's bender.

The deacons let that one slide, as well as the second and third. But the fourth, that was the one that landed me on my ass. I got an ultimatum; go to rehab and get sober or they would be getting a new pastor. I went with the latter. By that time, alcohol was the only thing that numbed me from the reality I was living.

It also landed me without a place to stay. Fortunately, my wife ensured we had life insurance. Blood money that I hated to use, but it was either that or the streets. And I wanted to save everything of my wife and daughter. Every picture, drawing, their clothing. I just didn't have it in me to part with any of it. So I packed it all up and moved into a one-bedroom apartment. But every piece of this town reminded me of Carmen and Bianca.

I saw their faces everywhere I looked.

The playground.

The school.

The library.

And the fucking church they were killed in, right by the pulpit. It's why I needed the alcohol, being that close to the spot where they took their last breaths. The red stained carpet where their blood poured from their bodies as they held each other tightly.

Lifting the glass to my lips, I tilt my head backward, letting it slide down my throat, no longer flinching from the harsh taste. I've become immune to it.

"Another!" I call out, slamming the empty glass back down on the bar top.

The bartender looks apprehensive, like he's debating his next move. But it doesn't take long for him to make up his mind, and in the process, pissing me off even more when I have to wait. Two large men in leather vests sit down on the stools to my left, tapping their hands on

SINNER'S CHOICE   11

the bar top, attempting to get the bartender's attention, which is firmly on me.

"I said, give me another!" I demand, my voice louder this time as I grit my teeth.

"Sir, don't you think you've had enough? You're in here every night, stumbling out at closing. I know what happened—"

"Shut your fucking mouth and do your job. Get me another round." I slam my hands down on the bar top, causing my glass to jump and fall over.

"We'll take a round of what he has. In fact, get us two rounds, drinks on me this time," the man beside me says, as the bartender nods his head at him, and I'd be remiss if I didn't say it looked like he had fear in his eyes.

Who the fuck are these two?

Turning my head, I take a closer look at them. One has longer hair with a bandana around his head, holding his hair back. He has a close-cut beard, one he's kept well groomed. Tattoos cover his exposed arms. There's a patch on his vest, but I can't make it out. The guy beside him is dressed much the same, only he's slightly younger, with short black hair and a pretty boy face, like that movie star, James Dean.

"You know who rides the black sportster out front?" the older one asks.

"It's mine." My voice is blunt and emotionless. I'm not here to chit-chat, just to get so drunk I'm numb and unable to think. It's been a year and today is the day I plan to end it all.

I know it may mean I go to hell, but I've been living in it every day since seeing that news report on television. As a spouse, you know the day may come when you have to bury your spouse. But a child? No. A parent should never have to bury their child.

"Man, that is one sweet ride," he draws out as he speaks, a huge toothy grin on his face.

"Yeah, I guess. But it doesn't matter anymore. I'm taking my last ride on it tonight." One final ride, right off the pier into the ocean, with me chained to it, so it just drags me right down to the bottom of its depths. I know there's a slight chance I'll back out, but at least if I do make it over the edge of the pier, there'll be no turning back.

The bartender sets two shots down in front of me and I pick up one, down it, then the next, before the men beside me even drink their first. "Two more," I bark out at the bartender. Shit, I can't even remember his name. I know I asked for it when I got here.

"Thanks for the drinks," I tell the bikers, turning to them.

"I'm Hawke and this knucklehead is Sundance, and you are?"

"Depends on who you're talking to. If it was my former congregation, it would be Pastor Adler. If it was my wife, it would be Mi Rey or Papi. My daughter called me Daddy. To my father I was Noah, but for everyone else, I'll just be another John Doe. So what does a name really mean, anyway?" *The bartender...Jake!*

Yep, that's it. That's his name. Jake refills my glass and I lift it to my lips and toss it back. "Another!" I bark out.

If this fucker stops serving me, I'll just find somewhere else that will.

"You said used to, so what happened to them?" *Damn, Hawke, you got a lot of questions.*

"They're dead. Anything else you want to know? My credit card numbers, social security, birthdate. I don't need them anymore." I reach into my back pocket and pull out my wallet, tossing it down on the bar in front of them. "I'll save you some trouble. Just make sure to cover what I'm drinking before you max the shit out."

"Shit, Preacher Man, you got a mighty grim look on life. What would your God think about all that?" Hawke asks me with a laugh.

"I don't have a god. If I did, he would've kept that fucker from coming into his house of worship and killing my family and members of my congregation."

Both go white at my words. Guess even bikers have a line when it comes to killing women and children.

"My ol' lady was killed, too. Fucker from the Grippers MC thought he was big and bad. Saw her and thought he could take what wasn't his. He waited until we were on a run, then broke in on her while she was closin' up her restaurant, raped her before he cut her throat. Used her blood to leave me a message. Thought he was being cute," Hawke tells me. His grip on his glass is so strong, it fucking breaks.

"What did you do?" I know if the man who killed my family was still alive, I would've murdered him.

"Cut his dick off. Then I fed it to him, made him eat every bit of it. Then, once he swallowed it all, I strung him up, and each day I went and stabbed him somewhere new, letting him bleed until he eventually died." I can't even see his eyes, but I know they're crazed. Hell, this man has to know he'd be given the death penalty.

"Did it make you feel better? Take away the pain of losing her?" Would I be sitting at this bar if I'd had the opportunity to kill him before he took his own life?

"See, that's a tricky question. It didn't take away the pain; time did that, makin' each day a little easier. But feel better? Well, yeah it did, cause I know that dick ain't out there screwin' with anyone else, or any of my brothers." He picks up the last glass with the amber liquid in it, lifting it to his lips and swallowing it in one gulp.

I just nod my head before motioning to the bartender and tapping my glass, letting him know I want more. The night is still early and I'm nowhere near feeling numb inside.

"Well, my pain will be gone tonight." My voice is flat as I watch the bartender fill my glass with Jack. He goes to leave, but I reach out, taking hold of his arm, stopping him. With my free hand, I pick up the glass, down the contents and slam it down in front of him, sliding the other empty glass over beside it. "Fill them both up."

"How's that?" Damn, you'd swear he was a woman the way he wants to gossip. Like that fucking comic from long ago that I can't even remember the name of with the two women at the fence.

"Bike, bridge, water. Perfect plan. So if you don't mind, I'd like to enjoy my drinks." Once again, I down both of the shots in front of me and motion for Jake to refill them.

He should just leave the entire bottle. Even asked him to, but the pussy claimed he couldn't.

"You see, I can't do that, Preacher man. I like you and I think we have the makin' of a beautiful future together. I can give you a way to work out all that anger and aggression while finding a brotherhood to surround yourself with. Plus, we got broads lined up givin' us all the pussy we want."

"You gonna help me find God again?" I ask, sneering at them.

"Or be God. So what do you think?" He reaches out, snatches the bottle of Jack from the bartender, and pours the three of us another round.

"Now take this wallet and put it back in your pocket. Come tomorrow, when you're sober, we'll talk about you riding out of this godforsaken town with us back to Kentucky to the Merciless Few clubhouse."

I don't say a word, just pick up the glass and drink its contents down, letting everything soak in. A chance to avenge my wife and daughter by fucking up others. Shit, God's forsaken me. Maybe I can do the same.

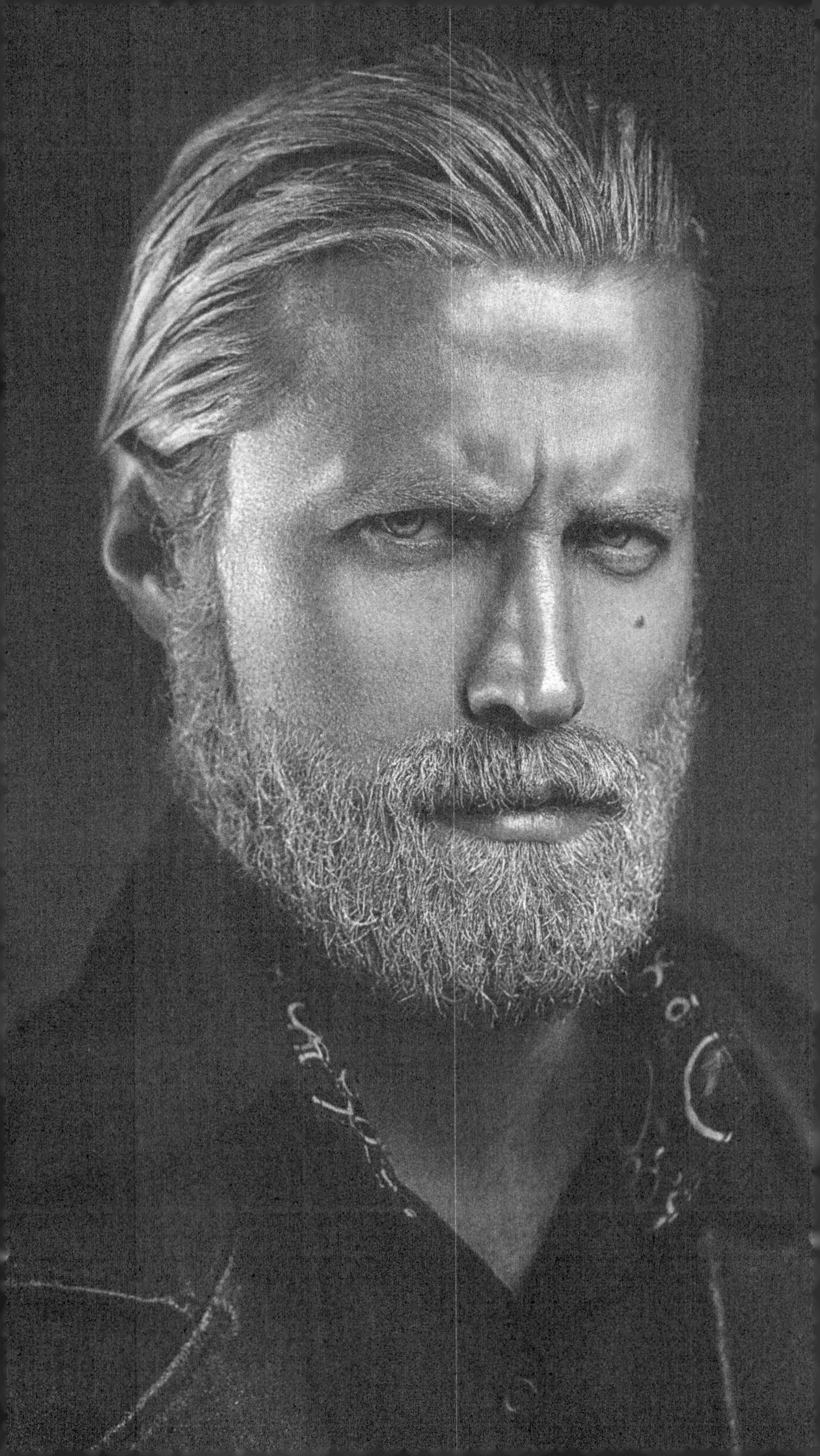

CHAPTER 2

Preacher

Present Day

"James, James, James," I chant as I walk back and forth in front of the asshole before me. "Did you think we wouldn't notice you were skimming money off the top?" I ask before a sadistic laugh rips out of me as I tap the metal Louisville Slugger baseball bat in the palm of my hand.

"Come on, Preach," he stammers as he looks at me with blood rimmed eyes, well, the one that isn't swollen shut. "I didn't mean to. It was a mistake and it won't happen again."

"Oh, a mistake, was it? You hear that Sundance, Prospect?" Then, for the sake of dramatics, I make my voice whiny and irritating, throwing some finger quotes in the air. "It was just a mistake. I didn't mean it."

I'm standing in front of where he's hanging from the rafters, chains attached to his wrists. His feet aren't even touching the ground while his arms are pulled from his shoulder joints. Taking the bat, I cock it back behind me and swing, like I'm trying to hit a baseball right out of the field, and smack into James' side.

His screams echo around me and damn if it doesn't make me feel good. The familiar tingles of excitement from making someone feel pain, just like I felt, courses through my veins. I swear I feel my cock twitching in my pants.

"You see, James, it wasn't a mistake, was it? Did you really think we were just some dumb bikers that wouldn't notice the accountant was stealing from us right under our noses?"

"I had to, man. Come on, Preacher. They threatened my family. Said if I didn't do it, they'd kill my little boy. Come on, surely you can see why I did it." He begs me, tears streaming down his face, a very visible yellow puddle underneath his feet and an obvious wet stain on his pants. *Guess that last hit was the water shot.*

My head snaps back up as I look at him. Curious now and pissed. I may have changed my view on faith, wielding God's word in a much different way now, but I will never be okay with the life of a child being threatened. But for him to imply his situation is the same as mine, that I would fall at his feet and allow what he was doing to go unpunished simply because someone killed my child? Hell no!

"And who is this 'they' you're talking about?" I ask as I flick my wrist, spinning the bat around in circles, ready to hit him again.

"Even you can't stand against their forces. They're psychotic, more than you are," he spits out as I sling my bat, cracking the other side of his body this time.

He cries out once more. "Who are they?" I ask again, annoyed as fuck by the fact I'm having to repeat myself. Over the last four years, I've come to hate having to do that.

He keeps his lips pressed together tightly, not giving me what I want, even though I've broken countless bones in his body. I'll give it to him. I thought he was just a spineless fucking weak man, but he's got more strength than I ever gave him credit for. I turn around and walk over to the table about two feet in front of me and let my fingertips skim along the various sizes of knives and guns laid out on it until they land on my silver Smith and Wesson set. Yep, this is it.

"Well, James, if you can't give me the information I want, then you're of no use to me. I was going to let you live a little longer, you know, out of gratitude for the years of service before you turned into a thief." I turn, cocking my hand back and throwing the knife. "But I've changed my mind."

The knife slices through the air, skirting across the distance within seconds, and the blade sinks straight into his forehead. Blood oozes down his face as he gurgles, choking on his own blood before he takes his last breath.

"Damn, Preacher, if you would've given him another lick or two, I bet he would've spilled the beans." Sundance snorts as he steps over to James' limp body. Straddling the puddle below him, he pulls a pair of gloves out of his pocket and puts them on, beginning to check James' pants pockets.

"Really? Gloves? Are we that damn prissy?" Rolling my eyes, I pull the pack of cigarettes out of my vest pocket. I never light them, simply pull one out and hold it between my lips.

When I was sixteen, Bianca caught me with one when I was trying to fit in with the cool kids, shortly before she brought me to church and I found my path to God. One that I've faltered on, but my promise to Bianca to never smoke is one I will never go back on. I know without a doubt she'd never approve of the man I've become. I can only hope that she'd understand.

"Yes, fuckin' gloves! It ain't got nothin' to do with bein' prissy. He's got mutherfuckin' piss on his pants. If the two of you assholes are all big and bad, then come check these pockets yourself!" he bellows out as he goes about seeing if he's holding anything useful, which turns out he isn't.

The only thing of any value is the wallet, holding a picture of his wife and son, two hundred and fifty dollars cash, and some credit cards. None of which are of any use to me.

"Burn the wallet, find a way to leave the cash for his family and get rid of the body. Remember to leave no trace; we don't want anything left for him to be identified by. Call one of the prospects to come help you do it," I order Sundance, who just glares at me with disdain.

Even though he's been a patched member of the club longer than me, I'm an officer and he's just a member. I know it eats at him every time he looks at me, but I don't give a fuck. He's the one that fucked up, not me. Now he has to pay the penance and earn that officer position that should've been his.

Turning to Cyrus, the road captain for our chapter, I see he's leaning against the wall, his leg flexed with his foot resting on the wall as he scrolls through his phone. "Let's get out of here, man," I bark at him as I head to the door. Whether he's ready or not, I am.

We head out of the garage into the brisk, dark night. The overcast sky blocks the moonlight, so the motion lights on the outside of the building are the only reason we can see at all.

"I'll see you tomorrow man, got me some pussy waiting on me," Cyrus calls as he mounts his bike, putting the key in the ignition and bringing it to life.

"Some, as in more than one?" I ask with a raised eyebrow.

"Exactly." He winks back, before peeling out of the yard, turning left after he passes through the gate.

I leave out behind him, stopping on the other side of the gate to talk to the prospect manning it.

"Keep your eyes and ears open. Anyone other than someone with the club tries to get in, shoot them," I instruct him before turning right, taking off to the clubhouse. The only thing I want right now is my shower and bed. In that order.

This is one of the few times I feel at peace. When the adrenaline of revenge courses through my veins and the wind beats against my body. I never wanted to be a killer and I know I'll go to hell for it. But it's the only way I've been able to come to grips with what happened. My way of being in control when I wasn't that day.

It's a warped way to think of it, I know. But yet it's my way of making sense of it.

I want to keep riding, but the need to shower and sleep wins out. It's Friday night, so I know there's going to be a party at the clubhouse. Shit, who am I kidding?

There's always a party. But every Sunday morning, the boys are up and in the clubhouse chapel, more commonly known as our common room. Ready to listen to my sermon.

Yeah, I found a way back to God in my own twisted way. I kill, then ask for forgiveness in hopes of one day, when this life of mine is over, I'll still get to see my wife and daughter again. It took three years to find my way back to him. If it wasn't for Hawke and Gunner, I don't think I would have.

I was looking down at the bottom of a bottle of whiskey on the second anniversary of their death, one year after joining the Merciless Few MC, when Hawke and Gunner stepped in. They sobered me up, dressed me in a Santa suit, and took me to the local county hospital, straight to the pediatric oncology ward. It ripped my heart out. Seeing them suffer but still have smiles on their faces brought God back into my life.

The visit didn't turn me into the same man who used to stand at the pulpit looking into the congregation, seeing the smiling faces of his family. That man is gone. But for lack of a better way to say it, they helped bring back the third cousin thrice removed from that man. Better than nothing, I guess.

Pulling up to the guard shack at our clubhouse, I see the newest prospect manning the gate. He's been showing his worthiness for the last six months and I like the kid. He's twenty, so still a baby, with shaggy black hair and a scar that goes down the length of the right side of his face. A remnant of an abusive father. One that me and Hawke plan to take care of as soon as we patch Steve in.

Pulling the bike to a stop in front of him, I ask, "Any trouble tonight?"

"No, sir." His voice is shaky as he tries to keep from looking me in the eye. He should be scared, but he doesn't need to let other people see it. A lesson for tomorrow, tonight I'm beat.

"Are you alone at the gate?" If he is, that's a problem; the gate is always manned in twos.

"No, sir. Sam is walking the perimeter. He should be back any minute."

"Good." I rev my engine and take off, riding up to the front of the clubhouse and pull into my spot by the front door. Yeah, I got a spot. Made it all official and put up a sign, daring any of these fuckers to question it.

I can hear the music blaring and laughter of my fellow brothers. Looking up at the sky, I take a deep breath and close my eyes.

I miss you, Bianca.

I miss seeing our girl.

I miss knowing I'll never walk her down the aisle.

I miss knowing I'll never bounce her child on my knee.

I miss knowing I'll never grow old with you.

Most of all, I hate myself for not being there for you when you needed me.

Bianca, can you forgive me?

I repeat the same thing every night. One day, I will find a way to forgive myself because I know she doesn't blame me. Once I finally do, then and only then will I be able to move forward in peace, with acceptance.

Turning off the bike, I dismount it and head inside. I make a beeline to the hallway that holds our living quarters and is off limits to anyone other than a patched member unless escorted by them. Or if one of the club girls is cleaning your room. No one ever comes into mine. It's how I want it.

I wave off the calls to join the party.

Sleep is all I want.

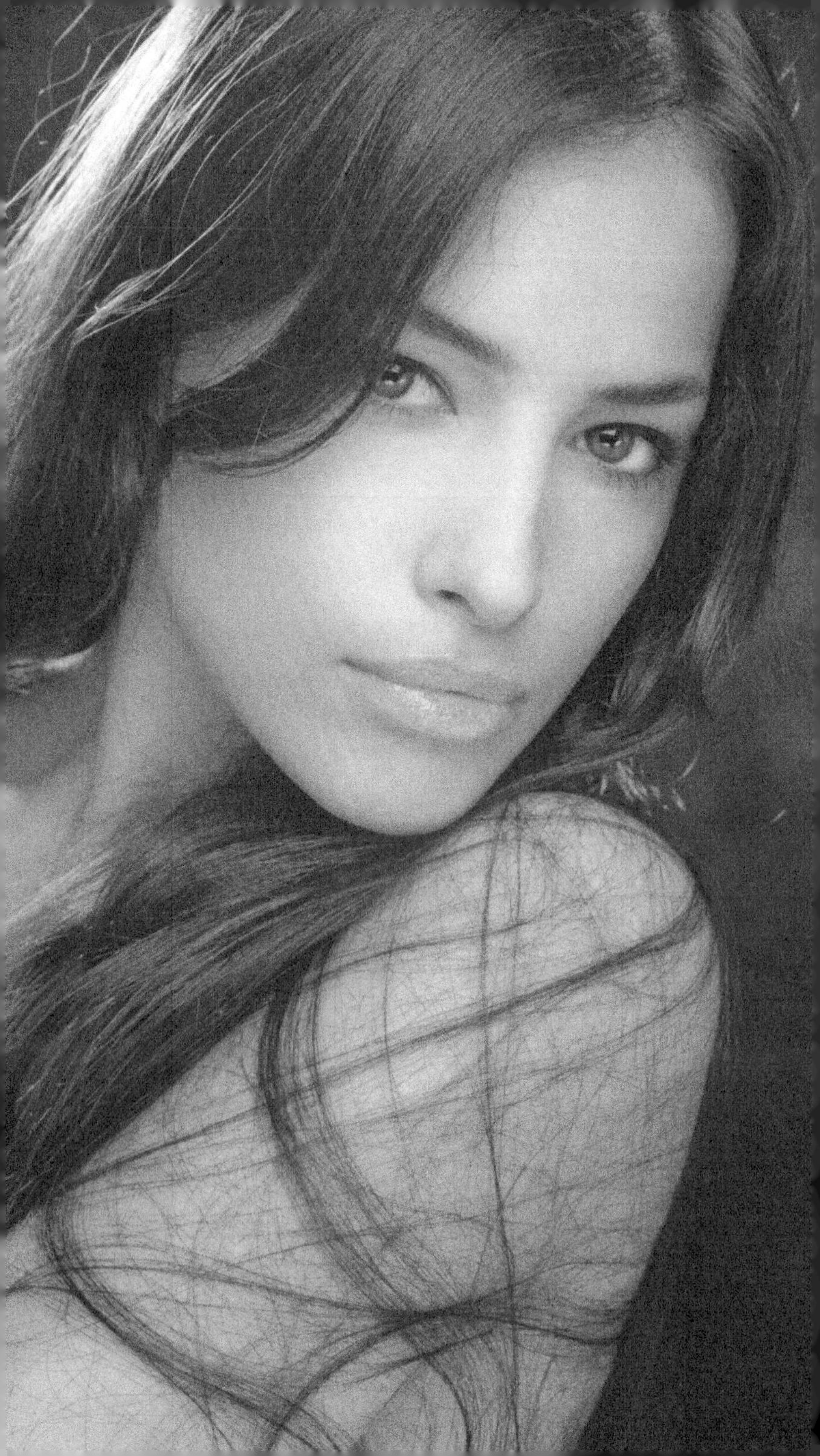

CHAPTER 3

Lucy

Today will be better than yesterday.
Today will be better than yesterday.

I repeat as I stand at the bathroom sink brushing my teeth. Just moving my arm sends pain radiating through my shoulder as bile works its way up my throat, begging to be released. It's my fault. I should have used my left hand, but I wasn't thinking, just like I wasn't last night.

Instead of handing over all the money I got from cashing my paycheck, I tried to hold on to a few dollars. How he knew I had stuffed a few twenties into my bra, I'll never know. Scott seems to have this unnerving way of knowing when I'm lying or hiding something. The sad part is, even knowing that he can tell, and what will happen if I do, I still do it, hoping to find some way to escape.

My parents.

It's all their fault.

Well, really it's not, but I can blame them for letting me marry this asshole right out of high school. They could have forced me to wait, and maybe if I had, then

I wouldn't be here today. Instead, I would've gone to college, met a good man and gotten married then. But nope, here I am four years later, a punching bag for a drug dealer, drug runner, whatever the hell it is he does for those men. I'm just a woman and I don't need to know, or as he likes to call me, a cum dumpster.

Stepping into the bedroom, I grimace when I see him still in the bed, face down and with his limbs spread like a starfish. Murderous thoughts run through my mind. It would be so easy to tiptoe into the kitchen, get a butcher knife and put it straight through his heart.

Prison can't be that bad, right?

Three meals a day, yard time, and a bed to sleep in.

I mean, I've watched Orange is the New Black. I'll need to make nice with the guards, go crazy or become someone's bitch, cause let's face it, I won't be winning any fights.

But that's not me. Bending over, I pick up my shoes from the floor, making sure to not use my right hand this time. Work is going to be a bitch today. I've only been there a few months, but I like it. The people are nice and it's time away from here. Maybe I can find a place to stash my tips at work; it'll be the only way I can save any money.

Stepping out of the room, I gingerly shut the door behind me so I don't wake him. Last time that happened, I had two broken ribs and a busted lip. Sitting down on the couch, I awkwardly attempt to put my sneakers on with one hand. When it becomes blatantly obvious it's not going to happen, I take a deep breath, clench my jaw and fight through the pain as I use my right arm.

I take one last look around the tiny house, making sure everything is in its place. When my eyes land on the oak wood kitchen table sitting in the dining room, I see a glass sitting on it and the chair hasn't been pushed underneath it. Rushing over, I push it in, pick up the glass and quickly take it to the kitchen to wash.

Once I've looked everything over twice and I'm confident everything's in its place, I slip on my jacket and finally step out into the brisk morning air. The temperature has started to drop and the cold air nips at my cheeks. Pulling my jacket around me, I begin the two-mile walk to work. Not a soul is out this early in the morning, and the only light leading my way is the streetlights.

Most women would be scared, I imagine, walking alone on a road with only the smallest hint of light. Not me. Sometimes I pray that something would happen to me. That my time here would be cut short and finally I'd have peace. I'd be away from him, but then he would just find someone else and their pain would be on me. So I stick it out.

Today will be better than yesterday.
Today will be better than yesterday.

I repeat as I trudge down the road. I guess I think if I keep telling myself that, it will come true. Getting closer and closer to the diner I work at, I know once I'm there, I'll plaster on the smile that has become my mask. No one can know what happens at home. What Scott does to me. If they did, he'd kill me. He wants the world to believe he's some sort of saint. Believe me, he isn't.

When the diner comes into view, I shake everything off. I need to be cheery to make tips, all without anyone noticing the pain ripping through my shoulder. There's only two cars in the parking lot. An old beat up '84 black Chevy Tahoe and a blue Ford Taurus. JD and Georgie are here.

I head to the front door instead of down the alleyway to the back, since I know it will be open. The bell dings over the door as I walk in, grimacing as pain hits me, since I stupidly used my right arm.

Georgie's head immediately pops up. "Good morning, Lucy," she calls out to me, before stopping when I let a wince slip out. She doesn't say another word, just looks. Her eyes roaming up and down my body like she's taking inventory. It's not the first time I've seen her watch me.

"Good morning, Georgie. Just let me put my jacket in the back and I'll be right up to help you." My words come out rushed as I speed past her to the back, hoping she won't have questions when I return.

Stepping into the back, I head toward the tiny hooks for us to hang our jackets and purses on. I don't carry the latter, just a small wallet that holds my ID and a picture of me and my best friend. Well, she was. I haven't talked to her since I graduated from high school. If I'm honest, even before then, really. It's like I never noticed how Scott slowly put a wedge between us, manipulating and controlling my actions, where I went, who I was with.

A smart person would have seen that for what it was. A huge red flag. Not me, though; I was dick whipped. He was my first, my only, and he made me believe he loved me. As warped as that love was. But that's something to dwell on another day.

Stepping back to the front, I hear JD's and Georgie's whispered voices, before I see them huddled together behind the counter. Not wanting them to think I'm snooping or to overhear something I shouldn't, I clear my throat.

"Good morning, Lucy." JD smiles back at me. "Guess I need to head to the kitchen and get ready for the morning rush." His fingers glide off of Georgie's and it's only then I notice they were holding hands.

I wait for him to leave before giving Georgie a once over. "Spill it. When did the two of you happen?"

She waves her hand at me. "There's no us. We're just friends. Now let's get this silverware rolled and coffee made. It's just the two of us this morning and Henry will be in around nine to bus tables. Cindy's out with the flu." She pushes the container on the counter between us. Looking inside, I see clean silverware in it.

"I hope she feels better," I mumble as I pick up a knife, spoon and fork followed by a paper napkin and begin to roll them, gingerly I might add. Today is starting off perfectly. Of course, someone would be sick on the day it takes every bit of energy in me to hold back the pain I'm feeling with every movement.

"Me too, but I hope she didn't spread those germs to us. You look a little peaked today. Are you feeling okay?" She looks at me down her nose, like she can smell if I lie to her or not.

"I'm fine. Just tired," I lie. Not about being tired, because I'm definitely that.

She stops folding the silverware, angling her body so she's looking right at me. Biting on her bottom lip, it looks like she's thinking about what she's going to say, formulating the words she wants to use.

"You know you can tell me if something is wrong, Lucy? We're a family around here."

I fight back the tears that want to fall, but I'm not going to break down in front of her. Nodding my head, knowing if I dare speak I'll be a sobbing mess, I resume rolling the silverware into the napkins.

She doesn't pressure anymore, just works beside me until the job is done, finishing in time for the first customer to step through the door. An older man, Mr. Jenkins, who comes in every morning for coffee, eggs and bacon, sits down in the booth in the far corner with a newspaper.

***

It's almost noon when I hear the roar of motorcycles out front. Excitement rips through me, hoping he'll be one of them. There's something about him that just draws me in, and I can't take my eyes off of him.

My prayers are answered when he steps through the door. He's tall, shit, he has to be about five foot ten or eleven, with brownish blond hair and gray sprinkled through it, giving him a distinguished look with a matching clean cut beard. His eyes are dark as coal and piercing, like they could cut right through you. His jaw is always clenched and his face is void of emotion. In the whole time I've been working here, I've never seen him smile.

Three other men are with him. Two who look around the same age as him and one a little younger. They're all wearing a vest with the same logo on the back. It makes me think of that television show about the bikers and I wonder if their club is the same as the one depicted on it. But I'll never ask, wouldn't want to end up buried in a hole in the middle of the fucking woods or something. The last few times he's been in, he's sat in Cindy's section or Georgie's helped him.

But today he's sitting in mine. Reaching up, I push the stray pieces of my chocolate hair that's come loose from my ponytail behind my ear and head his way. I've got my pad and pen ready to take their order, using it like a shield, holding it close to my chest.

"Good afternoon. What can I get for you?" I ask, my voice squeaky and shaky with each word that crosses my lips.

"Where's Cindy?" comes gruffly from the man I'm lusting over even though I have a husband, no matter how worthless he is, waiting at home.

"Cindy's out sick today. So it's just me and Georgie." I grip my pad nervously.

He just grunts, looks down at the menu, then orders. "Burger all the way, fries and Coke." The other three order the same, and I turn and rush away.

I give JD their order and quickly make their drinks. Instead of pushing them together and carrying them in my hands, like I've come to master over the last few weeks, I grab a small tray and set them on it. Pulling four straws from the container they're kept in and dropping them on the tray, I pick it up and head to the table.

Not thinking, I picked it up with my injured arm and almost drop it right on the floor. Thankfully, I acted quickly and was able to gingerly set it back down, rein in my nerves and then pick it up again, making sure the brunt of the weight was in my left hand.

I barely make it to their table, setting it down quickly on the edge of it. Some of the drink sloshes out of one of the glasses as he reaches out, catching it before it tips over, spilling its contents onto him.

"Shit girl, did you forget how to walk or something? You almost soaked me with it. Be more careful, or here's one for you—make two trips if you can't handle it!" he barks, and I feel the tears welling up in my eyes.

"I'm sorry." Turning, I rush off, but I can hear one of his friends before I make it out of earshot.

"*Shit, Preach, you made the cute little girl cry. You're fuckin' killer.*" Laughter erupts around them, only making me feel more like an idiot.

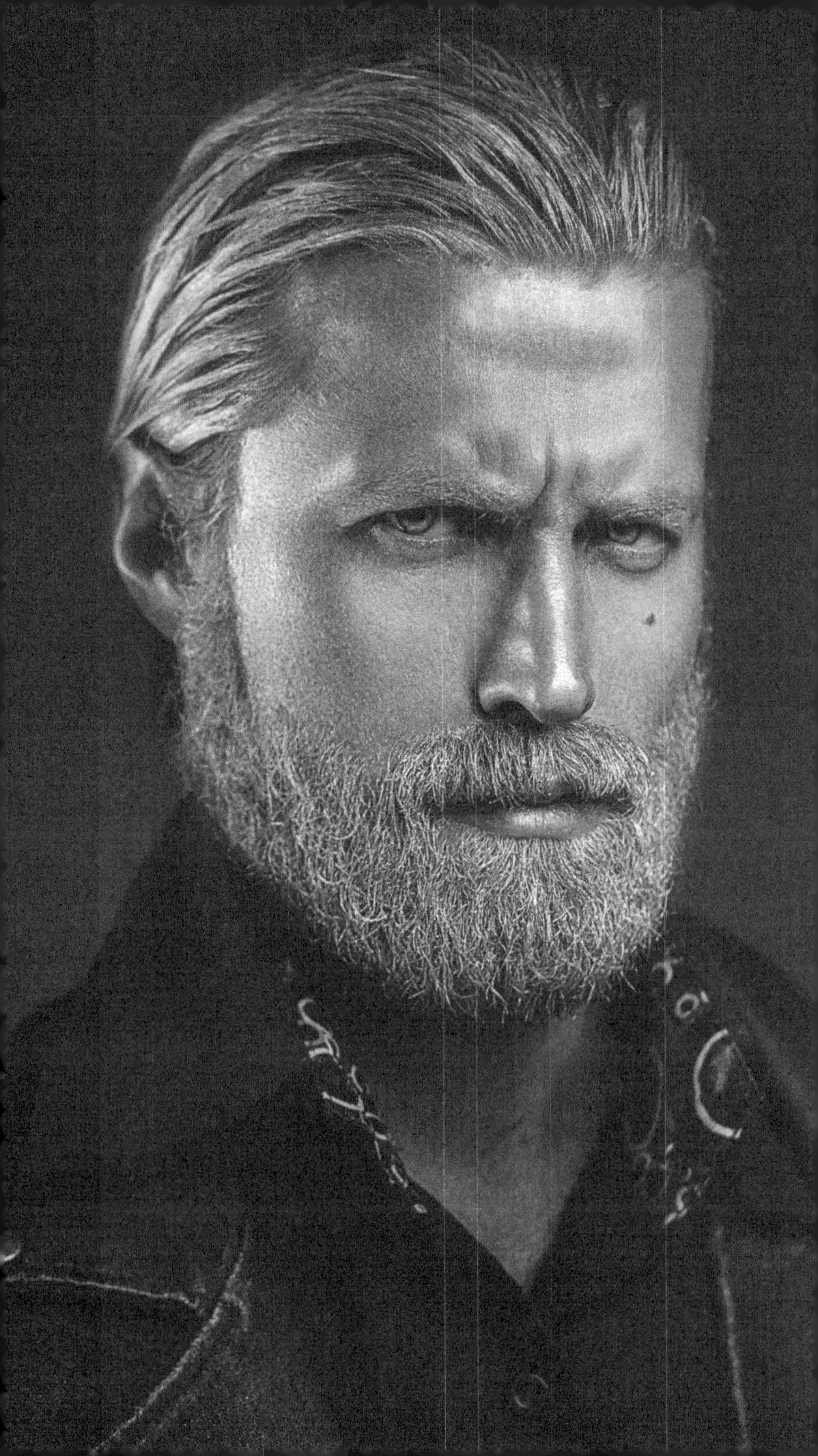

CHAPTER 4

Preacher

"Fuck off," I snap at them, while I watch her walk away out of the corner of my eye. I didn't mean to be a dick. It just came out before I could stop it.

"She's a hot piece of ass, I'll give you that. You think she's legal?" Hawke bumps my shoulder, nodding in her direction.

"Don't know, don't care," I bite out and quickly change the conversation. "Who do you think James was working for?" I'm curious, and not because we're hurting for money. No, we caught it before it got too bad. But we can't have people thinking they can steal from us and get away with it.

"No fuckin' clue. What has me worried is he seemed more scared of them than us." Hawke picks up his glass, taking a drink, while Gunner and Snake nod in agreement.

"You think we got someone tryin' to move in on our territory?" Snake reaches up, pulling his hair from the loosened ponytail and redoes it, while he looks around at us.

"I'm sending one prospect to his office, and one to his home, when the wife is out. Going to have them take all his files and computers. One way or another, we're goin' to find something out." Hawke's forceful voice fills our close space.

"Speakin' of prospects, are Davey and Nixon ready to patch in as members?" All eyes jump to me with Gunner's words.

"Why you all lookin' at me? The final say on that decision is this fucker here." I toss my thumb in Hawke's direction.

They just give each other a shit-eating grin before laughing. I fucking hate it when they do this stupid ass school kid shit instead of just saying what they're thinking.

"Come on man, you know you're our unofficial, official club chaplain. So we look to you to give us the final go ahead that they're ready." Hawke taps his fingertips on the table. He's done it ever since he found out I was a pastor in my past life, wanting me to take on that role in the club as well.

I'm about to say something when I catch movement out of the corner of my eye. It's the waitress from earlier. I lied to the guys. I noticed her. Fuck, how could I not? She's gorgeous. Long wavy brown hair, deep penetrating chocolate eyes, and curves that would make a man fall to his knees and worship her. But there are two things in the way. One, she looks like a kid—I bet she's barely legal—and the band on her left ring finger is very noticeable. I don't do married or jail bait.

She's struggling with the tray she's carrying and has stopped repeatedly to readjust it in her arms. I can see the grimace on her face, her clenched jaw and her glassed over eyes as she steps up to the table, almost dropping the tray as she sets it down.

Much of the same thing happened when she brought the drinks and that tray was far lighter than this one had to be. She goes to pick up the first plate, and it's then I see it again, the wince. She's hurt, yet not wanting anyone to know. Quickly switching hands, she begins to awkwardly set the plates in front of us. Hawke and Gunner's first, since they're sitting on the inside, then Snake and me.

Her face is scrunched up and I know she's fighting through some pain. From what visible skin I can see, which isn't much, just her face, hands and a small portion of her forearm, there's nothing. No bruising, scarring or any kind of cast or brace to show an injury from an accident.

She goes to turn and leave and something in me is calling to reach out to her, grab her arm and stop her. But I don't. It's not my fucking business. I can't always be the protector. Shit, that lesson was taught to me the hard way.

The guys continue on with muttered conversations as they eat, none of them waiting until they're done chewing their food like a bunch of heathens. I answer here and there with a grunt, so they think I'm actually paying attention, however it might end up biting me in the ass in the end. Last time I absentmindedly agreed to something, I was giving Tiny's daughter driving lessons. It was one of the few times in a long time I put my faith back in God.

My eyes can't stop following the brunette around the diner. Something is definitely wrong. She's putting on a valiant face, but her body is giving her away.

Fuck, why am I so worried about her?

I've slept with women since Bianca died. But they were nothing more than club bunnies, women with a willing hole for me to wet my dick. Nothing more. They know the score, though. Some try to up that status from club bunny to ol' lady. It rarely works and when they try to climb the ladder like that, we kindly show them the door.

"Hey Preach!" Hawke bumps my shoulder as he calls my name.

"What?" I bark, my eyes not moving from the girl before me. She's been back to the table a couple of times to refill our glasses. It's then that I see it. The pain in her eyes. Pain I know all too well. But her story differs from mine. At least, I hope it does.

"We're heading out. Are you coming with or are you going to decide to finish eating?" Looking down at my plate at Hawke's question, I realize I've barely eaten a bite.

"Yeah, I'm going to finish eating. I'll catch up with y'all at the clubhouse. Got some shit on my mind."

"More like some pussy. A fine looking one at that. Curves in all the right places." Snake moves his hands in an hourglass fashion as he speaks.

I cut my eyes at him, sending him into a fit of laughter.

"Ah shit, has our man been hit by the bug?" Gunner is the next to poke a joke at my slip in attention.

"I've not been hit by shit," I growl out, done with their antics.

"Okay, let's let him be. We got some shit to do. See you tonight at the clubhouse, Preach, and I need to know what you think about the prospects being patched in." Hawke's words put an end to all the chatter.

I stand from the booth, allowing him to slide out. Before he leaves, he pulls out his wallet and throws two hundred-dollar bills on the table. It catches me off guard and I look at him questionably.

"I saw the same thing you did. Something's up. If you want to look more into it, then I'll support you." The three of them walk away, throwing up a hand to wave at JD, who just stepped out of the kitchen as they go.

I should've known Hawke would see it too. He has this uncanny way of seeing the broken pieces in people. Hell, he saw it in me. He's what saved me from ending it all that night.

Picking up my burger, I take a bite, never taking my eyes off of her. Every move she makes, I watch, studying her, working through what could be wrong. I have a feeling it's whoever that wedding band is tied to.

I've taken the last bite of my burger, deciding to forgo the cold fries, when I see her moving toward me.

"Can I get you anything else?" Her voice is sweet like sugar.

I look up at her, her dark eyes gazing back at me. They're bloodshot and glazed over. "You can tell me who hurt you?"

Her eyes go wide in shock as what little color she had in her face vanishes. "N-n-n-no one has," she stutters, but it's all lies.

"Is that the story you want to stick to?"

Her face is blank as she stares back at me. Reaching into my pocket, I pull out my wallet, taking out a wad of twenties. A hundred and twenty dollars in total and toss it on the table, adding to the two hundred Hawke left.

"That's too much," her soft voice tells me, while she looks hungrily at the money on the table, leading me to believe that part of her problem is money.

"No, it's right." Standing, I nod my head to her as I head for the front door. JD pays well above minimum wage for a server, so what could be causing her to need money? It's a question I plan to come back and ask him later. I'd do it now, but she looks like a scared deer and I don't want to frighten her even more. It wouldn't give me the answers that, for some reason, I desperately crave.

"Sir," she rushes, calling after me, holding all the cash from the table clutched tightly in her fingers.

I stop dead in my tracks, turn and look back at her.

"I can't take this. It's too much." She extends her hand out to me with money in it, minus some in her other hand, which I'm sure only covers what the bill costs for the four of us.

"It's right. Keep it. Don't keep it. But I'm not taking it back." With those stern words, I turn, opening the door and stepping out into the cold, nippy air, heading straight for my sportster. The very one that was going to send me careening to my death four years ago.

Before I pull off, I take one final look back into the diner. She's still standing at the door, a look of awe on her face as she gazes at the money in her hands. Hopefully, it helps her and gets rid of the growing obsessive need in me to find out what's going on with her.

Revving the engine, I back out of the parking spot and pull out onto the road. I need to drive, to feel the wind beating against my face. It's one of the few times I feel like I'm flying and I can hear my wife and daughter talking to me. More like Bianca bitching at me for holding onto the pain of their death and not moving forward with my life. But I can't. I feel like I'd be replacing them and I never intend to do that.

My bike keeps moving forward down the road, all the while I'm consumed with thoughts of the brunette. My fragile little kitten. Hell, I don't even know her name. How can someone consume your every thought so quickly? It's a fatherly instinct. Yeah, that's what it has to be. It's not an attraction. It's not thoughts of her that have my cock growing hard in my pants. It's the vibration of the bike that's doing it.

Yeah, that's what I'm going to keep telling myself.

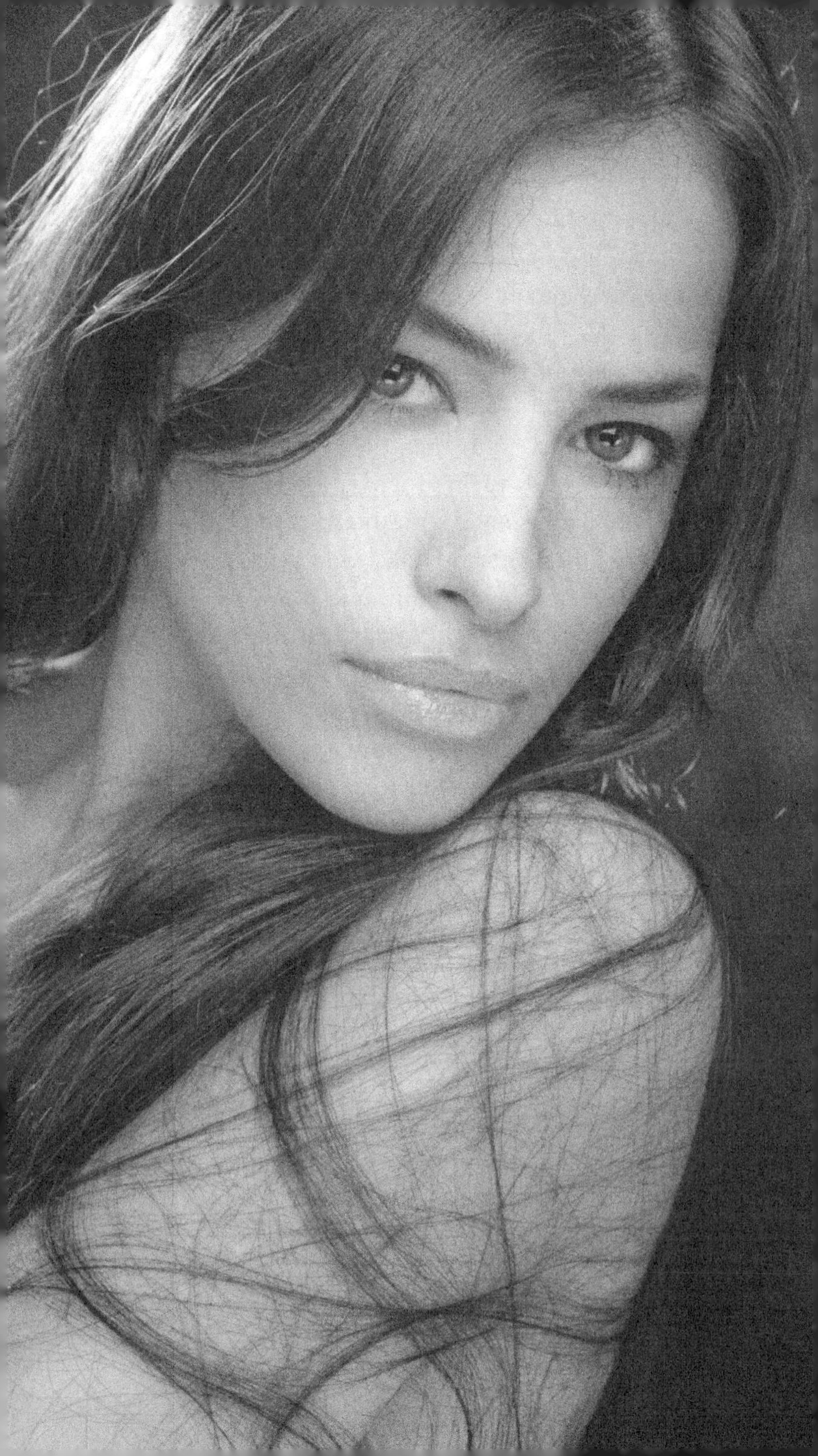

CHAPTER 5

Lucy

It's too much.

Almost a three hundred dollar tip. This can't be right. No one tips like this without wanting something. I'll hold on to it and give it back to them if they come back. My mind made up, I stuff the wad of cash into my back pocket and go back to their booth to clean it up, only to find Henry's already there, clearing it for me. Chewing on my lip, I bite the bullet and decide to ask Henry who they were.

"Henry, can I ask a question?" My nerves are eating me up.

He stops what he's doing, leaning against the table as he crosses his arms over his chest. "Sure thing, Lucy. What is it?"

"Did you see those men that were sitting here?"

"Yeah, the one that was sitting beside the one you were just talking to is Hawke. He's JD's cousin." He lifts his hand, wiping back the crimson strands of hair that have fallen into his face.

Shit.

"So, do they come in here a lot?" It's a stupid question, I know. I've seen them here before, except I've never had to serve them.

He just laughs. "Yeah, ain't you seen them before? I think Snake has the hots for Cindy and he's trying to make her his ol' lady."

"Ol' lady?" What the hell? Why would any woman want to be referred to as that?

"Yeah, it's what they call their women." Whatever facial expression I have on my face has him elaborating more. "It's the equivalent of a girlfriend or wife."

The light bulb goes off and I understand. "Oh. So they'll be back?"

"Yeah. Why, you got the hots for one of them? Be careful, Lucy. You're married and they don't give a shit about that. Plus, they're mixed up in some shit that just ain't above the law."

"No, it's not that. They just left too much money for a tip and I want to give it back."

"Shit girl, if you're giving away money, I'll take it." He uncrosses his arms and turns back to the table, resuming clearing it. One of my customers flags me over and I head their way. I'm so ready for this day to be over.

I go through the motions for the rest of my shift, taking orders, refilling empty drinks, reminding everyone to have a nice day and come back again. But my heart isn't in it. It's barely functioning at this point. The pain in my body has taken over and all I want to do is crash and forget the day. Maybe soak in a hot bath. But that won't happen, especially if he's at home when I get there. Which leads me to my problem. My tips. I need to save some of them, but I don't have anywhere to keep them here. Not that's safe, anyway.

"Girl, what are you still doing here? You got off about twenty minutes ago." Georgie sidles up beside me at the counter, where I'm rolling some silverware to get ahead for the evening rush. I was so caught up in my own thoughts, I didn't see Sutton come in to work.

"Oh, I was just trying to get y'all ahead for the night," I lie to her.

"Well, get on out of here. The night girls have this. Serves them right for not leaving us prepared this morning." Georgie reaches out and takes the silverware from my hand and places it back in the container.

I go to leave, then pause. Turning back to her, I clasp my hand and nervously pick at my cuticles. "Georgie."

"Yeah."

"Can I ask a favor?" She looks back at me, propping her hip against the counter.

"Of course."

Pulling the wad of cash from the bikers, as well as another hundred bucks I made minus what I kept, so I had something to give Scott, I hold it out to her. "Can you keep this money for me? I want to save it, and if I have it, then I won't be able to."

She looks at me with eyebrows furrowed, like she's trying to piece together why I'm asking her to hold my money.

"Of course, honey," she pauses, taking the money from me. "But are you sure that's the only reason you want me to hold on to it for you?"

Can I tell her?

No. She might try to do something to help me and it would only come back on me, or worse, her. Scott is dangerous and cruel. If he did something to someone as sweet as Georgie, I'd hate myself.

"I'm positive. Just wanting to save it." I mentally note I need to write down how much I gave her, and also what I need to give back to those bikers. Before I walk away, though, I ask for one final thing. "Is it okay if I give you some of my tips every day I work, so you can add to it for me?"

"Sure."

"Thank you. I'll see you the day after tomorrow." I rush to the back of the diner, taking my coat off the rack and putting it on. It takes me about forty minutes to walk home, after getting off the bus. I missed the connecting one and couldn't wait for the next one. Not that it matters, I'm already going to be late since I let time get away from me. Scott's already going to be ill as hell when I get there.

The weather's gotten colder since I left this morning, and my jacket barely keeps me warm. In fact, it's failing miserably. I wish I had a better one, but I don't, and I know better than to ask.

Cars pass by, some honking as they go and the occasional cat calls, but I tune it all out. Instead, I use this time to dream of a better life. One where I'm loved and cherished by a man. Funny thing. The man starring in my daydreams is none other than him, the man from the diner.

Fuck, I got it bad.

Fear rises as I get closer to the house. Stopping, I lift my head to the sky and let out a little prayer. Hoping like hell Scott isn't at home. Once I've said it, I continue on, turning onto my block.

Three houses away.

My heart rate increases

Two houses away.

Sweat begins to bead on my forehead.

One house away.

Bile rises in my throat.

Home.

I want to die.

Making my way across the overgrown front lawn, I take the steps slowly. I can hear the television on inside and I know he's here. Just maybe he's passed out and I can make my way to the kitchen, make sure I have some dinner ready for him, and head straight to bed.

It's what I'm hoping to do.

But it's not what happens.

Opening the door and taking my first step inside, I'm yanked to the side by my hair, stumbling to the floor. Pain radiates through my head as I'm dragged across the floor. My hands fly up, grabbing hold of the massive ones that are holding on to my hair and try to pry them loose, to no avail.

"Where the hell have you been? Were you whoring out your fucking cunt to anyone who would take it?" he growls as he finally drops his hold on me.

Tears stream down my face as he kicks me in my stomach, sending me into the fetal position. "I was at work, Scott!" I cry out. "That's it. I didn't realize how late it had gotten until Georgie told me. We were busy today and time got away from me."

He bends down on one knee and reaches out, taking hold of my chin. Turning my face so I have to look him in the face, he spits at me. "You think I'd believe that bitch? She was probably right beside you, selling that shriveled up pussy of hers, too." Then stars erupt behind my eyes as pain radiates across my face and blissful darkness takes over.

My eyes flutter open, unable to focus, but the room is dark and quiet. Eerily quiet. I roll over, getting onto my knees and stop. Waiting for the next blow, but it doesn't come. My body feels like a Mack truck ran over it. Even breathing hurts. It's more like I'm gasping for air than breathing.

But he hasn't done anything yet, which means he's not here, or passed out cold. I'm really hoping for the first. With every move I make, my body screams in protest. I need to get to the bathroom, both to pee and inspect the damage. The way my face feels, I know he must've gotten some punches in there. Standing slowly, I stagger toward it. It's something I've done many times, so I don't need lights. I have the schematics of the house firmly planted in my memory.

With each movement, I feel like I'm going to vomit. Why do I stay? Simple. He'd find me just like last time and I have no money. He sees to that. I don't have to slip my hand into my pocket; I already know all the cash that was there is gone.

Opening the bathroom door, I reach out, letting my hand run along the wall until I find the switch. Turning the lights on, I wince, the brightness causing more pain. Closing them gives me a chance to let the pain calm before attempting to open them again.

I gasp when I see my reflection in the mirror. My hair is in disarray, but what has me wanting to vomit is my face. Blood has crusted around my busted lip and swollen nose. The angry purple bruise covering my cheek will no doubt leave me with a black eye tomorrow.

Fuck me!

What am I going to do? There's no way this is going to fade by the time I have to go back to work.

One more place to check.

Looking down, I take hold of the bottom of my shirt and pull it over my head. My shoulder is in agonizing pain as I do. Once I have it off, I let it fall to the floor as I look down at my stomach. It's an ugly mess of black and blue with a very evident shoe print. Perfect.

Sliding off my sneakers, I undo my pants; I let them slip down my legs and step out of them. I opt to leave my bra on, too tired to try to fight through the pain to remove it. Opening the medicine cabinet, I pull down the container of pain medicine and take out two pills, and swallow them, praying they help just a little.

Picking up my washcloth from this morning, I wet it and clean the blood from my face. Once I've cleaned up as much as I can, I head to the bedroom and climb into bed. One that is thankfully empty. Pulling the blanket over me, I let sleep take over once more. Hoping to have dreams of perfect caring men like in the stories I read, versus monsters like the one I'm married to.

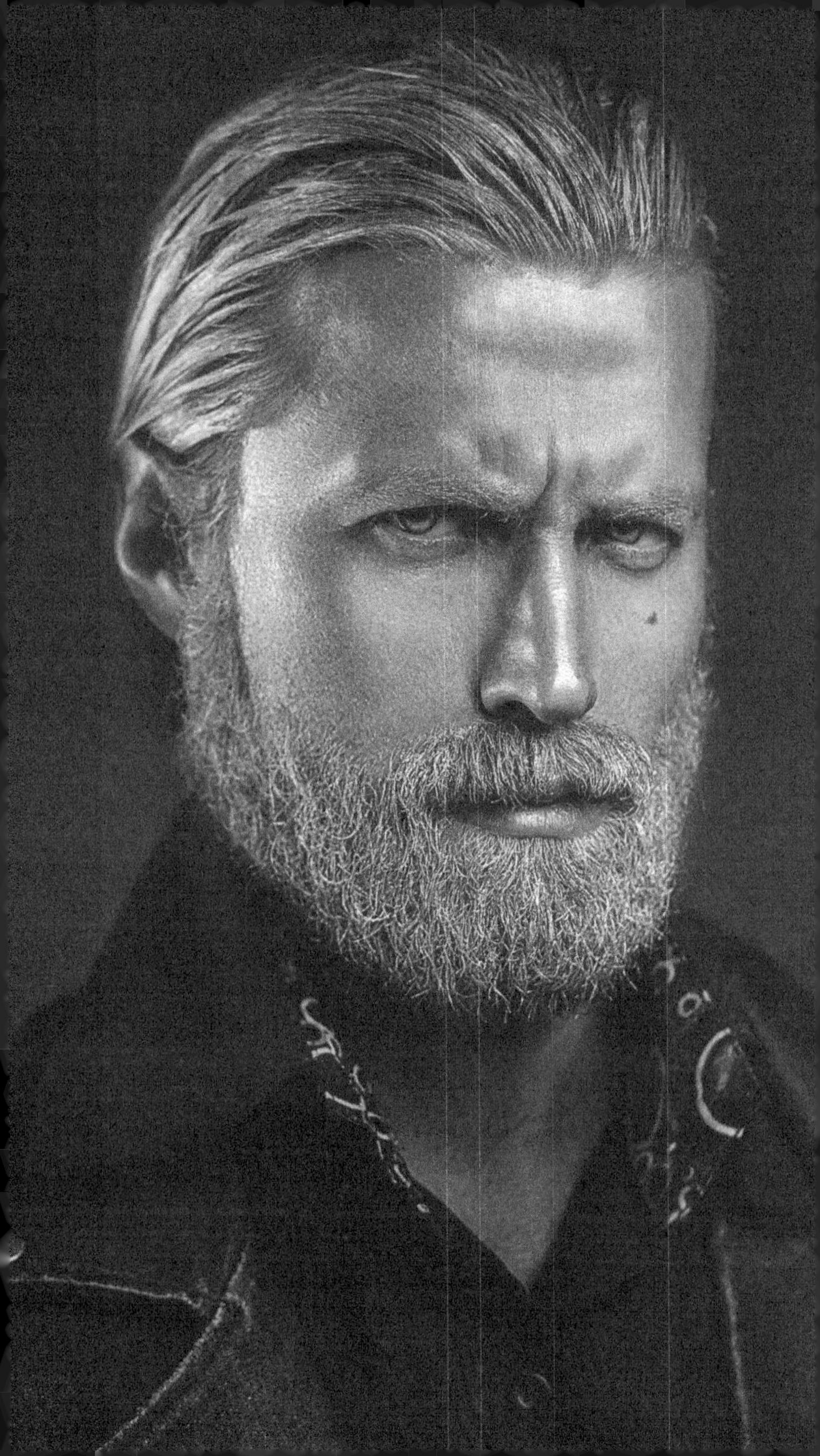

CHAPTER 6

Preacher

It's been two fucking days and I can't get that woman out of my mind. I went back the next day, only for her not to be there. When she still wasn't there the day after that, I got a nagging feeling in my gut. Something's wrong. And I can't get rid of it. It festers inside of me like a sore that just won't heal.

Snake's sitting in front of me, giving me a shit-eating grin. One that I'm ready to remove from his face. Cindy comes back to the table, stepping up beside Snake. She places her hand on his shoulder, and I can't help but see the gentle squeeze she gives it or the way he looks up at her like a lovesick puppy, while she refills his glass.

"Where's the other girl?" I ask gruffly, no longer able to hold it in.

"You mean Lucy?" she asks, a look of shock washing over her face.

"Yeah, the little dark-haired girl that was working the day you were out? Where is she?" And damned if she doesn't wink at me, but she doesn't give me the information I want. She's about to push me past my limit and right now I'm already teetering on the edge.

Why the fuck is this girl, this young ass girl, getting under my damn skin like this?

"Snake, I'd get your girl in line. I asked a fuckin' question and I expect an answer." Taking my fist in my hand, I pop my knuckles. I won't hit a woman, but damn if I wouldn't hit a man, and I got one sitting right in front of me.

Cindy must finally get the picture as she removes her hand off Snake's shoulder and takes a step backward. "I don't know. All I know is Georgie said she called in, that she wasn't feeling good. Really odd, since Lucy's been here for a few months and I know she's come in to work sick before. It must be really bad."

Pushing my plate away from me, I stand from the booth and storm into the kitchen, planning to get to the bottom of this. I need to get this girl out of my mind, because she's consuming my every thought.

Stepping into the kitchen, I catch Georgie and JD in an embrace, their tongues down each other's throat, none the wiser to my intrusion on their moment. Clearing my throat, they quickly jump apart as Georgie furiously tries to smooth down her clothing.

"Hey there, Preach. What are you doing back here?" rushes from her mouth as she picks up a rag and busies herself wiping down a counter. Is she really going to try to play off that I caught the two of them fucking making out? Who the fuck cares? It's not like they've done a very good job of keeping their relationship a secret.

"Where's the young girl that waited on us the day before yesterday?" My temper is flaring under my skin because I have to keep repeating myself to different people.

"Why are you wanting to know about her?" she asks, her eyes draw together in confusion.

"Because I fuckin' do. Now where is she?" What the hell is it with these women today, just thinking they can talk to me any fucking way they please?

"She called in sick." She pauses for a moment, wringing the rag in her hand, before speaking again. "Look Preach, I don't know why you're asking about her, but tread lightly. She's like a scared little puppy. One that's been caged up for far too long and doesn't know how to break free. There's something with that husband of hers, and I think he's the root of her supposed illness today."

"Is he fuckin' hittin' her?" I can feel my temperature rise, my rage boiling, and I know I'm going to need to let it out, preferably on someone.

"I can't prove it. But she's always limping or hurting. She tries to hide it, puts on a brave face, but I still see it. Lucy's a really good girl. I want to help her. I just don't know how without causing her more trouble at home."

"What do you know about the husband?"

"Not much other than he's a real piece of work. I have a sinking feeling he takes all the money she makes, especially after the day you came. She asked if I could hold some of it for her. She gave some lame excuse about wanting to save money. He came here once or twice. He talked sweet while someone was around, but the minute he thought they were alone, I heard how he talked to her."

"What's his name?"

"Scott. Scott Davis." Her voice is soft as she speaks the scum's name.

"Where does she live?"

"2264 Appleberry Lane."

I turn to leave when JD calls out to me. A name very few know and use.

"Noah. Be careful. I think he's mixed up in some bad shit. It could come back to bite Lucy in the ass if you go in guns blazing. I like the kid and I don't want her hurt as some piece of collateral damage."

Turning back to face him, I ask the important question. "What shit is he mixed up in?"

"Word on the street is he works for the Garcia gang."

Drugs. Fucking Drugs.

"Thanks."

Heading back out to the dining area, I head straight for my table, where Snake is still sitting. The only difference is Cindy has slid into the booth with him. I pull out three twenties and drop them on the table.

"I'm out of here, Snake. Got some shit to check on," I tell him before heading out of the diner and straight to my bike.

Scott Davis. Lucy Davis. It's time I find out about these two people. But first I'm going to drive by her house like a fucking stalker. There's no need for me to. I could simply go back to the clubhouse and have Jenner find all the information I need about the two of them, but nope, I'm a creeper. I'm going to drive by her house, hoping to catch a glimpse to satiate my need to know she's okay.

Mounting my bike, I pull out onto the highway, not even looking, as my body pulls me toward Appleberry Lane like a fucking madman. I'm still desperately trying to figure out why I'm drawn to this girl. One, I still don't know how fucking old she is. She's married, so she's gotta be at least eighteen. So it's not like I'm some fucking old man stalking a child.

I fought the urge that day to not let my eyes linger on her too long. She's been there for a few months, yet I never noticed. Was I so in my head I didn't see her? No matter what it was, the way she's hiding her pain has the need to be her savior, her knight in shining armor, taking over.

Fuck me. Why the hell am I letting a girl have this much power over me? Why is she consuming my thoughts when I have other shit to worry about? Like how that fucker thought he could steal from us and who he was more afraid of than us. That's where my attention should be, not on her.

But here I am, driving slowly down her street, stopping two houses down from her, just in the darkness outside the reach of the streetlight. Her house is dark, all but the faint glow barely illuminating the room, coming from the window at the back of the house. I can see the faint shadow of someone moving before it and the light vanishes.

Do I leave?

No.

I sit there.

Waiting.

Watching.

Needing to know more.

An older woman in a nightgown steps out onto her lawn with her small yipping dog, yelling that she's called the cops. Giving her the finger, I rev my engine and take off, still without the answers I craved.

Fuck, this slip of a girl is driving me mad.

I need to get laid, that's what it has to be. My cock is in fucking control of my mind, driving me toward this girl. All I need to do is get a bunny to take care of me.

Instead of heading straight to the fucking clubhouse, I play an enticing game of Russian Roulette. I make round after round driving by Lucy's house, playing with the odds that I could make just one more pass before the cops show up. For all I know, that old geezer was just toying with me, trying to scare me away.

When I finally realize the drive-bys are proving fruitless, I make my way to the clubhouse. Jenner can get me some answers. It's where I should've gone to begin with. When I pull up out front, brothers litter the yard, all with a beer in hand. Some have their arms thrown over their ol' lady, while others are with the club bunnies. All are in the middle of celebrating whatever the night has in store or merely the fact of simply being alive.

I hear my name, but I just throw up a hand and head inside. Hawke is sitting at the bar with his sister, Rizzo. The one girl in the club all of us members know not to touch. She is one hundred percent off limits, even though the vixen has tried to ride the cock of more than one of us. She got lucky once, with a prospect, and we haven't seen him since that night. It was a warning to any other man who thought he could have her.

SINNER'S CHOICE

"Where's Jenner?" I ask Hawke as I step up to the bar beside him. Reaching over the top, I grab a glass and a bottle of tequila, more than intent on drinking the thought of the buxom brunette out of my head.

"He's in the back going through James's computers, seein' if he can find a clue of who he was workin' with. Why?"

"Nothing. Just got something I want him to check into for me." Then I nod my head to Rizzo, wanting to rile Hawke up a little bit. "How you doin', baby?"

She smirks, deciding to play along. "I'm good, baby. Want me to stop by your room later? Work out some of that tension in your shoulders?" She glides her tongue over her bottom lip, as her eyes roam up and down the length of my body, while Hawke fumes beside her. His eyes are bugging out of his head, and I swear I even see steam.

We can't hold it in any longer and we both burst out laughing at his expense. "Dude, you are too fuckin' easy to mess with. She's like my little sister. No offense, Riz baby, but the thought of screwing you makes me sick."

"None taken. The feeling is mutual," she spits right back at me. Hawke is still silent, and I know he's pissed.

"You two are dead to me." He snatches the bottle of liquor that was sitting in front of him and storms off, grabbing a bunny by the hand and pulling her behind him.

"You know one day he's gonna kill both of us," I tell her, sending her into a fit of laughter.

"So whatcha need Jenner to check on? You know, I'm good with computers, too. Hawke just never gives y'all a chance to see my skills. He thinks he can protect me from this world, but what he doesn't realize is I'm already completely submersed just by being his sister."

"There's this couple I want some information on." I tell her.

"What's so special about them?" She tries to pull the real reason I want them looked into out of me.

"Nothing. I just need to know more about them. What the man does? Where they came from?" I pause, taking a deep breath. "That she's safe." I finish, saying the last part softer.

"Preach. Really? A married woman? Isn't there enough pussy running around here that you don't need to go out and get one that's already married? I know you abandoned your faith, but being married once, I at least thought you held that in regard."

"It's not that, Riz. Plus, she's too young for me. I just have a feeling she's not safe."

"What's their names?"

"Scott and Lucy Davis." I grab the bottle, forgoing the glass now, and head off toward my room. I stop after taking a few steps, not even turning around. "Thank you, Rizzo."

I don't wait for a response and I don't take a bunny with me. All I want to do is get drunk and pass out. To drink Lucy Davis out of my mind.

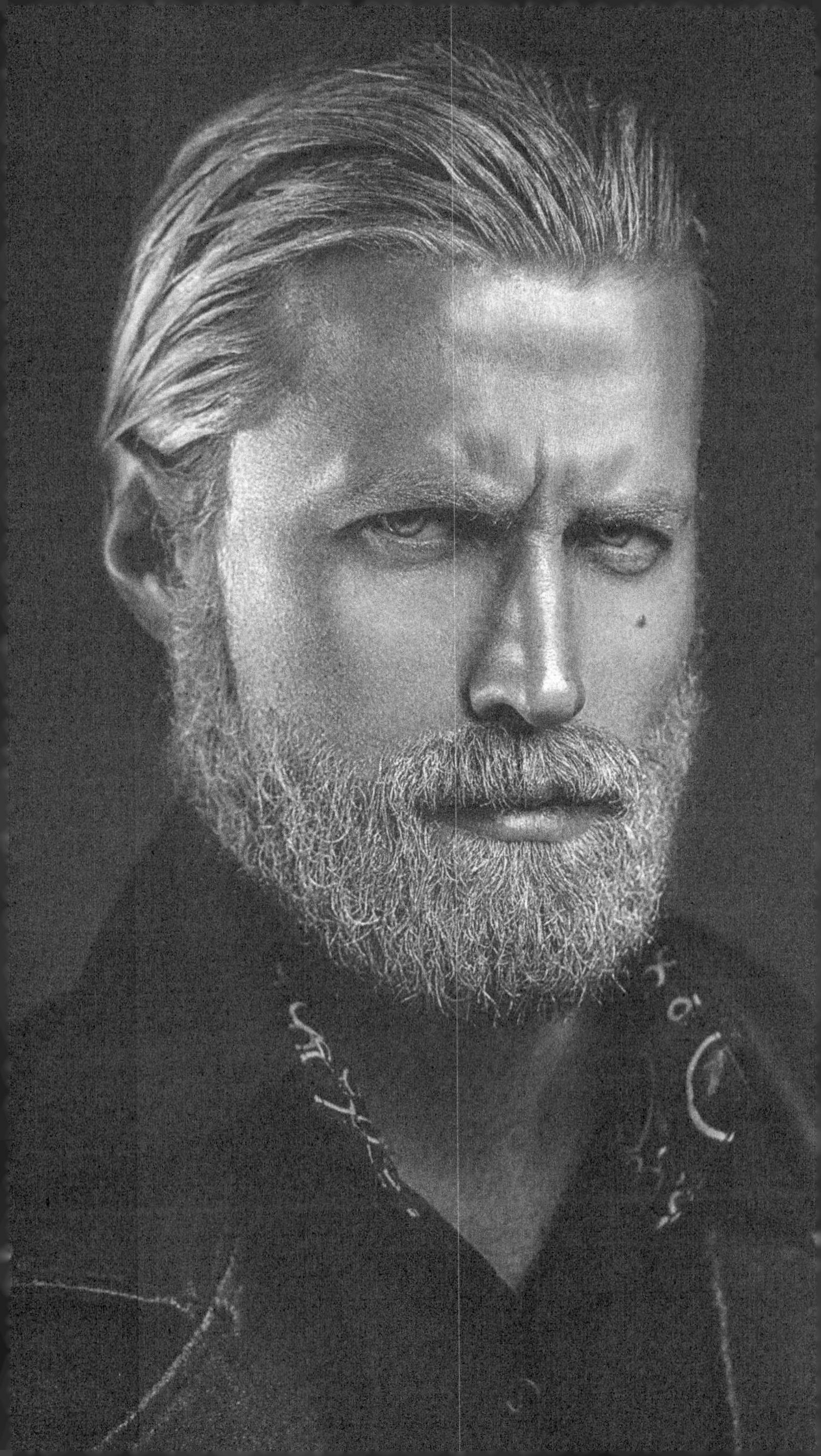

CHAPTER 7

Preacher

She didn't show up today either.

Why am I obsessed? It's like I'm a predator and she's my prey. Stalking her, ready to pounce and claim what's mine.

But she's not mine. She's married. And I don't do attachments. I don't do love or obsession. Not anymore. Not since Bianca and Carmen.

The more I sit here and watch Georgie, Cindy and Sutton bustle around the diner, my blood burns. She should be here. I need to know why she's taken up residence in my mind and firmly evict her from it.

"Georgie!" I call out across the diner, tired of sitting here stewing in my own thoughts.

"Look here, Preacher, you might be something in that club of yours and the boys come running when you bark orders, but I ain't one of them. I'm not scared of you and I'm not one of your fucking club sluts. Now, what the hell do you want?"

"Where. Is. She?" I ask through gritted teeth, enunciating every word.

"She's. Still. Sick!" she barks back at me the same way I did her, before turning and walking away.

Except she doesn't go very far. Instead, she turns around, storms back to my table and slams her hands down on it.

"Look here, Noah Adler." *Fuck, she used my real name.* "There's something going on with her and I'm trying to bring her out of her shell and find out what it is before it's too late. Don't you go barreling after her all caveman like and fuck up what I'm trying to do." With that, she leaves, disappearing into the kitchen.

Not even five minutes later, JD's standing in the doorway, arms crossed over his chest, legs spread wide, glaring at me. Yeah, she told him. I pissed her off somehow.

"Man, what's got you so worked up over this girl?" Sundance, one of the two enforcers under me, leans in and asks.

"I don't know. But she's gotten under my skin and I can't get rid of the itch she's causing. I'm going to head out of here and go back to the clubhouse. See if we've gotten anything off of James' computers." I drop some bills on the table, but Sundance puts his hand on them, sliding them back to me.

"I got it, man." He waves me off as he gazes across the room at Sutton. He's head over heels for that one, but he ain't the only one, and I hate to see how it's going to end.

"Thanks." I head straight for my bike, already knowing I'm going to take the scenic route back to the clubhouse. The one that will take me right by Lucy's house.

Turning onto her street, I slow my speed. My eyes locked on to her place. There's a car in the driveway.

A dark-colored Chevy Camaro. There's music blaring from her house. But no sign of her.

I'm here worried about the girl and she's throwing a fucking party. Guess she isn't too sick. See, this is what I get for listening to my heart and not my brain. She's fine.

Revving the engine, I speed up, racing by her house, catching a glimpse of someone stepping out onto the porch as I do. I know it's a man just by the build and size, so I assume it's her husband. Not wanting to wait to find out anymore, I head straight to the clubhouse. Right now I need to fuck someone up and hopefully whatever is on the hard drive will lead me to someone.

The clubhouse is relatively quiet when I pull up, aside from a couple of patched members and prospects hanging out in the yard. Hank is in the guard shack, along with one of the newer prospects, Alan. Boy's a little green around the edges, but he pays attention and does what he's told. In my book, that's a win.

"Yo, Preach!" is screamed across the yard, causing me to stumble slightly as I turn to see who it is.

"What?!" I call back, lifting my hand above my eyes to cut out the glare from the sun.

Now that the sun's out of my face, I can see Jenner running over to me. He comes to a dead stop in front of me, leaning over, placing his hands on his knees as he catches his breath.

"Damn, man, you that out of shape? You ain't even thirty." I joke, laughing.

"Fuck, you man. It's called I'm hung over as fuck. But if you want to be a dick, I won't let you know what I found on James' computer." He's standing tall now with a shit-eating grin on his face.

"Whatever. What did you find out?"

"Let's go inside to my office." He moves past me, opening the door to the clubhouse, and steps inside. He makes a pit stop at the bar, taking a bottle of whiskey with him. I scoff, to which he quickly responds, "What? Hair of the Dog, man. Best way to rid yourself of a hangover."

He laughs and keeps striding toward the room he calls his office. To me, it's more like a walk-in closet with no windows, and as cold as a walk-in cooler. But he likes it, so what can I say? Not a place I would particularly want to be cooped up in for most of the day.

He waits for me to step inside and shuts the door. Taking a seat in his chair, he opens the bottle and lifts it to his lips, swallow a good bit before setting it down.

"Okay, what do you have for me?" I'm growing weary of the way he's dragging this out.

"Jeez, Preacher Man. What, or should I say, who's crawled up your ass? Wouldn't have anything to do with what you were talking to Rizzo about, would it?" Confusion mars my face at him knowing. How does he know I talked to Rizzo about Lucy? Well, her and her husband, but she caught on quickly. Lucy is the woman who has my interest.

"How—" He cuts me off by laughing, as he nods his head toward the row of four televisions on the wall, all showing different parts of the clubhouse and compound. Then, flicking a button, the screen goes to one picture with the audio.

"Big brother is always watching. There's not a thing goin' on in here I don't know about. Learned it from my buddy in the Memphis Hellions MC, after they had that mole issue. Ain't no way in hell we're gonna have the same issues."

"Fair point and good thinking. Just don't tell me if you got them in the public bathrooms."

"Fuck nah, man. I don't want to see, nor hear what goes on in there. But if anyone asks, I do have cameras there. Wouldn't want anyone havin' that as their new place to plan their takeover of the club." He laughs, causing me to have to work hard to contain mine, needing to maintain my stoic stance.

"Okay, well, what's this news you got for me?"

"So I was lookin' through James' shit and I came across his calendar. Seems every time he skimmed some money off the top, he had a meeting set up for three days later with someone named Sal."

"Okay. And how does that help us?" I'm getting bored with having to drag the information out of him versus him just telling me.

"Well, he has an appointment set up for three days from today, which means today would have been the day he took some money." He stares at me, a huge ass grin on his face reminiscent of the joker.

"And what fuckin' good does that do us? It ain't like we know where this meeting is takin' place."

"Oh, contraire mon frère—" he starts, but I'm at my boiling point with him.

"Look here, asshole, first off you need to stay off those fuckin' movies you watch. No one uses that fuckin' sayin' in real life. Second, you have one more chance to tell me everything without the riddles, otherwise you're goin' to be feelin' the force of my hands on your face before your head hits that wall behind you," I growl out. I'm too fucking old for this shit.

"Fine. Damn, Preach, you suck all the fun out of life. Just so happens, an email came in confirming the drop time and place. I went back and looked and he got one every time, and each time the place changed. Fortunately, the asshole never deleted any of them and I was able to find out how the drops went down and how he spoke. So we're confirmed for it. Hawke has a meetin' planned in the mornin' to go over the plans."

"Well, well, well. Guess this is our lucky day. Keep me posted," I tell him before heading out of his room, in a little better mood than when I entered. Three days and I'll have someone to fuck up. It will be a brief reprieve to pull my thoughts from the brunette who's taken over them.

Stepping into the common area of the clubhouse, I scan the room, taking in the bunnies here. I'm a man on a mission, and I don't stop until my eyes land on Lacey. I need to relieve the tension built up in my body and she'll do. Letting my eyes roam up and down the length of her body, I take in every inch of her. She's about the right build, height and has almost the same curves. Her hair is shorter and not quite the same color brown, but If I close my eyes or dim the lights, I can let my mind envision her. Lucy. Hell, even her name is close enough.

Moving across the room, I make my way to her. She's sitting between two brothers, but fuck them. I want her and she's mine. Rank always takes precedence. Stopping in front of them, I hold out my hand to her.

"Lacey, let's go." She doesn't question me and neither do the brothers. She slips her hand in mine as she stands, showing me even more of her shapely body, barely covered by the crop top and skirt she's wearing. A skirt dangerously close to showing her pussy. One I bet is already wet from whatever they were doing to her.

I practically drag her behind me toward my room. There's no talking needed. No foreplay. I want to fuck her and fuck her hard. Once we're behind my doors, she tries to kiss me, but I quickly shut her down.

"Clothes off and on the bed on all fours. I want that fat ass up in the air, ready for my cock," I order, and she quickly obeys.

I sit in the chair and slip off my boots before standing and undressing. She squirms on the bed in front of me, eager to have me stuffing her greedy little cunt. Gripping my cock, I stroke it up and down. Visions of Lucy fill my mind and I imagine it's her on the bed in front of me and my dick quickly jerks to attention.

"Play with your clit," I command her, happy when she does as I ask.

Opening the drawer at my desk, I pull out a condom. I don't waste time putting it on. Climbing on the bed behind her, I line the head of my cock up with her hole and thrust in. I'm not slow, tender, or giving. I fuck her furiously. She cries out and I can't seem to find it in me to care. I only have one thing on my mind; to fuck this woman from my brain.

It doesn't take long and I'm shooting my load inside the condom, holding onto her hips as my cock jerks. My grip is firm as I ride out my high. Sweat is rolling down my chest as I try to catch my breath. Once my heart rate slows down a little, I pull out, making sure the condom stays firmly in place.

Standing up, I tie the condom and toss it in the trash, then turn around. Lacey now lying on her back, playing with her clit and moaning. "Out," I demand.

"But, baby, I'm not done. Surely you want more." She spreads her legs, thrusting her finger in and out of her pussy.

"I said get the fuck out. Do you really think I give a fuck if you come?"

She looks at me wide-eyed. Shocked by how I'm treating her. If I'm truthful, I haven't ever treated them like this. It's just this shit with Lucy has me all fucked up inside. Lacey thinks she's something, and at one time I would've agreed, but now, I don't. She's merely a poor substitution.

What the hell am I going to do? I cannot be obsessing over a married woman.

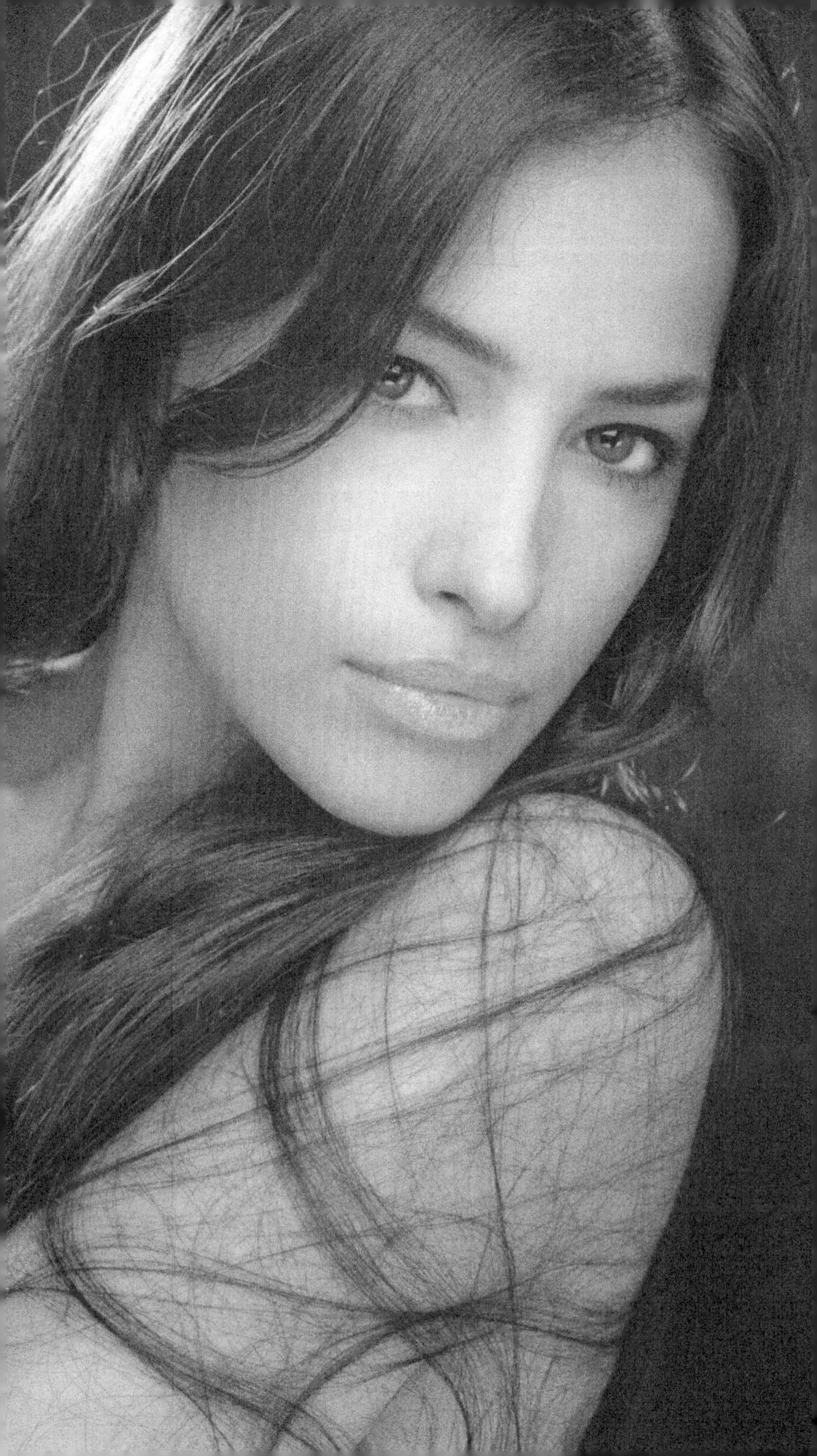

CHAPTER 8

Lucy

"You're taking your lazy ass to work," Scott bellows from the living room.

When I talked to Georgie yesterday, she told me to come in for the lunch rush today instead of my normal early morning shift. I want nothing more than to go to work, but I have no clue how I'm going to hide all my bruises. Shit, I'm barely able to move around without wanting to scream. "Did you hear me, bitch?" His voice raises, the anger clear in his tone. The sound of it instantly makes me shake.

"I heard you," I call back. It comes out with a bit of attitude, not meaning for it to, as I continue to wash the dishes he left piled in the sink from last night. As soon as the words slip across my lips, I know it was a mistake. The slapping of feet on the floor comes storming toward me, just as my head whips back and I stumble into a hard body. *His to be exact.*

"Don't ever fucking talk like that to me again, you fucking cunt bitch. Seems to me like you've forgotten your place."

"No, I'm sorry. Please." I beg. "I know my place."

He lets go of my hair, then shoves me forward. I fall onto my knees, my face barely missing the sink. Pain radiates up my legs into my back, matching what I feel in my head. But I don't cry. I won't give him the pleasure of seeing a single tear fall.

"Finish getting this shit cleaned up and get to work. I ain't driving you, so if you're late and they fire your fat ass, don't think about coming home until you find another job." He turns and leaves the room, but not before making a pit stop at the refrigerator to grab another beer.

His phone rings and he pulls it out of his pocket. When he answers, he immediately starts talking about plans he has with whoever is on the other end. As soon as I know he's gone, I release the breath I had been holding and my muscles relax.

Slowly trying to get up, I wince as a wave of pain hits again. It radiates through my legs when I put any weight on them. I make it about halfway before I collapse to the floor and throw my hands down in frustration.

I can do this! I scoot my body over to the counter and pull myself up, bearing all my weight on my good arm. When I'm finally standing, I take a moment to breathe. Taking a couple of deep breaths, my body slowly adjusts to all the weight I'm putting on my legs. I have to be able to handle it to make it through the day

Okay, now to dress and walk to work. I highly doubt Georgie or JD would fire me, but I don't want to push my luck. I've been out for two days. It doesn't take long to dress. Jeans and a long sleeve shirt with the diner's name written across the chest. Normally I wear a short-sleeve shirt since it gets hot with all the moving around I do, but today I need to hide the bruises. I don't need any more questions asked than normal. The real problem is my face.

Looking at my reflection in the bathroom mirror, I wonder what happened to the happy girl I used to be. I know I lost her in high school as soon as I started dating Scott. You could say Lucy died the day she met Scott Davis.

Looking underneath the counter, I pull out the container that holds my makeup. Normally I don't wear any, preferring the natural look. But when I have to hide traces of my home life, I do. I hurry about applying a heavy coat of concealer, foundation, and anything else I can think of to hide the bruises mottling my skin. I also opt to wear my hair down, trying to hide the marks on my neck.

When I'm fairly confident I have everything hidden, I leave for work. Stepping out of my driveway, I get a prickling sensation down my spine and look around, but see nothing. *No wait, is that a motorcycle at the end of the road? And is the person on it staring in my direction?* No, that's not possible. Shaking it off, I wrap my jacket tighter around me, holding my head down to block the wind from hitting my face.

By the time I make it to the diner, I'm frozen to the core. It's days like today I wish I had a thicker, more insulated jacket. But that costs money, which I don't have.

Georgie's smiling face greets me as I step inside the diner. I give her a quick wave since she's helping a customer, but her scrutiny of me doesn't go unnoticed.

She's definitely going to be cornering me later with a barrage of questions. It's getting harder and harder to lie to her

Moving gingerly, I pull the apron over my head and reach around to tie it in the back, then slip a notepad into my pocket. Taking a deep breath, I plaster a fake smile on my face and head back out to the front, ready to get to work. Hoping like hell I stay busy, so Georgie doesn't get a chance to question me and I don't have to add any lies to the ones I've already told her. Every time I tell her one, it kills me a little more inside.

This person I've been forced to become is not who I envisioned myself to be. But then again, there's nothing I can do about it now. Scott's already threatened me that if I ever left him, it would be in a body bag. I'd never be with anyone else. Ironic, since for him, a wedding ring means nothing and is just a decoration. I know he's cheated on me. The only bright spot in it is that if he's fucking someone else, then his dick is out of me.

But the sight at the counter has me stopping dead in my tracks. What is he doing here? Why is he in my section and not Cindy's? That's where they normally sit. Noah's alone today. And he looks pissed. More so than he normally does. But he's in my section and I need to take his order, even if he does look terrifying. I make my way over, pulling out my notepad, ready to ask what I can get him when he speaks first. Speak is a generous word, more like he growls. "Why are you fucking walking to work when you have a car?"

"How did you know I walked?" My voice shakes as I speak. *Was it him at the end of my street? I know I saw a motorcycle.*

"Don't worry about that. Just answer my damn question," he snaps back.

"Because I don't have a car." I turn to leave the table, tears fighting to escape, and I don't know why. I can handle everything that Scott throws at me, yet this man, talking to me like this, has me wanting to curl in on myself.

"Stop," he bites out. "Aren't you goin' to take my order? I mean, do I need to tell Georgie you are refusing to?"

Fuck me!

This fucking asshole of a man knows I walk to work, which means he must have followed me. And now, after being a dick to me for no reason, invading my personal life, he wants to threaten my job. One I desperately need to survive, no matter how poorly that is.

"What can I get you, sir?" I ask in a sanguine voice. I've always been told to kill them with kindness. It doesn't work on Scott; the asshole just keeps on breathing. I swear he must be part cockroach. He'll be living long after everything else is dead.

"I want to know why whoever has that car in your driveway didn't bring you to work?"

"That's none of your business, and why are you following me?" I ask, scared now. *Is he planning to hurt me?* I've heard rumors about that club, but I choose to treat them as that, rumors. Not believing them.

"Why are you avoiding my questions? You've been sick and yet you walk to work in the freezing cold, with barely more than a sweater on. Seems like someone needs to be following you and asking questions."

"Well, lucky for me, I have a husband. Something you know since you've been stalking me?" I go to turn away again, but he grabs hold of my wrist, causing me to flinch as his hands dig into my skin, sending pain shooting up my arm. I go to jerk away, but it causes my shirt to move up my arm, exposing the bruises.

He lets out a massive growl as he quickly stands, knocking the salt and pepper shaker off the counter. "Who the fuck did this to you?" His eyebrows furrow and he clenches his jaw.

"No one. I'm just clumsy. Please let me go?" I stare at him, my eyes telling him more than they should, but his hold on me lessens and I swear I see a softness come into his eyes. One that tells me that maybe he's been through his own shit. But it doesn't lessen the fact that he's still holding onto me and not to mention the stalking.

"That is not from being clumsy." He lifts his free hand, using it to push the hair away from my face as he inspects me, letting his eyes roam over me. Slowly, he takes in every inch of my face. "Why are you wearing makeup? It's dark. Are you covering something up?" His questions never seem to end. Not only that, my heart and mind push me to answer him, to tell him the truth. *Could he be my savior?* The one to get me away from Scott, so I can run to the other end of the world and hide, finally building a life where I can be happy.

I've always promised myself if I can get away from Scott, then I'll never let another man have control over me again. I'd rather go to my grave alone than be with someone like him again.

"Is it a crime to wear makeup?" I ask, feigning a laugh, needing to get him to stop asking me questions.

"Preacher!" a feminine voice calls out from across the diner. A very familiar voice. *Georgie.*

He looks at her, and immediately releases his hold on my wrist and sits back down. "I'll take a burger and fries. Just tell JD it's for me. He'll know how I want it." I turn and take two steps away before he's calling my name. "Lucy, this isn't over. You're goin' to tell me what happened." It's not even a question. He's telling me how it's going to be. And shit, if I don't want to tell him. What the hell is wrong with me?

The whole time I'm giving JD his order, I can feel him staring a hole into my back. I take a chance and glance over my shoulder, and sure enough, his soulful dark eyes are laser focused on me, scrutinizing my every move. I work hard to make sure every movement is smooth, fighting back every grimace, trying not to show the pain.

Georgie steps up beside me as she pours a cup of coffee, her soft voice fills the space between us. "Are you okay, sweetie? Preacher can be a little overbearing, but he has a good heart buried underneath that gruff exterior.

"Oh, I'm fine," I lie, and I don't have the energy left in me to even wonder if she buys it.

"If he bothers you anymore, let me know." She picks up the cup of coffee, but before she leaves, she looks back at me. "Lucy, both me and JD are here for you when you're ready to talk. I know you missing had nothing to do with being sick, but more about the fact of why you look like you do today. But the thing is, it's not just today. So when you're ready, my door is open. We can help you."

She doesn't say another word, just leaves, and I can hear her jovial voice as she speaks with the patrons of the diner on the way to the table she's delivering the coffee to. My heart bursts with love, but I can't and I won't risk Scott doing something to her for helping me.

I finish filling the glass with tea and take it to Preacher. "You didn't say what you wanted to drink, so I took a guess."

"Thank you."

I don't stay to give him time to question me, instead, I make my rounds, checking on all my tables while his food cooks. But his eyes are always watching me.

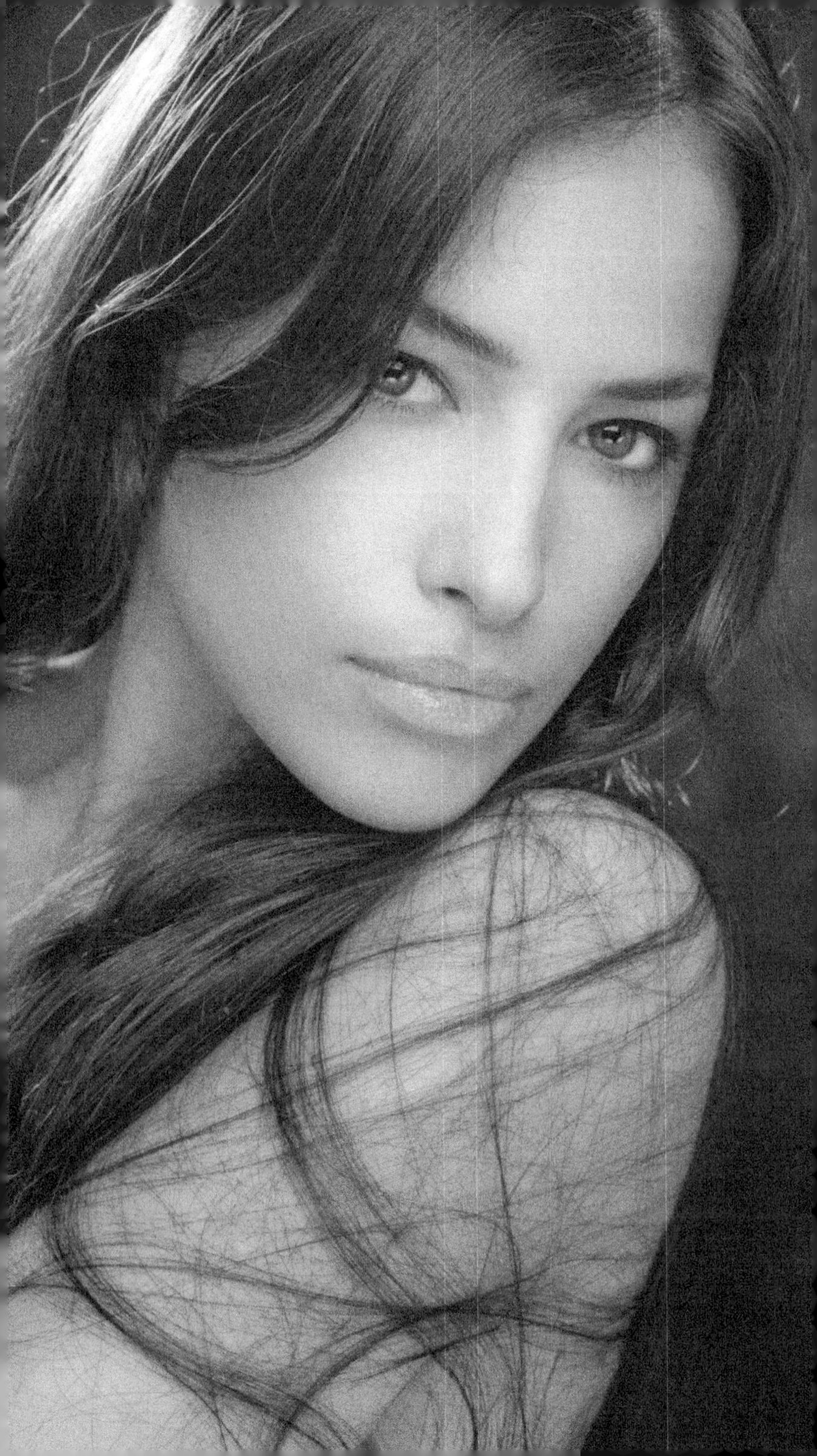

CHAPTER 9

LUCY

"So, are you ready to tell me what happened?" At least this time, he's not asking like a crazed lunatic.

"I have. You just don't want to listen to what I said," I tell him as I place his food in front of him. Picking up his glass, I head back over and refill it, then set it down in front of him.

He's still staring at me like he's some kind of telepath or something, and he can read my mind if he focuses hard enough. His eyes unnerve me, not in a bad way, but more 'I'm ready to shed my clothes and fuck you'.

"Preacher, is it? Honestly, I think that's a weird name."

"It's my road name. Not many know or have the privilege of knowing my real name," he butts in, his voice lacking any warmth.

"That's all well and good. I wasn't asking for it. It's none of my business. Just like my personal life isn't any of yours. It's evident you have some kind of issue with me, so maybe next time, you go back to sitting in Cindy's section." With that, I turn and leave, not letting him know how much he affects me. That there's something about him that makes me want to spill my guts and beg him to save me. Because I know if I don't get away from Scott, one day soon, one of his beatings *will* kill me.

"Lucy!" his gruff voice calls after me. I pause for a moment before continuing toward the bathroom. I shouldn't be in here, especially when I have customers, but I needed a moment of peace. Away from him and those eyes that have my stomach turning in knots.

There's a knock at the door and I quickly wipe away the tears that have started to fall without me noticing. Turning on the water, I wash my hands.

"Just a minute," I call out to whoever is on the other side.

"Lucy, are you okay?" Georgie asks from the other side of the door.

"Yeah, I'll be right out."

"Are you positive? If Preacher is bothering you, I'll kick his ass." Her voice is soft but firm. I think this woman would move mountains if I asked her to.

"No, it's okay. I can handle him," I tell her as I step out of the bathroom, then turn and walk away, mumbling under my breath, "I've handled worse." She doesn't hear, not unless she has super hearing.

When I go back out, he's still sitting there, but I keep walking past him. He has his food, and his glass is full. That's all he's getting from me. After checking on my other guests, I total up his check. My plan is only to drop it in front of him and keep going. I make my rounds quickly, making small talk with my regulars and smiling with warmth to those I'm not familiar with, always chasing a bigger tip. I've got two days' worth of money to make up for, plus still trying to stash some with Georgie. It may cause another beating, but it'll be worth it in the long run.

For the last two days, I did nothing but think. Trying to figure out how far away from here would I need to go before Scott would give up looking for me.

Taking a deep breath, I rip his check from the pad and walk his way. With each step, my feet feel like lead, as if the ground beneath me is quicksand, pulling me down. Even breathing becomes hard, almost as if my brain has forgotten how to tell my body to do it.

How can this man, who's acted like a dick every time I've seen him, have this effect on me? Scott should be my warning to stay away from men, especially those who act like him and this Preacher. The only good thing the motorcycle god has going for him is he hasn't hit me. Instead, he seems concerned about what has happened to me. Maybe he has a heart. *Maybe?* But I still can't let anyone know what truly happens at home.

He looks up at me, his eyes going straight to my soul. "Here's your check. Will you be needing anything else?"

Laying the check down on the counter, I wait for a moment, giving him the chance to say something. He opens his mouth, but quickly clamps his lips shut. Whatever he was going to say a flittering thought, already not worth the breath.

"Thank you, Lucy. Can I get some more tea, please?" His voice is calm, soothing, not an ounce of venom present, and I almost gasp. This is the first time he's ever talked to me like a normal human being.

"No problem, Preacher." I give him his name right back. Well, the name I know.

He smiles, a genuine smile, flashing all of his beautiful pearly white teeth.

Nodding my head, I pick up his glass and take it with me, straight to the beverage station. His ice has melted, so I add some more, then pick up the pitcher of tea and fill his glass. Glancing over my shoulder, I peek back in his direction, only to come face to face with him staring right at me. I quickly turn around, my face burning at being caught.

I inhale deeply, then blow it out. Trying to calm my nerves before I head back over to him. Once I've gotten myself under control, I pick up the glass and head his way, setting the tea in front of him. "Here you go, Preacher."

"Noah. My name is Noah. I want to apologize for coming across the way I did. It's just seeing you hurt, has me wanting to make sure you're okay."

"Oh! Okay." I feel like an idiot. He's apologizing and exposing himself to me and I just say okay.

"Well, I'll be seeing you, Lucy. And I promise to sit in Cindy's section." He goes to stand, picking up the bill, and looking at it before reaching into his back pocket and pulling out his wallet.

"Noah, it's okay. If this is the person you'll be when you come in, then you can sit in my section. If the asshole returns, then sit in Cindy's section." I turn and rush off quickly, not waiting to hear his reply. His laughter rings out, filling the diner, but I don't look back.

When I hear the jingle of the bell on the door, then the subsequent rev of an engine, I turn around and look. He's gone and oddly, I miss him. What the hell is wrong with me? Heading back over to where he sat, I pick up his plate and glass, placing them in the basin behind the counter.

Picking up his check, I see a wad of cash, more than what the bill cost. I count the bills until I get the amount for the check and slide the remaining money into my pocket. Again, he paid well above the bill, but this time it makes me happy. More to add to my stash to help me run from Scott. To be able to have a life where I can be happy and live. No longer fearing if the next beating he gives me will be the one that finally ends my life.

"I think he likes you," Georgie's voice comes out of nowhere. I didn't even notice she had sidled up next to me.

"No, I think they just like to tip big," I tell her, then reach into my pocket and pull out the money. Best to give it to her now, so I don't make a mistake and forget. "Here, can you add this to the rest that you're holding for me?"

She takes it from my hand, then slips it inside her bra. "Sure thing, darlin'. But one day you'll tell me the real reason I'm holding this money for you and not the bullshit story you gave me."

I give her a tight smile and scurry off toward the table that was just vacated. If she finds out the truth, Scott would hurt her if he found out. It's best she knows as little as possible.

The rest of my shift is filled with thoughts of Noah. Oddly, they make me happy.

"Nice to see your ass is home on time tonight. Now get in there and cook me something to eat," Scott's gruff voice barks out from where he sits in the recliner in front of the television, beer bottle in his hand.

"Okay, Scott." I hang my coat up on the rack and scurry toward the kitchen.

"Stop right there, bitch. Don't you have something to give me?" I knew it was coming, just wasn't expecting him to want it as soon as I stepped in the front door.

Reaching into my pocket, I pull out the wad of twenties, fives, and ones and hand it over to him. I kept back forty, hoping to ride the bus home for a couple of days this week and get some personal things I need.

He lifts his eyes from the money in his hands and glares at me. "Is this it?"

"Yes, Scott." My voice cracks, already fearing the hit that's about to come.

"Not a whole lot here, is there? I don't think you're making enough money at this job. I got you an interview at the House of Puss tomorrow. When you get done at the diner, head straight there if you know what's good for you."

House of Puss, that's a strip bar. A seedy one at that. "You want me to strip?"

He doubles over in laughter. "Are you fucking stupid? Who wants to see your fat ass dance? I barely can stand having sex with you. That's why we hardly do it and when we do, the lights are out."

"But why can't I just get a job at the grocery store or pick up more shifts at the diner? Please don't make me work in a strip club," I beg him.

He lowers the footrest of the recliner, and before I can blink, he's up and across the room, standing in my face. "You'll do it because I fucking told you to. For some fucking reason, Cal likes how you look and wants you there."

"Who's Cal?" My voice trembles as I ask.

"That's none of your fucking business. You're to be there tomorrow by three pm and ask for Cal. Now I'm going out to find me a real woman to fuck." He shoves me backward, causing me to fall to the floor, my injured arm taking the impact as I hold back a scream.

I want so badly to just end this hell of a life I'm in. It would be so simple. Some pills, then climbing into a tub of water and slicing a knife across my wrist. I'd slip away into the darkness, free from the hell I'm living in. No one would miss me.

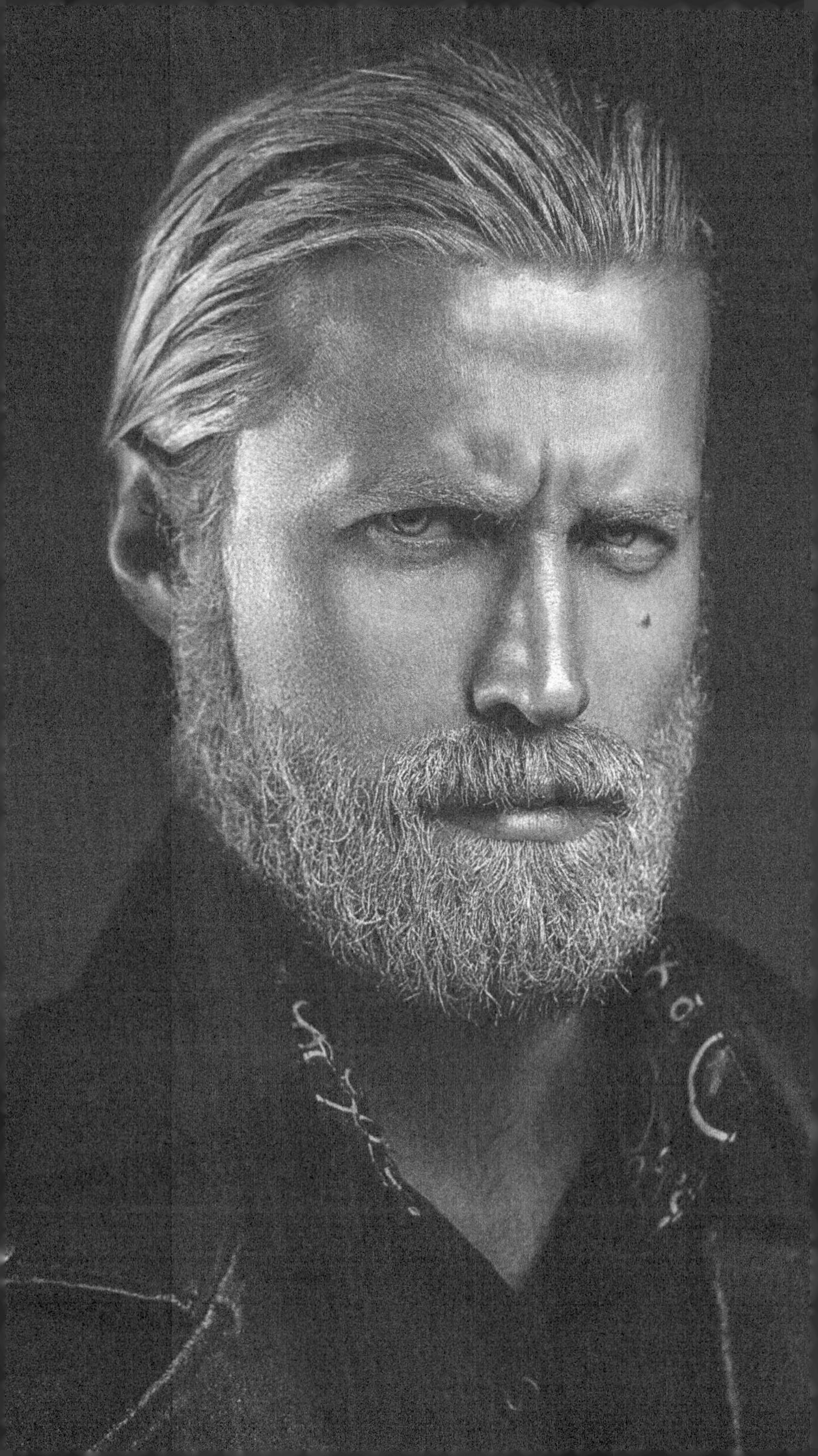

CHAPTER 10

Preacher

I drag myself into Hawke's office at the ass crack of dawn. He called a meeting at this godforsaken hour because he wants to have it before he heads out. He and Rizzo are mysteriously leaving for a few days. It's been happening more often lately and I'm beginning to suspect something is up. I just need to find the right time to ask.

All night I dreamed of the brunette holding my attention. I think I broke past the first barrier of the bubble she has firmly around her. At least if I bite my tongue and don't push, I can sit in her section. It's baby steps, but I'll take them to find out what's going on with her, get her out of my system, and move on with my life without her.

I thought I'd be the first in the room, other than Hawke, of course, but I was the last. What the hell kind of alternate world am I in right now? Hawke's seated behind his desk with Jenner sitting at his side, his laptop positioned on the edge of the desk. Cyrus, Gunner, and Snake are all standing, backs against the wall as we wait to hear Hawke's plan.

"Now that his highness has graced us with his presence, we can get on with this shit. I've got stuff to do, and I need to get out of here. Now we know from what Jenner pulled from James' hard drives, two days from today he would've been makin' a drop to someone. So, this is our chance to find out who. I don't suspect that it'll be the ones in charge, rather just another flunky. But it's the best lead we got at the moment."

"So, how we handlin' it, Prez?" Snake's deep voice asks, as he sits down in the free chair.

"We're goin' in. Just a small team, one or two max, the rest will wait outside. Jenner's gonna wire us, so we can keep in contact. Once we spot our mark, we grab him and take him back to the warehouse. Preacher, it's up to you, once he's there, to get all the information you can. Do we all understand?" He looks around at each of us, as we all nod in understanding. "Good. I need to get out of here, but I expect a full report, Gunner."

"Do we know what the mark looks like?" I ask the magic question no one has seemed to. How do we track someone if we don't have a clue who they are or what they look like?

"Was wonderin' when someone was going to ask that?" Hawke gives a stern look at the others, especially Gunner.

"I got that answer. Apparently, the person sits in the same booth every time. Now, as far as the sex, from the way the person is talking, I'd deduce it's a man. So we have the time, the place, and the exact spot. Should be a breeze." Jenner sits back in his chair, crossing his arms over his chest as he gives us all a smug ass look.

"Okay, seems we got it all handled. Keep me updated and get out of here. Me and Rizzo need to hit the road." Hawke doesn't even blink an eye as he dismisses us.

I hang back, allowing the others to leave before pushing off the wall I was leaning against. Hawke is closing up the laptop on his desk and putting things away into the drawer as I step up toward him.

"I said y'all could go," he barks, his jaw clenched and brows furrowed.

"I know ya did. But I want to know what's goin' on?"

"It's nothin'." He keeps his head down as he continues to clear his desk. *Something is fucking wrong!*

"The others might buy that bullshit line you're giving, but I'm not. Now spill."

He drops down in the chair, raking his hands through his hair. It's then I see it. The worry lines etched on his forehead. The bags under his eyes. The tenseness in his body, more so than normal.

"I promise I'll talk to you. Just let me get through this trip. I'll know more once it's done, and depending on the outcome, I'll come to you for your particular brand of guidance." His answer is vague, but tells me enough about who it may revolve around and it can't be good if it involves who I think.

I take a wild guess when I ask, "Is it Rizzo?" He just nods.

Fuck!

"Let me know, man, and I'm here day or night. As soon as you know whatever it is, call me."

"I will." He stands and moves around the desk, stopping only long enough to place his hand on my shoulder. "Thank you, brother." Then he heads out of the room, leaving me standing there to process what I was just hit with.

As I leave the room, shutting and locking the door behind me, my heart is heavy. Not only am I worried about what's happening with Lucy, but now I have this on top of all the whole club shit.

There's nothing I can do about the last two at the moment, but I can go and check on Lucy today. Just being able to see her will help ease some of the weight that's on my shoulders.

I bypass the brothers and head outside. I don't know her schedule, but it's seven am now, so if she's not there, I can check with JD about when she works again. Stepping outside into the brisk morning, I head straight for my bike and make my way out of the parking lot. There's only one place I want to be right now.

Taking the long route which takes me by her house, I slow down as I get near it. The car I saw the last time is in the driveway and the house is dark and quiet. So either she's safe and warm in bed or she's at work. It had better not be anything else other than those two options.

I speed up, taking the route she would to get to work. It's not even a quarter of a mile down the road when I see a figure walking in the distance. I don't even have to see their face. I know who it is.

She's walking with her head down, and she has something over her head, but her long brunette hair is blowing in the wind. Fuckin' christ. It looks like she has that shitty coat on again. I speed up even faster, pulling up beside her, and she still hasn't looked up to see who's beside her. *Is she fucking crazy?*

"Lucy!" I holler over the rumble of my bike.

She jerks her head to the right, shock on her face as she looks at me. "Noah?" She seems confused about seeing me.

"What the hell are you doin'?" I start, but quickly get control of myself. "It's freezing, Lucy. You'll catch pneumonia out here in what you're wearing. Why didn't your husband drive you to work?"

She just looks everywhere but at me and I know she's getting ready to tell me some bullshit lie.

"He... he was asleep," she stammers.

"Why didn't you wake him? You shouldn't be walkin' in this weather."

"I'm fine. He... umm... he worked late, and I didn't want to wake him. I'll be fine." She pulls the coat tighter around her, her hands shivering as she does, not even any gloves covering them.

I stop my bike, then hold my hand out to her. "Climb on behind me, and I'll take you. It'll get you there quicker, and then you can sit and have some coffee with me while you warm up." She hesitates at first, turning her head, looking up and down the road, almost like she's checking to see if she's being watched. Just when I'm about to ask again, she reaches out and takes my hand. It takes her a minute, but she climbs on behind me. Reaching up, I take off my helmet and hand it back to her. "Put this on."

She does as I ask, not giving me any pushback. "I've never ridden on a bike," she says softly, but just loud enough that I can hear.

"You'll be safe with me. Just wrap your arms around my waist and hold on tight. If you need to tell me something, then tap me twice with your right hand. If you need me to stop, tap once with your left hand. Lean with me when we turn. Got it?"

"Yes." Her warm breath skirts across my neck, sending shivers up my spine and causing my cock to twitch.

I rev the engine and pull off slowly, not wanting to scare her. But all I can think about is how close her hands are to my cock and how good it feels having her body against mine. Picking up speed, we move down the road, and I release one of the handlebars and place my hand over hers. I leave it there until I need to turn.

The ride is over before I know it as we pull up into the parking lot of the diner. Once I've parked and turned off the bike, she releases her hold on me, and I miss it. Shit, what's happening to me? She climbs off from behind me, swaying slightly once she has both legs on the ground. "You okay?"

"Yeah, my legs are still vibrating, and they feel like jelly. I can only imagine what yours must feel like after riding." She laughs, a rich, happy laugh that warms my heart. It reminds me of how Bianca used to laugh after one of our rides.

"Guess I'm just used to it." I can't help but smile at her. She's gorgeous, but too young for me and, most of all, she's married. She'll never be more than an image to jack off to. "You owe me coffee," I remind her as I reach out and take my helmet from her, then get off the bike.

It takes everything in me, not to take her hand, or put my hand around her waist, and lead her inside of the diner. Instead, I walk behind her, forcing my eyes to look forward and not down at her ass, or focus on the way her hips sway with each step she takes.

But my dick takes control, and my eyes slip down the length of her body.

Fuck me! All I can think of now is my hands gripping her hips as I bend her over and fuck her from behind, thrusting my cock in and out of her tight, wet pussy.

She clears her throat, pulling me out of my head. Shit, I got so lost in my damn daydreams I didn't open the fucking door for her. She's standing there, holding it open for me instead. "Thank you, darlin'."

"You're welcome. I'm just going to take my stuff to the back," she says quickly before taking off. I'll give her a couple of minutes, but if she isn't back, then I'm going back there and dragging her ass back to me.

Looking around, I see a booth in the back corner vacant, and far enough away from everyone that we can have a private conversation. I head that way, setting my helmet on the seat as I slide in, making sure I'm facing the front door and the counter so that I can see everything taking place. It's a lesson I learned the hard way not long after becoming a prospect for the MC.

I keep glancing at the clock, watching the seconds tick by, until another minute passes, and I get antsy. She's trying to ride out the time until she has to clock in for work. I know it, but it ain't happening today. Just as I go to stand up, I see her step out of the back and head straight to the counter. Lowering back in the seat, I watch, waiting to see what she's going to do.

She has her back to me, so I can't see everything, but I can see her pick up two coffee mugs from the rack. *Good girl!* Damn, my cock twitches at her obedience. No, no, I don't want to sport a boner in here, not with people around and not in front of her.

A moment later she turns, her hair fanning out as she does, and heads my way. Lucy smiles sweetly once she steps up to the booth and sets a mug down in front of me. "I didn't know what you like in it, so I brought a little of everything." It's not until she's reaching into the pocket of her apron do I notice she's wearing it. She puts a variety of creamers on the table in front of me, along with sugar packets.

"Normally take it black, if nothing's around. But since you took the time to bring me all these fancy flavored creamers, I guess I'll try one of them out." Lucy stands there nervously, shifting back and forth slightly as she holds her cup of coffee still. "Sit, let's talk."

She glances back over her shoulder to where Georgie and JD are standing before looking back at me and sliding into the booth. Setting her cup on the table, she looks down, trying to avoid eye contact. It's cute, but it won't fly. Not today. I need to get some answers, even if it's only one. I need something to keep me from going insane.

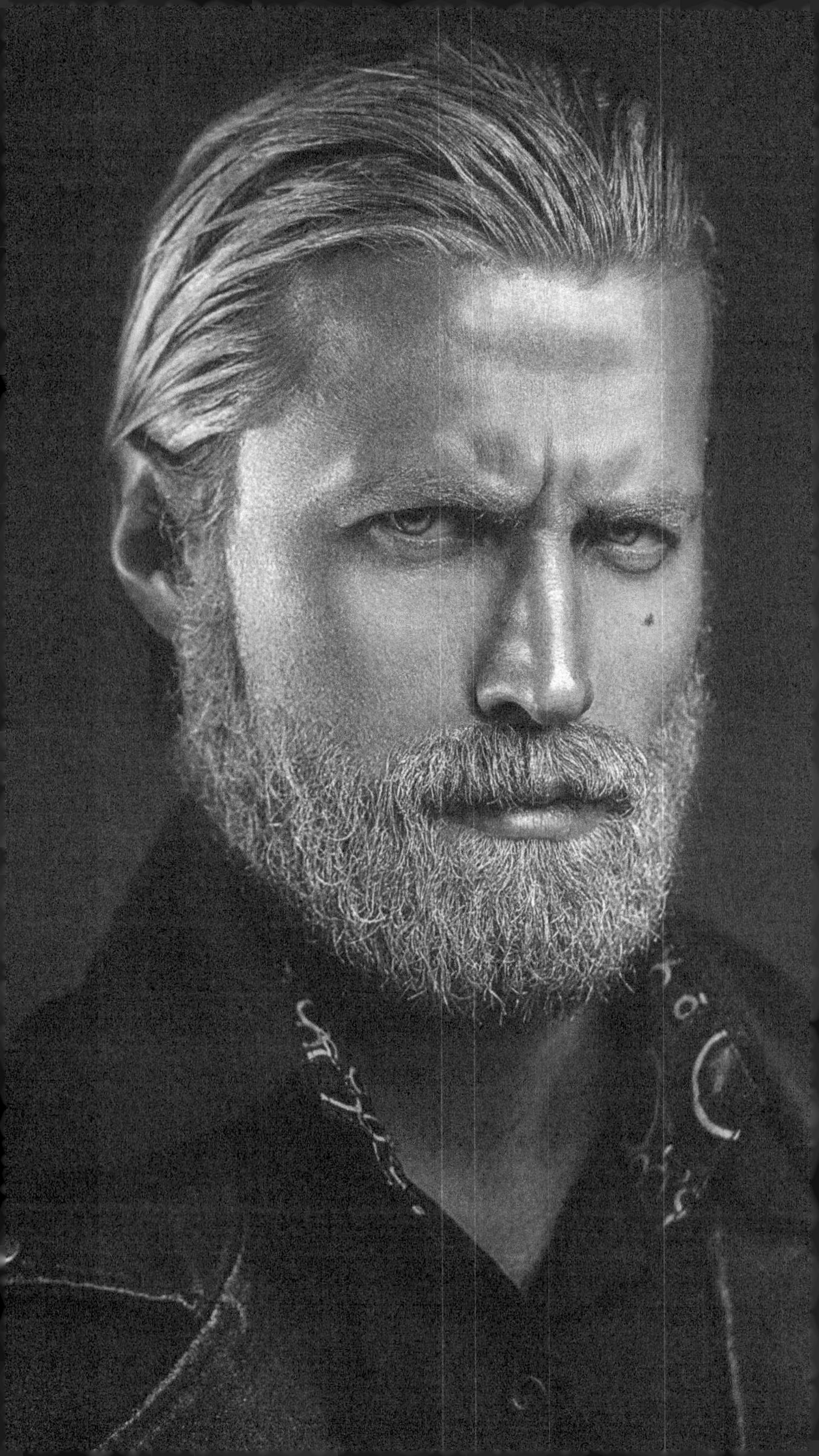

CHAPTER 11

Preacher

"So, are you sticking with the story about why you were walking to work this morning?" I try to keep my voice calm and free of harshness and anger. I'm not sure if I succeeded, but I sure as hell hope I did.

"I am." She keeps her head down, not looking up at me. Her voice is soft and void of emotion. It's a voice I remember well. It reminds me of my own five years ago. Except, I had anger in mine. It's then, at that moment, in that memory of myself, that I begin to wonder if she's headed down the same path. Is she having the same hopeless thoughts I was? My gut clenches in agony, and I know I need to be here for her. Be her savior if nothing else, like Hawke and the MC were for me.

"You don't think I know that's bullshit? I won't press you on it, though, but I need to know if you always walk to work this early." I tap my fingertips on the table, making my own little beat as I wait for her answer.

She lets the tips of her fingers glide around the rim of her mug before she lifts the cup to her lips, taking a small sip of the hot liquid.

Setting it down, she lifts her eyes, barely looking at me, and nods her head.

"What—" I stop and clear my throat, trying to control my temper and keep my tone calm. "What days?"

"Umm, the days I work the morning shift. I'm going to be asking for more days. I need more hours, so I'm not sure," she replies timidly.

More days. What the fuck is she having to work so hard for if she has a damn husband? How can he even be okay with his beautiful young wife walking to work? Not only in the early hours of the morning, nor the distance she walks, but that she barely has on what could be classified as a coat when she's doing it.

"Okay, let's start off easy, then. Do you work tomorrow mornin'?"

She takes another sip of her coffee before answering. "Yes. I got to be here at seven."

"Okay then, what time will you be leavin' for work?"

"To get here on time, around five." She looks everywhere but at me. I can tell she's nervous the way she's fidgeting in her seat. My questions are making her uncomfortable and as much as I hate it, I still need to ask them.

"No, you won't be, not tomorrow. Leave your house at six. Meet me at the corner. I'll pick you up there, so your husband doesn't get suspicious. Then we'll meet here and have coffee again and talk about the next day you work. Do you understand?"

"Yes." That one word means everything. It's giving me more time with her, and a chance to get closer, to help her.

"Where were you born, Lucy?"

She looks at me with confusion. My question is so out of left field, she wasn't expecting it. But she laughs and answers.

"Here actually. Well, the next town over. My husband and I moved here after we got married. So, I've been in this town for four years."

Okay, so she's newer here than me. We sit in silence for a few more minutes before I blurt out another question at her.

"How old are you?"

"Twenty-one."

She's legal, that's good. At least I'm not going crazy over a kid. But still, there's a fourteen-year age difference.

"When's your birthday?" I ask her, then take a sip of coffee.

"January twentieth."

At her words, my jaw drops. No, this can't be. No. A chill runs down my spine and I need to get out of here. Standing up in a hurry, I knock the table, causing the coffee in my mug to spill, since I've barely drunk anything.

"Sorry, I got to go, Lucy. I'll see you in the morning, at the corner of your street at six." I rush out of the diner, straight to my bike and climb on, then speed out of the parking lot.

No. This cannot be. It's like everything is crashing in on me at this moment and Hawke isn't here to help me control what I'm feeling.

💀 💀 💀

Lucy

I've been wracking my brain all day trying to figure out what made Noah run out of here like he did. But I can't come up with anything other than it had something to do with my birthday. I'm still nervous and unsure about tomorrow morning. I didn't know what to say when he said he was taking me to work. I know if I had said no, he would still be there, waiting for me. But it beats walking in the cold. He was right about that.

The minutes ticked away, and it's almost time for the end of my shift and I'm dreading it. I know where I have to go after this, and it's killing me. I finish up with my last customer, making sure they have everything they need. They'll probably still be here after I leave, but Georgie will be sure to give me their tip tomorrow. I made decent money today, but not enough to skim any off the top.

Taking in a deep breath and blowing it out, I head over to Georgie. "Hey, I'm all done except for the couple at table four. They're just finishing up their dessert and having some coffee, and I already topped them off."

"Sure thing, Lucy. You heading out?"

"Yeah. Scotty's expecting me." She looks at me with sadness. I know she has a suspicion and I've done one hell of a job at avoiding her questions, but I won't be able to forever.

"Okay, want me to put their tip with the other money I'm holding for you?"

"Please." I turn to leave, then look back. "I'll see you tomorrow."

Heading to the back, I take off my apron and remove my jacket from the hook, and put the apron in its place. I've got thirty minutes to make it across town and as much as I hate it, I'm going to have to get a cab. Making my way across the room to where the phone hangs on the wall, I take it off the hook and dial one of the few numbers I have memorized. I have a cell, but Scott will only give me a prepaid one, and it's by minutes. So, I make sure to keep them available to receive his calls. Otherwise, he'll be pissed if he can't reach me.

Once I tell them where I am and where I'm going, I slip into my coat and head to the front door to wait. The dispatcher said it should only be a few minutes and I don't want to miss it.

I keep my focus out the door, only taking casual glances over my shoulder, and I see Georgie and JD huddled together, whispering. I know it's about me.

Five minutes later, I see the yellow cab pull up in front of the diner and I rush out to it. Opening the back door, I climb inside as the driver repeats back the address to me of where we're going for confirmation. Once I agree, he takes off. Thankfully, he isn't one that needs to fill the time with idle chit-chat. Instead, we make it to our destination with the radio filling the silence between the two of us, playing the local country station.

When we pull up in front of the House of Puss, he clears his throat and looks back at me. He's an older man, probably in his sixties, doing this for extra money.

"Are you sure this is where you want to go, sweetheart? You look like a good girl, one who shouldn't be here."

I pull out the cash from my pocket to cover the cost of the fare as well as a tip and hand it to him. He takes it, still looking at me with concern in his eyes. Reaching out, I take hold of the handle and open the door. Before sliding out, I look up at him, my eyes already beginning to water.

"Unfortunately, it is. Thank you for the ride, sir." Exiting quickly, I shut the door behind me and make my way the short distance across the parking lot to the entrance.

Reaching up, I smooth my hair down, trying to look a little presentable. I've got to make a good impression on this Cal, because if I don't get this job, then I know I'm in for another beating when I get home. Because I'm sure Scott will know it before I step in the door.

It's just an average-looking building, except the windows on the front are blacked out, so no one can see in. There's a sign on the door that everyone entering must be over eighteen and have a valid picture ID. The sign on the building was as vulgar as it could be without being banned. A woman in a bikini that barely covers her breasts with House of Puss in bright neon letters.

The number of cars in the parking lot only amplifies my anxiety. Reaching out with shaking hands, I grasp the handle and pull open the door. The sound of heavy bass and laughter, along with smoke and sweat, assault my senses. I'm shocked that there's anyone here at this time of day. I thought for sure the building would be empty.

A large, bald, muscular man, with a form-fitting black tee, stops me. I had to take a second look because he reminded me a little of Dwayne Johnson.

"What can I do for you, babe?" The way his eyes are slowly trailing down the length of my body as his tongue slides along his bottom lip has me queasy.

"I'm here to see Cal." My voice trembles in his presence as nerves and fear take over. Everything in me is begging for me to turn and run out of here and never stop.

"Umm, I could help you warm up for him." He steps forward, and I move backward, not wanting to be close to him. He's bad news. I feel it in my bones.

"No, that's okay. If you could, please direct me to Cal or let him know I'm here."

He looks at me, then laughs, pointing to the bar, where I see a man sitting with his back to us. "That's him." I step to the side to move past him, a small amount of relief hitting me until I feel a heavy weight on my shoulder and my body being pulled backward until I crash against a hard body. "I'll let you go for now. But you're going to be mine. Wait and see. I always get what I want, and baby, I want you."

He lets go and I rush across the room, trying my hardest to fight back the tears that are threatening to break free.

Stepping up behind the man, I clear my throat.

"What?" he says loudly, laying down whatever was in his hands and turning around to face me. "Who are you?"

"I-I-" I stutter.

"Spit it out. I ain't got all day."

"S-s-sorry." I take a deep breath and continue. "I'm Lucy. My husband Scott told me you were expecting me."

He looks me up and down, then smiles. "Take off your jacket."

My hands shaking, I do exactly as he says, then I hold it in my arms in front of me.

"No, put it in the chair, or drop it to the floor, then turn around in a circle for me. But do it slowly."

Taking a step closer, I fold my jacket and place it on the stool beside him. Then I do as he says, going slow. Fear courses through me, knowing that if I don't do exactly as he says, he'll tell Scott.

When I turn back around to face him, he's standing with his arms crossed over his chest and one arm raised at the elbow as he slides his thumb back and forth across his bottom lip. He looks at me so intently, as if he's taking every part of my body and committing it to his memory.

"Scott was so wrong about you and in the best of ways. You're far too valuable to be just a waitress. For tonight, we'll train you on that, but you're going to be on that stage behind me. Especially if he wants to pay off the debt he owes me."

No. Wait. What the hell did he just say?

"No, I can't dance," I rush out quickly. The thought of men seeing my body makes me want to puke.

"Are you saying no? I'd hate to call Scott and let him know," he says, smirking at me, knowing he has me right where he wants me. There's no way I'd ever tell him no.

"No, I'll do it." I feel a piece of me dying inside.

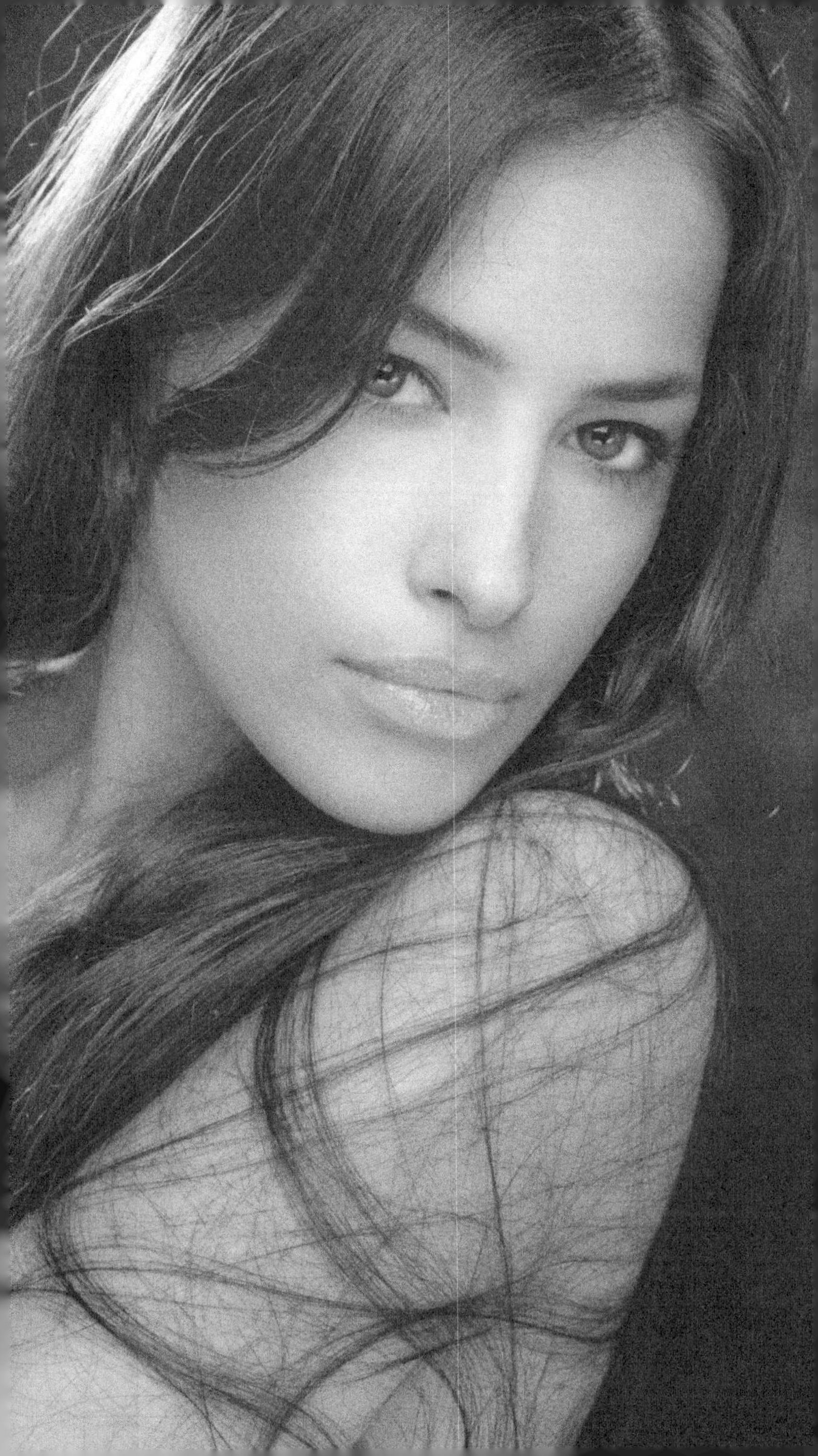

CHAPTER 12

Lucy

"Come with me and I'll show you where to put your stuff. I'm going to have Candi and Jazmin show you the ropes tonight." He heads toward the back of the club, but I just stand there in shock because of what's about to happen.

He stops about fifteen feet away from me and turns. "I said come on, I ain't got all day."

"I'm sorry," I squeak out, as I rush across the room to catch up with him. The whole time, I'm taking in everything I didn't pay attention to when I first entered the club. There are two round stages on either side of the room, with a tiny walkway connecting to the stage in the center. Around the main stage is a bar, with chairs along the length of it. At the outskirts of the bar are booths along the wall, and throughout the space in between are small round tables. There are men already in the bar, with three half-naked women on the stage, two of which are grinding their bodies against each other, while the men shout, urging them on. The lights are low, but not so low you can't see anything, while there's a spotlight on each of the girls on the stage. The waitresses are dressed in skimpy panties and a bra. And I grimace, knowing I'll be wearing that as well.

He leads me down a hallway before stopping by a door. He opens it, pops his head in, then steps inside. When I don't immediately follow, he calls out, "Siren, get your ass in here!"

Who is he talking to? I look around but don't see anyone behind me. "I ain't got all day. If Scott had told me you were this bad at following directions, I wouldn't have offered this as an alternative to his money situation."

I rush into the room, confused at why he called me that. Looking around, I see it's a very large dressing room. There are vanity tables throughout, with a row of tall lockers where it takes up the top and bottom space into one. There are three women in the room, all barely dressed, with either their tits or their vaginas on display. "Sorry, I thought you were calling someone named Siren." I try to pacify him as to why I didn't follow right away.

"It was you. That's going to be your stage name. I pick one for all the girls. This is Candi and Jazmin," he tells me, pointing at two of the women in the room. "She's learning the floor tonight, then she's going to learn the stage on her next shift. Make sure she knows all the ins and outs. If you get offered a private dance, then let her sit in and watch. I'm sure all the horny men out there will eat it up." With that, he smacks one of the women on the ass and turns, leaving the room.

They wait for the door to shut behind him, then after a few minutes, they go back to getting dressed. Not saying one word to me. I stand nervously, unsure of what to do. When they're both dressed, they finally turn to look at me.

"Shit, girl, you look nervous as hell. You can't let those men out there see you looking like that," the redhead tells me. She's dressed in a very short, skintight skirt that has both her ass cheeks peeking out from below it. Her skintight white tank top cuts off just under her breasts, showing a sparkly bra peeking out from underneath. "Just in case you missed it, I'm Jazmin."

"I'm nervous. Sorry, I'll try to rein it in."

"What are you wearing?" the other one that I now know is Candi asks.

I look down at my clothes before looking back at them. "This. I don't have anything. I just found out last night I had this interview here today, and I wasn't expecting to be put right to work." A lone tear escapes my eye and I quickly lift my hand to brush it away.

"Wait. Hold on a minute. What are you saying?" They both speak at the same time, so I'm not sure who said what.

"Um, my husband told me I had to come here today. From what Cal just said, I guess my husband has a debt that I'm going to be paying off working here." I clench my jacket, pulling it tighter to my body, as if it were some magical shield that could keep me safe from everything around me.

"Shit, girl. And I thought my old man was bad, but from the sound of it, yours is worse." Candi steps over to the lockers as she speaks, opens one of them up, and begins moving stuff around.

"Come sit over here and I'll do your face and hair," Candi tells me as she pulls out a chair from one of the other vanities. "You'll have one of these for yourself. Some of the girls here are real bitches, so just stick with us and we'll show you who to avoid." I just shake my head as I sit down in the chair she pulled out.

"I think I got something you can wear. We look to be about the same size. What size shoe do you wear?" Jazmin asks as she pulls out a couple items of clothing and a bag.

"Seven."

They talk amongst themselves, trying hard to include me, which I appreciate, but I'm so frazzled I wouldn't have cared if they did or didn't. Once she's done with my face and hair, Jazmin tells me to look in the mirror. She has a huge ass smile on her face like a kid in a candy store.

When I look in the mirror, I'm not expecting the reflection looking back at me. I used to wear makeup long ago before I started dating Scott. He didn't like it, so I stopped. But what I see stuns me; I look gorgeous. Hell, I knew I wasn't completely ugly, but she transformed me into one of those cover girl models. She has my hair in ponytails and made my curls even more massive and full.

"Thank you," I sob.

"Nope, none of that. You'll ruin my masterpiece. One day, I hope to raise enough money to open up my own salon. Hair and makeup, I'll do the works," she announces proudly, her face beaming.

"Okay, now the clothing. I thought we would go good old catholic school girl. I even have some platform Mary

Janes for you to wear with it. Sadly, the only thing I don't have to fit you is a bra. You look to be smaller than me but bigger than Candi, but I have a solution, and since you're not stripping tonight, it will work. I'll bring in some of my costumes I don't use anymore for you and see what I can do for the bra. What size are you, anyway?"

I can feel the heat on my face, embarrassed at the question, but still reply. I need all the help I can get, especially if I want to make Scott happy. "36 D."

"Yep, I'm clearly enhanced, as you can see. Just got them about six months ago. Let's just say that was a learning curve with dancing and walking." She cackles at her own joke.

"Okay, sweetie, we need you to strip out of your clothes. You can put your stuff in my locker for now and then we'll help you get one for yourself." I turn my back to them as I pull my shirt over my head, careful not to mess up all the work Jazmin just did. I leave my bra on for now until I know exactly what they're putting on me. I unbutton my jeans, pulling the zipper down. Slipping off my shoes, I shimmy out of my jeans, then turn around to face them in nothing but my ratty bra, panties, and holey socks. The bruises from Scott's last beating are on display for them to see.

"Okay. So, I have these for you. I promise they are clean, cause what you have on isn't going to work." She hands what she has in her hand out to me. Taking it from her, I see it's a very skimpy pair of panties.

Candi just stares at me, and I hold my breath, but she smiles. "I have this great cover up for tattoos, I bet it would cover those bruises too. Let me get it for you." She rummages through her bag before coming back over to me, putting some on her hand and rubbing it in. Sure enough, it does.

"Thank you," I whisper softly.

"Go ahead and put those panties on while we piece together the rest of your outfit." When I still stand there frozen, she sighs heavily. "Siren, you're going to have to get used to being naked, especially if you're going to end up on that stage. Best to start here with us where it doesn't matter first." She gives me a pointed look, and I set the underwear on the vanity before slipping my fingers underneath the seam of my panties and sliding them down my legs. Once I'm out of them, I pull the others on.

I haven't worn a pair of underwear that fit like a glove and weren't all stretched out in ages. Thankfully, as I stole a peek at my backside in the mirror, I saw they were high cut, with my ass cheeks poking out of them, but they looked good on me. I folded my old ones up and placed them on top of my clothes.

"Now for the bra. I think this will work." She hands me a skimpy top, so I pull it on. It was a tank top very similar to hers but made of spandex, so it fits tightly, holding my girls up and in place, even causing me to have cleavage poking out over the top.

"Now the skirt." The skirt she hands me is plaid with suspenders and I really want to laugh, but I don't.

I put it on, slipping my arms through each of the straps, pulling them up on my shoulders. As I turn to look in the mirror, it's like seeing a totally different person.

"Here's some stockings." Jazmin hands me some thigh-high stockings with that sticky band along the inside, so they don't slip down and some shoes. "These are for you and we're set. We both dance tonight, so when I'm dancing, you'll be with Candi and vice versa."

I nod my head at her as I pull off my socks and put the stockings on. Once I'm done, I make sure I have all my belongings in a pile and Jazmin places them in her locker. Standing slowly, I try to balance, not use to wearing heels, especially ones this high.

"Okay, let's go," Candi announces excitedly as we leave the room. I'm walking slower than them, trying not to break my neck.

They give me a brief tour of the club, pointing out where the rooms for the private dances are, the VIP section that's off to the left of the bar, which is where Cal has his special guests sit. They both remark on how well they tip. Once they've covered everything, Candi heads to the back of the stage while Jazmin and I head to the bar, where Cal is still sitting. He must have a low jack on me because as soon as I get near him, he turns around to face me.

"Shit, Siren. You look hot as fuck, baby. Want to go in the back and give me a test dance? I bet I can do more for you than that sorry ass husband of yours." My eyes go wide at his blatant offer of fucking me. "Calm down, baby. I want you to learn some moves first, but you will be dancing for me. All the girls have to in order to do a private dance." He winks, then turns back around in his chair, picks up his pen, and goes back to work.

Jazmin picks up two trays from the bar and takes hold of my arm, pulling me away gently. Once we're out of earshot, she leans in and whispers to me, "Watch out for him. Overall, he's not bad, but when he sets his sights on you, he's relentless. He means it when he says you'll have to dance for him. Just try not to be left alone with him."

"Okay. I'll remember that," I whisper back to her.

"Now, let's get to work and make some money." She hands me a tray and I follow her to a table with a middle age, potbelly, balding man seated at it. I stand back in awe and listen as she showers him with charm that he eats up.

She and Candi may just be the best parts of this place.

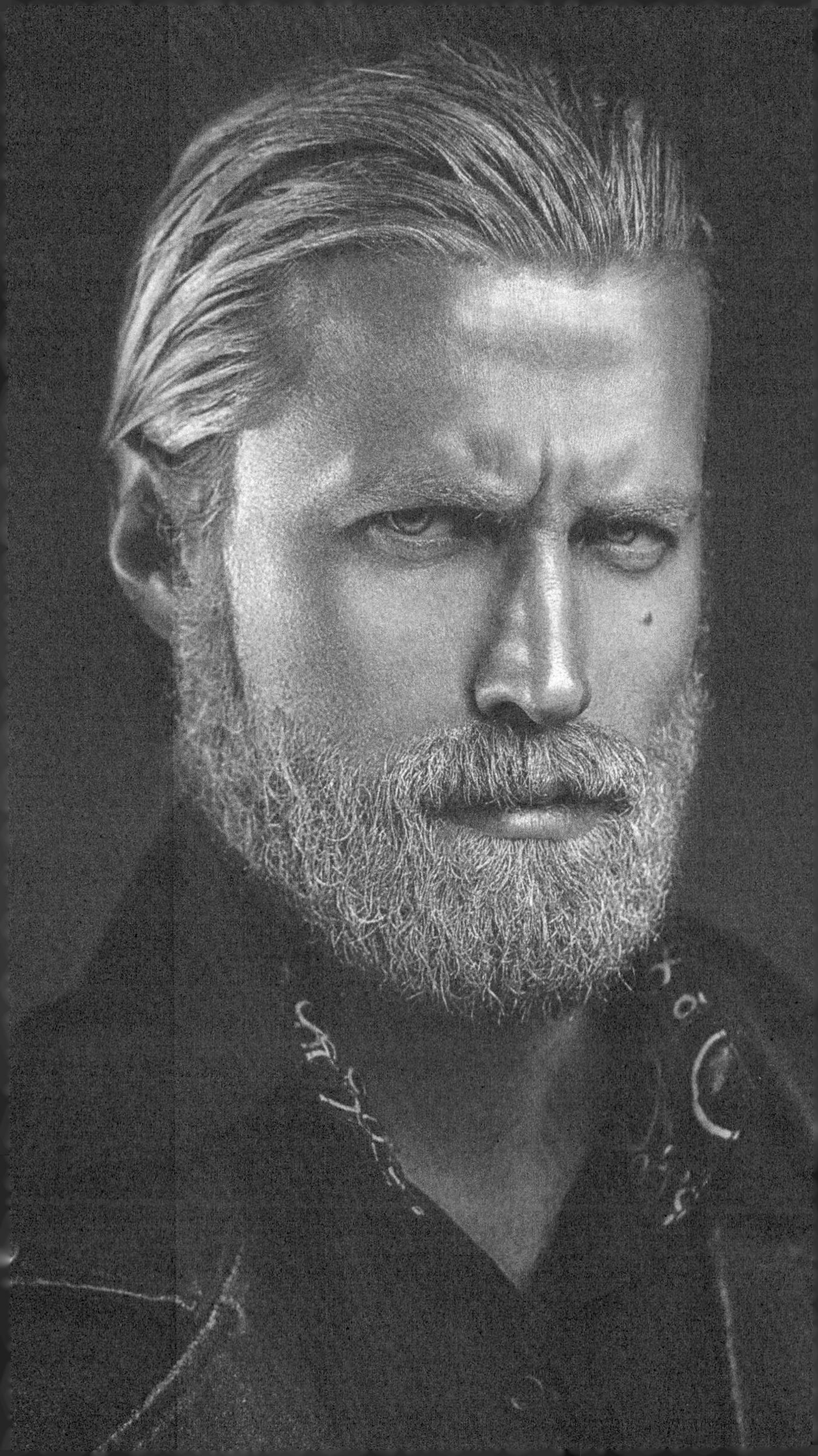

CHAPTER 13

Preacher

Lucy needs a jacket. God, I wish that Rizzo was here. If she was here, I'd send her to get Lucy a jacket or maybe she has an extra one laying around that would work. But she's not, and that's just something else for me to worry about. I need to know what's wrong with her. Rizzo may be Hawke's biological sister, but she's mine by choice.

I do the only thing I can, and go to the damn mall by myself. The coat is first, but I plan to find out everything she needs. Stepping inside the mall, I'm hit with chatter from all the people milling around. Sounds of laughter, fighting, children crying, all hit my ears and I already want to turn around and walk right back out. I head for one of the department stores, Jankins, that sells clothing and accessories for men, women, and children, as well as some household supplies.

I head straight back to the women's department as memories of shopping with my wife and daughter flood my brain. Moving between the racks of clothing, I finally find the one I'm looking for. Reaching up, I begin moving the hangers, the sound of the metal sliding along metal grating my nerves.

My eyes stay locked on a dark black coat with fur around the hood and around the cuffs of the sleeves. It'll keep her warm, so I take it from the rack and head over to look for some gloves for her. I pick up a pair, then put them back down, going through this process over and over until I find a pair that has the same furry material as the jacket. Oddly, it has a matching toboggan attached to it.

Happy with my choices, I make my way to the register and pay for them. The woman behind the counter bats her eyes at me and I smile, trying to be nice, but don't speak. I don't need this woman thinking I'm interested in anything she has to offer. She's one of those plastic girls. All fake, nothing real on her body, and it's nothing I'm interested in.

Bianca had substance. She was beautiful naturally, only wearing makeup for special occasions. She had the heart of an angel, making her the perfect choice for the wife of a pastor. Then Carmen came along. Motherhood suited her, and we even had plans to have more kids, a houseful of them. Now I'll never know the joy of a child calling me dad again. Worst of all, I'll never see my daughter grow up. It eats away at me, not as much as it did those first few years, but it's still there, right below the surface, festering like a sore.

"Will there be anything else, hun?" she asks, her high-pitched voice grating on my nerves.

"No," I answer her curtly, not even looking her in the eye as I hand over my credit card. She looks at it, then back at me. Guess she wasn't expecting to see someone dressed like me with a black card.

"I need to see identification." I let out a bold laugh, then pull it out of my wallet and hand it to her, smirking, when she sees the name matches and the picture is me. People and their prejudices. Makes me sick to my stomach.

She finishes the sale and hands my card and ID back to me, then bags the clothing. I didn't think about it before, but I should have driven my truck, now I have to carry this home on my bike. Tomorrow morning, I definitely need to drive it instead of taking my bike. Lucy won't know it's me. I'll have to make sure to look out for her and get out, so she'll see me.

Getting on my bike, I put the bag in front of me between my legs and stick my arm through the bag's handles. It's a bit bulky, but it'll work to get back to the clubhouse. I'm sure I'm going to catch some flak from the brothers for the shopping I've been doing, but they can all fuck off. At least now I know Lucy will have a good jacket. I'm just doing what any friend would. But are we friends? Is that all I am to her?

The whole way to the clubhouse, I mentally argue with myself about how she is nothing more than some girl I'm trying to help. Hell, I used to help people all the time when I was a preacher. Didn't mean I was trying to get in their pants, but I was also married.

Pulling onto the property of the clubhouse, I stop at the gate to check in with the two prospects inside. They're newer, Dallas and Cole. "Any trouble tonight?"

"No, Sir, been quiet. No one other than brothers have been through tonight."

"Good. Make sure to stay awake. Last prospect to fall asleep on the job didn't like what the punishment was." I leave them with the threat and drive on up to the clubhouse, parking my bike beside Hawke's, inside the garage. I parked my truck just outside of it.

Taking the bag, I head inside. Brothers are scattered throughout the common area, most with a drink in their hand and a club bunny on their lap. Others are playing pool. It's going to be an early morning tomorrow, so I keep walking, and head to the hallway in the back that leads to the sleeping quarters for the officers, going straight to my room.

Once I'm inside, I lock the door. Taking the few steps across the room to my bed, I sit down, placing the bag on the floor, then remove my boots, setting them off to the side. I need to get some rest, and hopefully, my dreams won't be plagued with a certain brunette I can't get off my mind. There's too much going on with the club that needs my attention to be distracted by a woman.

💀 💀 💀

The buzzing of the alarm on my phone wakes me up. I run my hand up the length of my face and through my hair before sitting up, slinging my legs over the side. My eyes are heavy, and I strain to open them. The clubhouse is quiet; all the brothers must still be sleeping. My room is dark, except for the glow from my phone. Standing slowly, I make my way to the bathroom inside my room, piss, brush my teeth and hair, and then head to my dresser to get some clothes.

Once dressed, I pick up the bag, grab my truck keys, and head out. The brisk, cold air hits me as soon as I step outside, and I'm thankful I'm picking Lucy up. The thought of her walking in this sends rage running through me. I'd love to meet this husband of hers and give him a piece of my fucking mind.

As I'm heading her way, I decide to make a pit stop at the nearby fast-food restaurant and order us both the largest cup of coffee they have. I remember her putting cream, but no sugar, in hers yesterday, so I have them add only that. Hopefully, she likes it.

It takes a little longer than I expected, so I hope she isn't walking, but rather waiting, like I asked her. As I turn onto her street, I begin looking, creeping slowly past her house. When I see that fucker's car in the driveway, my vision turns hazy and I see red. What a worthless sack of shit. If Lucy was my woman, I don't care how tired I was, she wouldn't be walking to work.

Her house is dark, but it always is, and it gets me thinking. Does she have power? I need to ask without seeming intrusive. I pull to the end of the street, doing a U-turn at the intersection, so I can face her house. She's not here, but it just turned six. So, I sit and wait.

The time ticks by. Five minutes pass, then ten, and I begin to worry. Did she foolishly walk to work, thinking I wasn't coming because it was so close to six? Then I see something. Someone's running this way, hair flying in the wind. It has to be Lucy.

Opening the door, I step out of the truck and move to the front of it so she can see me. She comes to a screeching halt in front of me, completely out of breath, with bags under her eyes. God, she looks exhausted.

"I'm so sorry, Noah," she rushes out as she doubles over, putting her hands on her knees as she breathes heavily.

"It's fine. I was bout to leave to go lookin' for you. Figured you were stubborn and started walkin'," I tell her as I take her by the elbow, once she stands back up, leading her to the passenger door. "Got you a cup of coffee inside. It might have cooled off some, though." She flashes me a smile that has me wanting to see more. She's gorgeous. A fucking angel. I rush around and climb into the driver's seat before turning the car around, heading to the diner.

"Oh, you didn't have to. You've been sitting here waiting this whole time?" She looks shocked, like no one has ever done anything nice for her.

"I told you I was goin' to be here to take you to work. Though I did think you left and walked. I was contemplatin' going up to your door and knockin'." She shoots her head around to me, fear in her eyes. "But I figured it wasn't the best thing to do."

I reach back into the backseat, pick up the bag, and hand it to her. "This is for you."

She takes the bag from me. Her eyes widen as she opens and looks inside. "What's this?"

"It's a jacket. Better than the one you're wearin' and some gloves and a hat." I keep my eyes on the road as I tell her, picking up my coffee and taking a swallow of it. I can see her from the corner of my eye, holding the jacket in her hands and staring at it. A lone tear slides down her cheek and she doesn't try to wipe it away.

"Why did you do this for me? You don't even know me." She just keeps looking at the coat in her hands, rubbing her fingers over the fur around the trim.

"Because you needed it and I wanted to. I have the money; it ain't a big deal."

"But it is. That's why it kills me that I can't accept it. My husband would be furious."

"I've already thought about that. Even though I don't condone lyin', just this once, tell him Georgie gave it to you. I'm gonna talk to her and have her say it if he ever asks."

She just nods her head as more tears fall. All I want to do is pull the truck over to the side of the road and pull her into my lap as I soothe her, making sure she knows how special she is. But I don't. She's not mine, and it wouldn't look right.

She sits in silence as we continue the drive to the diner. Before I know it, we're pulling into the parking lot. I should leave, forget about having coffee with her this morning like I said we would, but I can't bring myself to do it. Instead, I put the truck in park and turn it off. "We still got some time before your shift to have some coffee, maybe even a muffin."

Climbing out of the truck, I make my way around to her side and open her door, helping her out. She puts the bag on the floorboard and goes to walk away, but I'm not having it. "You forgot something, darlin'."

She turns around, moving her gaze between me and the bag. When she sees I'm not going to cave, she marches back to the truck and picks up the bag. "I expect to see it on you the next time I bring you to work, which you need to tell me when that is."

"Tomorrow, same time," she mumbles, before heading inside. I smile a little at that and follow her. Same as before, she heads to the back, and I go and sit in the same booth as yesterday and wait for her to join me. This morning, in the short time we have, I plan to ask her about her. What she likes, dislikes. Trying to find out all that I can about her. Then, after a few days of this, I'm going to hit her with the hard shit. I want to know how that dick of a husband of hers is treating her. And kill him if I need to.

A couple minutes later, she's heading my way with a tray in hand. I noticed it earlier, but she looks like she hasn't slept a wink between yesterday and today, and I intend to find out why.

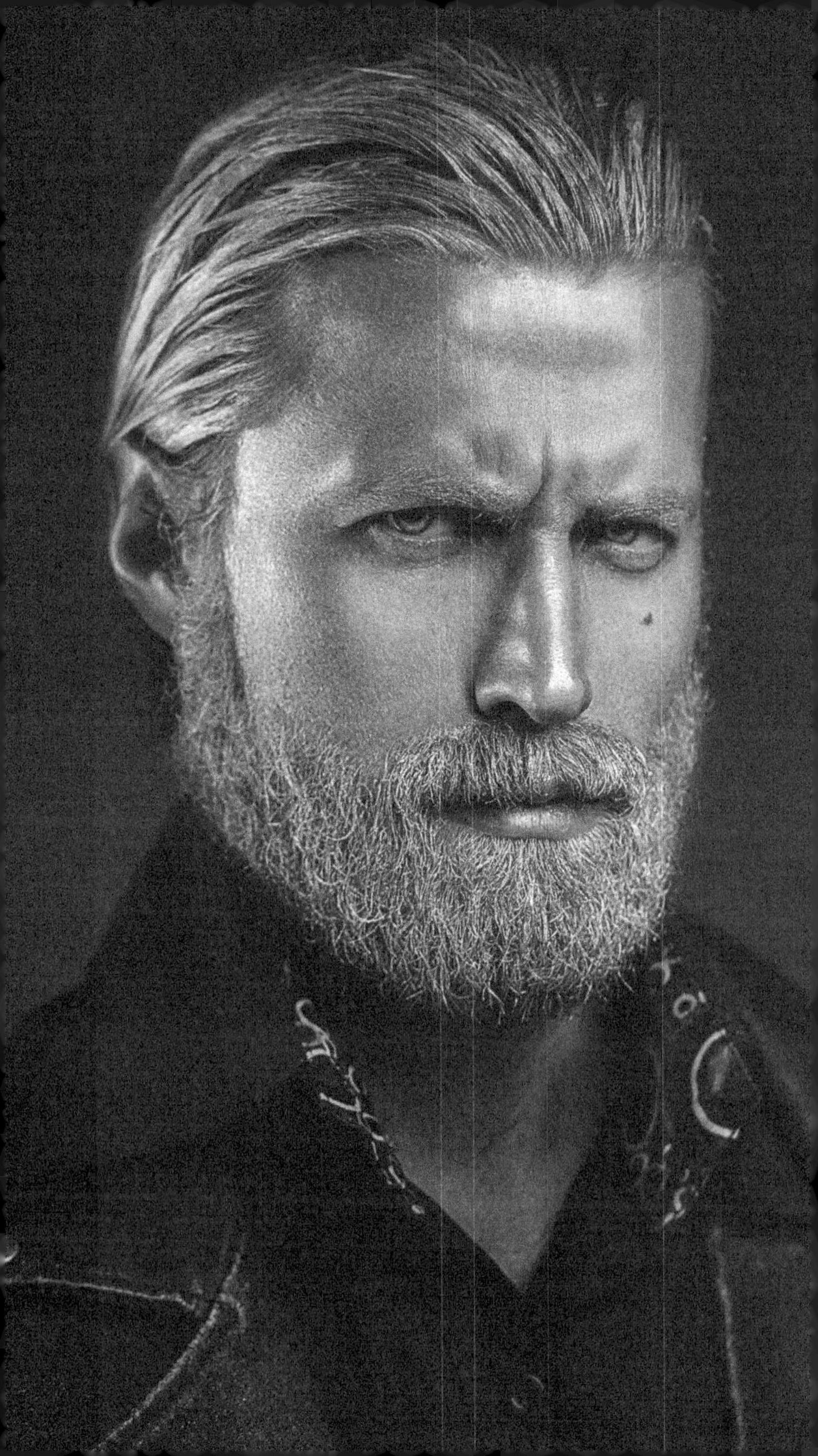

CHAPTER 14

Preacher

I left about twenty minutes after Lucy went to work. I don't know why, but I couldn't leave. Instead, I just sat there, drinking coffee, watching her like a creepy stalker. She kept glancing my way every once in a while, turning the corners of her lips up in a smile, flashing it my way. In return, I gave her one. It felt weird having these feelings for her. I haven't had them for anyone since Bianca, and it's killing me. It's like I'm cheating on her, forgetting her for someone else.

Standing up, I toss the money for the coffee and muffins on the table, along with five more twenties—she best not try to give them back either—then give her a wave before heading out of the diner. I'm going to try to make it back later today and find out when she's getting off, so I can give her a ride home, too. If I don't make it, hopefully she has the good sense to use some of the money I gave her for a taxi, so she doesn't have to walk.

Once I'm in the truck, I head back to the clubhouse. I need to meet with Gunner and make damn sure I'm one of the two people going inside the meeting place tomorrow. There's no way in hell I'm letting this fucker, whoever he or she is, slip through our fingers. We need to know who the hell had our accountant skimming money from us and why he was more scared of them than us.

I tap my fingers on the steering wheel to the metal song playing on the radio, some old school Ozzy. Got to love that man. He may have done some crazy shit back in the day, but man can he sing. It's just going off as I pull up to the guard shack, the prospect inside jumping to attention when he sees it's me. That's right, you should be scared, boy.

Just as I park the car, my phone buzzes, letting me know I have a message.

Rizzo: Hey preacher man!
Me: Riz
Rizzo: Got some info you might like
Me: Okay
Rizzo: What you gonna give me for it?
Me: Nothing
Rizzo: One day you'll have to tell me how you kept your congregation riveted to your sermons, cause you aren't much of a conversationalist.
Me: Sorry, what is it?
Rizzo: Got some info on your girl. Gonna email it to you later.
Me: Thank you. How did you find all this out?
Rizzo: We can talk, and I could tell you my ways, but I'd have to kill you.
Me: Thank you.
Me: Are you okay?
Rizzo: I don't know.

Rizzo: But if you're still on good terms with the big guy, can you put in a word for me?
Me: Already have, sweetheart.

I let my head fall back on the headrest as I close my eyes and do something I haven't done much of lately. Pray. I've reconciled my anger with God for allowing what happened in the church that day, but I haven't returned to a fully committed relationship with him. I don't pray for help, but today I do. I need Rizzo to be okay. I pray for her, for Hawke, and for this club.

"Amen." I hope he's listening. Taking a deep breath, I head inside to find Gunner. I don't have to look far; he's seated on the couch, legs spread wide, as Cassie, one of the club bunnies, sucks him off. Not wanting to have the conversation with him while a whore's around, I opt to go to the bar and make a drink.

It's common to see someone fucking, having their dick sucked, or eating some pussy in the clubhouse right out in the open, but I don't care to be having a conversation with them while they orgasm. Makes me wonder if I'm considered the prude out of all the brothers.

I can see the look of frustration on Gunner's face when I glance over my shoulder to see if he's done. Either she's doing a crap job, or she's trying to slink her way into getting him to choose her as an ol' lady. He never will. We all know he's got his eye on someone in town. Someone he's not ready to approach yet. The whores here are merely a way to pass the time until he makes a play for the woman he wants.

Looking closer, I can see her saying something to him each time before sliding her mouth down the shaft of his cock. Gunner must have had enough of it. When she comes up this time, he pushes her back, causing her to fall onto her ass and tears stream down her face. He stands, shoves his dick back in his pants, and zips up. Stepping over her, he heads my way with a scowl on his face.

"Fucking whores. All I want is my dick sucked and I can't even get that shit done right," he growls as he steps up beside me and sits down on the stool.

"She still tryin' to be your ol' lady?"

"Fuck yeah!" he says through clenched teeth.

"Then why do you keep goin' back to her? You need to cut your losses with her and keep her mouth off your cock, and keep it out of her pussy. Damn, Gunner, thought you were smarter than that."

He laughs loudly before slapping his hand down on my back. "I did too, Preach. What's goin' on with you? You were out of the clubhouse early this mornin'?"

"Took someone to work. That's all." I try not to look at him, afraid he could read any sliver of emotion on my face.

"Oh, really. She wouldn't be the same someone working at a diner, would she?" When I clam up and don't say anything, he gets the answer he wants. "Fuck, Preach, ain't she married? I never took you as one for messin' with a taken woman."

"I'm not, just helpin' her. Her dick of a husband makes her walk to work before the sun's up, in freezin' weather, with nothing more than what I'd call a damn sweater on." I can feel my blood pressure rising as I talk.

"Shit, what an ass. Even I wouldn't do that." We both just nod our heads.

"Tomorrow, I'm goin' to be the one on the inside." I don't ask, I tell him.

"Was there even a chance you wouldn't be? Come on, man. You're our best guy. We just need to make sure we get somethin' useful from this one. We need to know who out there has people more scared of them than us." We both pick up our beers and take a swallow.

We sit there in silence, drinking. Finishing the one I have, I reach over the counter and pick up two more, sliding one to Gunner. Popping the top, I take a sip before lowering the bottle and setting it back on the table.

"Do you know anything?" Gunner asks from beside me.

"Huh?"

"About these trips Riz and Hawke are takin'." He looks over at me, his eyes holding so much sadness.

"I don't know the details, except it's about Rizzo, and not good. Hawke said he'd talk once he found out."

"Yeah, he told me the same thing. I'm worried. They're family and it's killin' me not knowing, especially if I can do something to help." He keeps his hands busy trying to pull the label off the beer bottle without ripping it while he speaks.

"I know Rizzo messaged me about something else, then asked me if I was still on good terms with the big guy, and if so, if I could pray for her. That tells me all I need to know."

We both sit there in silence as the sounds of music and the other brothers laughing and joking around fill the room. We're the only two who look like they're at a funeral and I'm hoping like hell we won't be going to one.

I'd lay down my life for Rizzo. If it wasn't for Hawke, I wouldn't be here today. I'd be attached to a bike at the bottom of the ocean. Nothing more than food for the inhabitants of the ocean.

We sit there and drink the rest of the day. Neither of us had anywhere to be, and drinking seemed like the right thing to do. Drinking our sorrows away, at least for the moment, until we know more. It wasn't until I looked at my watch and saw that it was six did I realize not only didn't I go back to give Lucy a ride home, but I never checked my emails. Pulling out my phone, I open it up and see an unread email from Rizzo. I've drunk too much to read and comprehend anything, so I choose to wait until the morning. Right now I need food, then to shower and go to bed. I can't be the least bit late to get Lucy in the morning, plus tomorrow night we're getting our mark.

Standing up from the bar, I sway a bit, and have to reach out and grab hold of the counter to steady myself. "See ya later, man. Going to get some food, then to my room. Gotta be up early in the morning."

"No problem, man. I'm going to go find another girl to suck my dick right and make damn sure she knows I don't want to have a fuckin' conversation. Just stuff her mouth with my monster." He laughs as he heads over to the pool table where Sundance and Snake are playing a game.

Heading to the kitchen, I luck out, finding carryout boxes of pizza on the counter. I take out a few slices, then get a bottle of water from the fridge. I stick the bottle under my arm and make my way to my bedroom while eating the pizza. I didn't realize how hungry I was until the first bite of greasy, cheesy goodness hit my tongue.

It doesn't take long to eat and shower. Climbing into bed, butt ass naked, I close my eyes. My mind is going a mile a minute as I try to think of what Lucy is doing right now. Is she in bed? Is she alone or is her dick husband with her? It's then I wonder if she's fucking him, which pisses me off.

Shit, I need to stop obsessing over her. She's unavailable.

Something my heart and my already hardening cock need to fucking learn before I go insane. Eventually, thoughts of her recede, replaced with worry about Rizzo.

One thing at a time. I think of it as a sequence, a to-do list, so to say.

1. Take Lucy to work tomorrow, especially since I got too drunk today to go back and pick her up.

2. Read the email and see what information Riz found.

3. Get the fucker tomorrow night and torture the shit out of him until I get what I need.

4. Find out what's going on with Rizzo.

Now that I have a firm plan in place, my thoughts calm and I drift off to sleep, blissful darkness taking over me. Visions of a dark-haired goddess wrapped around me fill my dreams. In them, she's single and all mine.

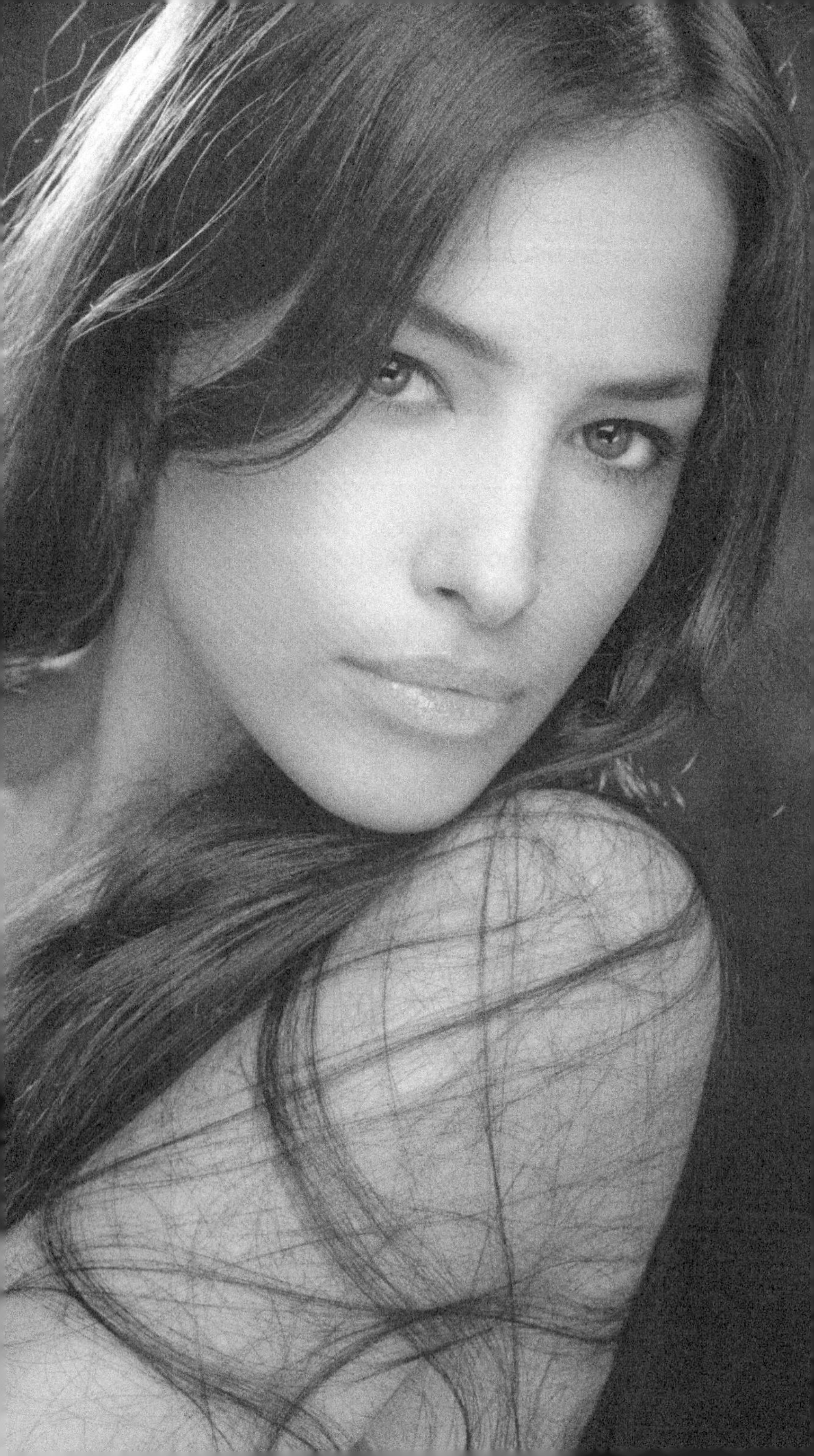

CHAPTER 15

Lucy

Tonight has been hell. Cal has me working tables and I feel like a chicken running around with my head cut off. I've already screwed up orders, spilled drinks, even once on a customer, and now I'm having to wait to be scolded by Cal like a fucking kid. It's like I've gotten in trouble and I'm waiting for the principal to enter the room to punish me.

I begin to pick at my nails, hating how much skin I'm revealing to everyone. I'm really starting to rethink my decision about being married, but I need to hold on a little longer. Once I have enough money to escape, I'm gone. I'll run so far; he'll never find me. Lucy Davis will be as good as dead to anyone who knew her, including my parents. Once, I tried to talk to my mom about how Scott treated me and she had me believing I was the problem.

The door opens behind me and I can smell the distinct smell of his cologne. It's overpowering, almost like he took a whole bottle and dumped it over his head before coming into the club. Last night I thought it was a fluke, an accident, but when I came in tonight and it was just as strong, I knew I wasn't.

"You're costing me money tonight, girl. How do you plan to repay what you've spilled or for the client we had to compensate with free alcohol and a private dance with the dancer of his choice?" He moves across the room and sits down on the desk in front of me, spreading his legs wide, causing his pants to pull tight against his crotch.

"I...I...I... can pay for it. I'm sorry. Take it from what I make here," I stammer out, afraid of how much everything is going to cost.

He lets out a roaring laugh, one that has him throwing back his head, before he calms himself, settling his gaze on me. "What you make here? Really? I already told you that everything you make here is going to pay your husband's debt to me. So, rethink my question. How do you expect to pay me for the loss of revenue incurred by your negligence?" He crosses his arms over his chest as he lets his eyes trail down my barely covered body, causing my skin to crawl in revulsion.

"All of it? I didn't realize that," I respond, shocked at this new bit of information. "Honestly, Cal, I thought some of what I made would still be mine."

"I think we can find a way we can work it out in trade. You can take care of some of my needs, and in exchange, I'll take some off of what you owe me. You can start by dropping to your knees and sucking my cock." He reaches down and begins to undo his belt.

"No!" I cry out. "I'm married, I can't. I'll do anything else." Tears well up in my eyes. How could this man be this crass?

"Then be prepared. Tomorrow you're on the stage. You will strip for not one but three shows and then do private dances in the back room. You will allow every man to touch you in any way they want. If the debt isn't paid by the end of your shift tomorrow night, then your ass is mine." Then, to make matters worse, he adds, "Literally."

I begin to shake. My body and mind are exhausted and not able to handle everything being thrown at me.

"Now get out of here and don't fuck up anymore." He shoos me away as he stands and moves behind his desk. I'm still sitting there in shock, my mouth hanging open, not knowing what to do or say. He looks up at me, dropping the pen he just picked up back down. "Changed your mind? Ready to suck my fat cock?"

"No." I stand quickly and run from the room, nearly stumbling over my own feet.

I'm not paying attention and run smack into Jazmin, almost causing both of us to topple over and fall onto the floor. "Girl, what's got you all worked up?" She gets her balance, then reaches out, placing her hand on my shoulder.

"Umm, Cal—"

"What the hell did he do to you? Did he make a pass at you? Force himself on you?" She pulls me in close, wrapping her arms around me, hugging me tightly. I barely catch the glare she sends down the hallway in the direction of Cal's office.

Pulling away from her, I wipe the tears from my face, knowing I've smeared my makeup.

"Come on, let's get you fixed back up. Ya still got about four hours left of work." She takes my hand and pulls me down the hallway to the dressing room. Once we're inside, she leads me over to a vanity and has me sit in the chair in front of it, taking a seat across from me.

She picks up her makeup and begins to touch up my face. "Siren, you got to stay away from him. He's our boss, but he's bad news. He'll try anything in his power to get you in his bed."

"He wanted me to suck his cock to make up for the money I cost him with my mistakes tonight."

She drops her hands in her lap in anger. "That asshole. We've all made those mistakes. Hell, I dropped a tray of drinks two days before you started. Siren, did you do it?" She doesn't stop, but continues retouching my makeup before closing up the compact and placing it back on her vanity table.

"No, I didn't. But now I have to dance tomorrow night and do private dances and he's going to take all the money. If I don't cover how much I cost him, then I have to." I can't even look her in the eyes, I'm so embarrassed.

"He's slime. Don't worry. I'll help all I can with the dancing. Just when you get up there, move. It doesn't matter if you can dance or have rhythm, it's all about the skin. Take your clothes off slowly, tease them. Then with the private dances, just grind on them. There's nothing to worry about there; they can't touch you."

My head jerks up to look at her. "But they can. He said they can."

I can see it already. The pity in her face.

"It's going to be okay, Siren. You have me and Candi. We'll help you. Now let's get back out there."

The taxi pulls up to the front of the house and I see Scott's car already sitting in the driveway and every light in the house is on. My anger builds that I had to spend money to get a ride home when he could have come and picked me up himself.

Pulling some cash from my pocket, I hand it to the driver and slowly walk across the yard to the front door. I'm thankful for the jacket Noah gave me, as it's keeping me from freezing in the bitter cold.

I pull open the screen door and take a deep breath before stepping inside the house. Scott is sitting on the couch, butt naked, with his cock out while the sounds of moaning come from the television. He's holding a blunt in one hand and stroking his dick with the other.

"Good, you're home. Get over here and suck my cock, bitch."

Taking off my jacket, I hang it on the rack before making my way over to him. I know better than to refuse or complain about how tired I am. Walking quickly, I make my way over to him and kneel down, replacing the hand around his cock with mine. I place my mouth at the tip and slide down until it hits the back of my throat, gagging me.

His hand comes to the back of my head, as he wraps the long tendrils of my hair around it and pushes my head further down on his shaft. Each time I pull my mouth back up, he slams my head back down, pounding into the back of my throat. He doesn't care that there are tears streaming down my face, he just wants to come.

My stomach churns and I feel like I'm about to puke, so I try to pull away, but he holds me still. "Don't you dare, bitch, you're going to swallow every last drop of my cum."

I try to plead with him that I need to stop, but my words only come out in a mumble, sounding like the teacher from the Charlie Brown cartoons. It gets harder to breathe and I feel the bile working its way up my throat until I'm throwing up all over his dick.

"What the fucking hell?" he screams before shoving me off of him, causing me to fall backward, hitting my head on the coffee table. He storms from the room, as I sit there, the room spinning, trying to pull myself together.

The sound of the shower has me looking around, knowing I need to get up. But I can't move, my body feels like lead. A door slamming down the hallway has me looking up, my vision blurry as I make out three Scotts heading my way, except now he has shorts on, and his hair is wet.

"You're fucking useless, Lucy." He reaches down, grasping a handful of my hair, and begins dragging me down the hallway.

"Scott, you're hurting me," I cry out as I reach up, taking hold of where he has a grip on my hair while I kick my feet, trying to stand.

He stops dead in his tracks, turning to face me, before kicking me hard in my stomach, knocking the air out of me.

"Shut your mouth. You'll speak only if I want you to." He continues down the hallway until he pulls me into our bedroom and drops me down on the floor. He steps over to the bed, taking hold of the belt laying there, before he begins to beat me with it. He catches me a few times across the head before I'm able to lift my arms to shield myself.

I don't know how long he does it, but eventually, he stops, drops the belt to the floor, and moves to the bed. I can hear the squeak of the springs as he sits down on it, then the lights go out. The thought of getting up and moving over to the bed occurs to me, but I don't. I stay there, lying still until I hear his soft snores.

I roll over, getting on my hands and knees, and crawl over to the bed. Taking hold of the edge, I pull myself up, slowly standing, then crawl on top of it. I move up, making sure to stay on my side and not touch Scott. The room is spinning from everything that just happened. Once my head hits the pillow, my eyes close, and I fall to sleep, praying this is the beating I don't wake from.

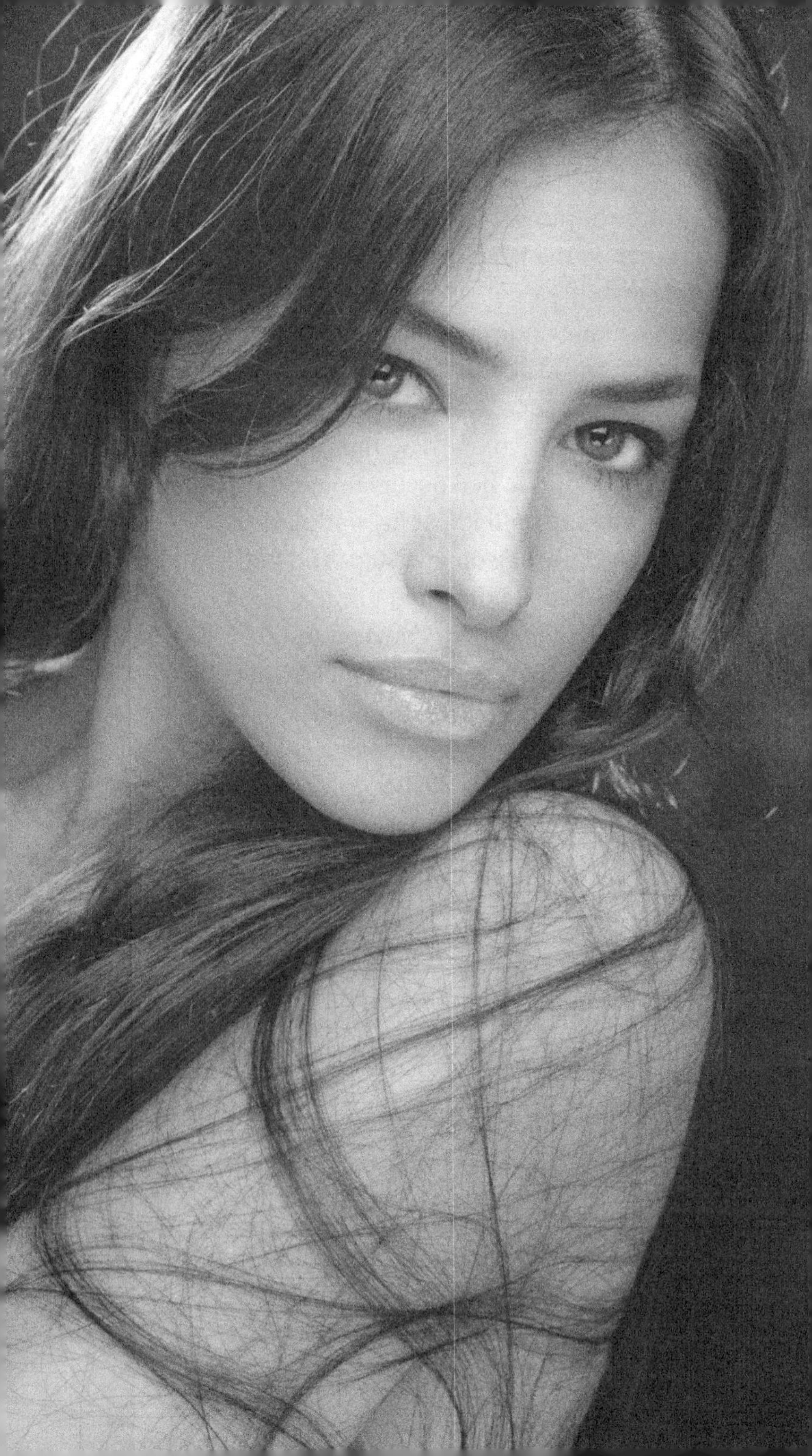

CHAPTER 16

Lucy

The beeping of the alarm sitting on the nightstand wakes me the next morning. It feels like I've just gone to bed, and when I manage to pry my eyes open, I see the time; five-thirty. Reaching out, I turn it off, not wanting to piss off Scott, and slowly sit up. Every muscle in my body screams in agony, hating me for everything it's been put through.

I sit on the edge of the bed, trying to figure out how in the hell I'm going to be able to work all day, and then go to that fucking club tonight and dance. I've barely gotten six hours of sleep in the last forty-eight hours and my body is already feeling like I'm going to pass out from exhaustion.

Standing slowly, I fall back onto the bed. Taking a deep breath, I do it again, this time staying upright, so I head to the bathroom to quickly shower and dress for work. Scott was smart this time. He didn't hit me in the face, so there are no marks there, but there is bruising on my arm where I attempted to protect myself from the belt. As I pull off my clothing from last night, I see my body didn't fare as well as my face. It's riddled with ugly bruising and welts. It's so bad that even with all the makeup in the world, I'll never be able to cover them all up. How the hell am I supposed to work tonight to pay back the debt that I now owe Cal? Just the thought that I may be forced to suck his dick has me sick.

I can't think about that now, though, it's a worry for later. Now I need to shower and dress for work at the diner. That's the first thing on my list. Turning the water on, I step under it, flinching as the first drops of hot water hit my battered and broken body. It stings, but also feels good, if that's possible. It slowly helps relieve the ache that's settled deep in my bones. Knowing I need to hurry, I quickly pick up the sponge, squeeze a little body wash on it, and scrub myself, trying to be as gentle as possible.

Once I feel clean, I turn the water off and step out, pulling the towel from the rack as I go. Drying quickly, I get dressed and opt to leave my hair down, when pulling it up into a ponytail proved painful. Stepping back into the bedroom, I quickly gather up some clothes to wear, making sure not to wake the sleeping beast in the bed. His snores fill the room, and all I can do is envision how easy it would be to smother him with his pillow or tie him up and tightly wrap plastic around his head. I quickly shake off the heinous thoughts. Hating myself for even having them.

Reaching down, I pick up my shoes that I somehow took off before climbing into bed last night. Pain courses through my body at the movement. Gritting my teeth, I snatch them up, then tip-toe out of the room, swallowing all my screams of discomfort and pain.

Looking back at his sleeping form as I step out of the room, I flip him the bird before pulling the door shut behind me. Heading out to the living room, I gingerly lower myself onto the couch and put on my shoes. It's only when I look up at the clock on the wall, do I see the time. I've got about ten minutes to make it to the end of the street and I know with the way I'm feeling, it's going to take that long, if not more, to get there.

Standing up, I move over to the rack by the door and pull off the beautiful coat Noah bought for me. I let my fingers trail over the soft fur around the collar and take a moment to imagine what it would be like if he were my husband. How it would feel to be cherished and loved instead of ridiculed and treated like a piece of property. Slipping my arms into the sleeves, I wrap myself up in the warmth it provides, then pull on the gloves and toboggan before picking up my wallet and keys and heading out into the cold morning air.

Taking my time, I walk down the quiet road. All the houses are dark, except for a few who have their porch lights on. There's frost on the ground and the air is nippy, cutting straight through to my bones, making me even more thankful for the coat.

Looking down the street, I see his truck parked underneath the streetlight. He must see me too, because I see his door open and he steps out. He did it yesterday too, and I'm coming to realize that after the first couple of dates I had with Scott, he never opened any kind of door for me again. It should have been my first clue of what a damn loser he was.

As I walk closer to Noah, I wish more and more that I was with him. Then guilt hits me. I'm married. I shouldn't be having thoughts like this. Before I know it, I'm stepping right up in front of him, trying my hardest to hide my pain.

"Good mornin', Lucy. The jacket looks good on you." His voice is deep and his southern drawl is even more prominent this morning.

"Thank you again for getting this for me. It's a lot warmer than my other one." As I head to the passenger side, I hear him mumble behind me, *'Anything would be better than what you were wearing,'* and I can't help but feel a little bit of embarrassment. How many other people thought the same thing, but never uttered a word? What did they think of me wearing something so ill-fitting for the weather?

I climb into the truck, barely containing the agony I'm feeling. Noah closes the door for me, and I turn my head, fiddling with the seat belt so he can't see the pain etched on my face. He doesn't need to know. He'd ask questions, one's I couldn't give him the answers to. Hell, if Scott knew he gave me this jacket, not to mention the rides to work, he'd kill me and Noah.

"How was your night, Lucy?" Noah asks as he settles into the driver's seat.

"Uh, it was okay. Nothing to write home about." I give him a forced smile, hoping he doesn't ask anything else.

"Yeah, neither was mine. I hung out at the clubhouse, drank a little too much." It seems like he wants to elaborate on it, like there's something more he wants to tell me, but he doesn't.

"Sounds fun. I've only drunk a couple of times, but it's been years since I have. Probably wouldn't even know what I'd like anymore." I give a snort, especially since

I work in a bar, so you'd think I'd know of something that sounded good to drink. In my defense though, most get beer or hard liquor, and I always liked the sweeter drinks.

"You don't need to drink, darlin', it ain't all the hype they make it out to be." He rests his forearm on the armrest as he begins to crack his fingers with his thumb.

I keep my head down, stealing glances at him as he drives. Suddenly, my eyes catch the glint of silver on the ring finger of his left hand as he grips the steering wheel. A wedding ring. Shit, he's married and here with me. What would his wife think? My heart begins to race as I start to panic.

"Pull over, Noah!" I shout, as I start to pull my arm out of the jacket, shoving the pain I'm feeling deep down inside of me.

"What the hell are you doin' woman?!" he shouts right back.

"You need to let me out. I swear I didn't know."

He pulls to the side of the road as my hand grasps the door handle. He must've caught my movement because he hits the door lock button and holds it down, preventing me from opening the door.

"Calm the hell down, Lucy. What are you going on about?" He looks at me, concern in his eyes about my erratic behavior.

"I shouldn't be in this truck with you, and you shouldn't have bought this jacket. It's bad enough that I'm married, but so are you. I won't be the cause for any trouble in your marriage." I'm fighting back tears, and I already know he must think I'm a blubbering pathetic mess. I'm always about to cry when I'm around him. Hell, it's become a common occurrence for me.

His face doesn't look like a man who's been caught in his infidelity, but it holds a sadness. He huffs as he twists the ring around his finger with his right hand.

"Lucy, first off, we haven't done anything wrong. We haven't kissed or said anything inappropriate to each other, so your husband has nothing to be angry about. Should I have bought you a jacket or be bringing you to work without his consent? No, I shouldn't. But he should also be stepping up to the plate and doing these things for you. If I've made you uncomfortable doing these things, I apologize, but I won't stop doing them."

I sit there dumbstruck as he speaks the words so eloquently, but it doesn't escape my notice that he has yet to acknowledge his wife. It makes me sad. Does he think that little of her? Is she that replaceable? He seemed like such a good guy.

"My wife is not a factor in this, Lucy. She's dead." It's all he says, before turning back to the steering wheel, shifting the gear, and pulling back onto the road.

I feel like shit. Utter horseshit. He's doing these things for me out of the kindness of his heart, and I just threw it in his face about his wife and how what he's doing is wrong. When it isn't. It's me who's in the wrong.

The rest of the ride to the diner is full of awkward silence. When we pull into the parking lot, I turn to look at him. "I'm sorry, Noah, I didn't know."

"Of course you didn't. It's okay. You should go on in to work. I got some stuff for the club I need to go handle."

I sit there, shocked. He's angry, I can see it in his tense posture and I did that to him.

"No—"

"Lucy, really, it's okay. Forget about it, she died a while ago. I was just being nice, now go on in and work."

Opening the door, I slide out of the truck and make my way inside, my head hung low in shame. A man who has been nothing but nice to me and I made him feel like he was a cheater. It's like a knife has ripped my heart in two. I've got to find a way to make it up to him, to apologize.

Georgie is standing at the counter, pouring a cup of coffee for the older man perched on the stool in front of her. She looks at me, her eyebrow raised, before her eyes glance behind me to the truck pulling out of the parking lot.

"No Preacher this morning?"

Shaking my head in response to her question. "I think I pissed him off with a comment I made." My voice is soft and shaky.

"What could you have possibly said to piss him off? I mean, it's you, Lucy, you're as sweet as they come."

"I saw his ring and made a comment about how it wasn't right. Him driving me to work and buying me a jacket, questioning him about what his wife would think about it."

Her eyes go wide, and her jaw drops. "Oh, I get it now. Sweetie, you didn't know. He's not mad, he just needs time to process. Trust me." Her eyes hold sympathy for me as she goes back to her customer.

I really hope she's right.

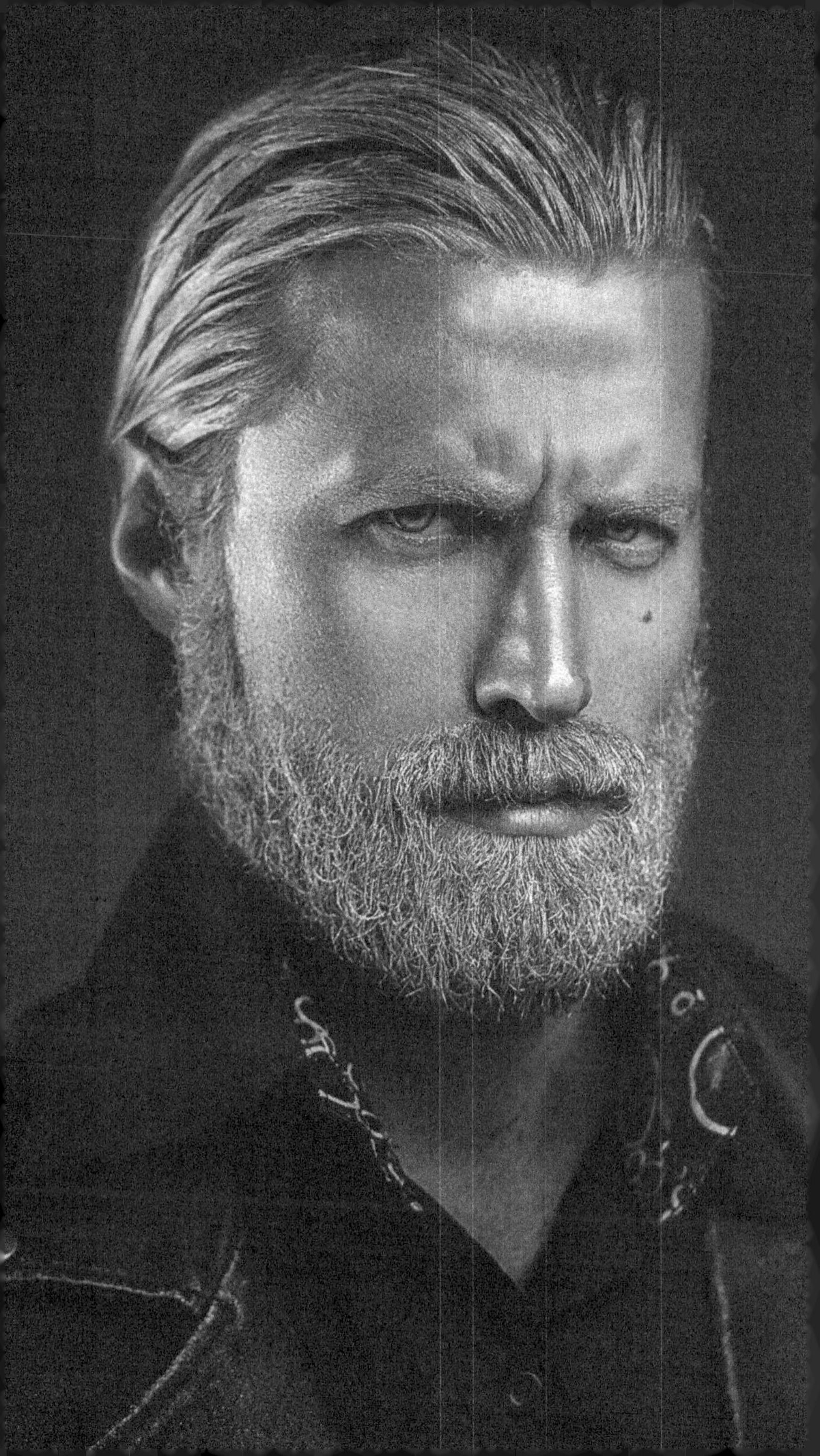

CHAPTER 17

Preacher

I upset her.

But I couldn't stay. I needed to get away, to let the shock of what she said pass. Gunner often asks me why I continue to wear my wedding band and I never have an answer for him. I know why; if I take it off, I feel like it would be saying goodbye to her forever and I can't do that, not yet anyway. It's been six years since she and Carmen were killed but, in my heart, it was just yesterday.

An hour and a half later, I pull back into the diner parking lot, ready to apologize to Lucy. Once I park, I sit there for another fifteen minutes, just watching her through the window. She's moving slowly, and I can tell each step is killing her. What happened to her this time? She needs help, and it's time I stopped pussyfooting around and offer it to her. Clearly, no one else is going to. Just before I'm about to get out, my phone buzzes.

Picking it up from where I have it in the console, I see it's a message from Rizzo.

Rizzo: Never heard back. Thought I would have after you read the email.

Me: Got sidetracked and never read it.

Rizzo: Go do it then. I have nothing but time right now to wait for you to text back.

Me: Where's Hawke?

Rizzo: Sour puss is sitting across from me, looking like someone stuck a corncob up his ass.

Me: Opening it now.

Flipping over to my email, I scan through the recent ones. There's one from one of my old Deacons and I open it first to read. It's been a while since I've heard from him.

Hello Noah,

It's been more than a year since I messaged you, but I wanted to let you know the exciting news. My daughter, Mariela, had her first child, a daughter. She loved your wife and daughter so much and she wanted to honor their memory. Attached is a photo of her, Bianca Carmen Santos.

My eyes go blurry and it hits me. I miss her so much. Carmen would be eleven. I try to picture in my head what she would look like now, but all I can see is the sweet angelic face of my five-year-old.

I go back to the email, wanting to read the last few lines before I see what Rizzo sent me.

I want you to know we all miss you. We understand how hard it was for you, more so than the rest of us. But know you always have a home here with us. Mariela has not planned the baptism, but in her heart, she would love for you to do it. Just tell me you'll think about it and get back to me.

Samuel

My fingers hover over the keyboard but it's just not in me to respond. Instead, I close it, and scroll until I get to Rizzo's, ready to see what has her all worked up for me to read.

Hey Preacher Man,

So I told you I was better than Jenner, why all you men seem to doubt my skills is beyond me.

But here you go, next time maybe you men won't be so stupid.

Lucy Jane Davis, born January 20th Lucy Hales, 2001 graduated from Calgary High School in Alaster, Kentucky. Married Scott Jason Davis right after she graduated. He was her high school boyfriend. They moved here four years ago.

Now to the good stuff.

This guy is a real piece of work. Lucy has been in and out of the ER with multiple broken bones, contusions, and falls. All are the result of some type of fall and are always close together. She has not only been to the ER here, but also in surrounding cities. It doesn't stop there. Even in high school, she was a victim of accidents.

He has a standing room at the seedy ass motel out on 11th Avenue and has been there with different women, so yeah, a real gem.

He doesn't seem to be employed by any local company, not paying any taxes yet, and his bank account gets a sizeable deposit on the 16th of every month. The interesting thing is he's behind on his mortgage and car payment and just had his electricity cut off two weeks ago, before paying to have it turned back on. Each time the mortgage or car comes up to be taken, he mysteriously gets caught up. He apparently also owes a debt to the owner of House of Puss.

Yep, I can see your face now. We all know Cal is a sleazy motherfucker.

Getting you more, but thought you'd like to know that your girl is living in a hellhole, and I expect you to have her out of there by the time I get back, which is in a couple days.

Rizzo

I have to take deep breaths in and out, because it's taking everything in me not to drive over to Lucy's house and kill that asshole she calls her husband. To beat his wife so badly that she needs to go to the emergency room is punishable by death in my book. How could her parents allow it to happen? I don't even know her that well, but I knew right away that something was wrong.

Rizzo: Well, is the reason you haven't responded because you're bathing the streets in blood? If you are, pictures or it didn't happen.

Me: All this is true, every word?

Rizzo: I wouldn't have sent it if it wasn't. The club needs to save her. I need her to be saved.

I can feel the desperation in her text. Rizzo doesn't really have female friends and has always grown up under the shelter of the club. The whores at the club steer clear of her, unless they're trying to get in with one of the brothers. She was used once before, and after she beat the whore to within an inch of her life, they tend to not use her as a gateway to any of the men any longer.

Me: Are there any answers about you?

Rizzo: Yes.... but I don't want to talk about it yet.

Me: I'm here. In another lifetime, I was a good listener.

Rizzo: You still are in this lifetime. Now get out of your truck, go inside, and save your girl.

Me: She's not my girl and I've told you to remove that tracking app from my phone.

Rizzo: Told you I wasn't going to, besides Gunner likes the idea of knowing where his brothers are, even plans to put it on everyone's phones, especially if he can do it without them knowing. That shit with the Hellions hit hard, and it wasn't even our club.

Rizzo: And she is your girl, you just haven't realized it yet, or better yet, you haven't come to terms with it yourself yet.

Me: She's married.

Rizzo: That can change. Make it change, GTG.

I love her, but she can be infuriating at times. Turning off the truck, I open the door to head inside. The bell jingles over the door as I open it and her head immediately turns in my direction, calling out a good morning.

Her face drops, not knowing why I'm here or the reaction I'll give her, seeing how I didn't leave her on the best of terms just a short while ago.

I head straight back to the booth, our booth, and take a seat. A few minutes later, she heads my way, stopping at the end of the booth. "Noah—"

"No, Lucy, please sit for a minute." She glances over her shoulder, checking on the other customers, before looking to Georgie, who gives her a nod.

She slides into the booth, placing her hands on the table.

"Okay, first I'm not upset with you. I know you didn't know when you saw my ring, and you assumed what any logical person would. I was married, even had a daughter, but they were killed six years ago. It gutted me. I even wanted to die myself. It's one of the reasons I wear the ring. It's like if I keep it on, a piece of her is still with me. If I made you feel uncomfortable, I'm sorry. But, seeing you, I see a broken flower and I want to help fix you. I'm here to help you in any way you need. It hasn't slipped my notice, the bruises and the painful way you move. You can say it's from a fall, but it's not." Reaching into my pocket, I pull out the slip of paper that I had written my number on earlier and slide it over to her. "Call me anytime you need me, Lucy. I'll be there day or night." She picks it up, holding it in her hands like I've just given her the winning lottery ticket. "Now, do you work tomorrow?"

"Yeah, same time."

"Okay, I'll see you at the same time and place." Standing, I head right back out of the diner. I need to think about how I plan to proceed with Lucy, but most importantly, I need to have my head on straight for tonight.

Once I'm inside my truck, I head back to the clubhouse. I need to get some rest before we meet to discuss tonight. Drinking yesterday and getting up early this morning haven't done any favors for me.

I've no sooner stepped a foot inside of the clubhouse, not even fully in the door, before Gunner is calling my name, ordering me to Hawke's office. He says nothing more, so I know it's about tonight's sting.

"Shut the door," he tells me when I enter the office.

He steps behind the desk and takes a seat. "Okay, so it's you and Cyrus goin' inside tonight. Snake, Sundance, and I, are goin' to be outside. We'll be in the van waitin' for you to deliver the package to us. Just make sure he's breathin' so we can talk to his ass and find out who he's workin' for. We know he isn't the big dog, but he's trusted enough with the drop. Best of all, we can get some of our money back from the fuckers."

"Sounds good to me. I'm goin' to my room to get some sleep. I'll be back down before we head out."

I go to leave, but he calls out, stopping me. "Have you heard anything yet?"

"All I know is Rizzo said they got the answer, but it wasn't good. They'll be back in a couple of days. I don't think it's good though, so we all need to be prepared. I got a feelin' whatever it is will break Hawke. She's all the family he has other than us."

"We'll be here for both of them. Get some rest. You look like shit."

I just flip him off and shut the door behind me, heading straight for my room and the bed that's calling my name.

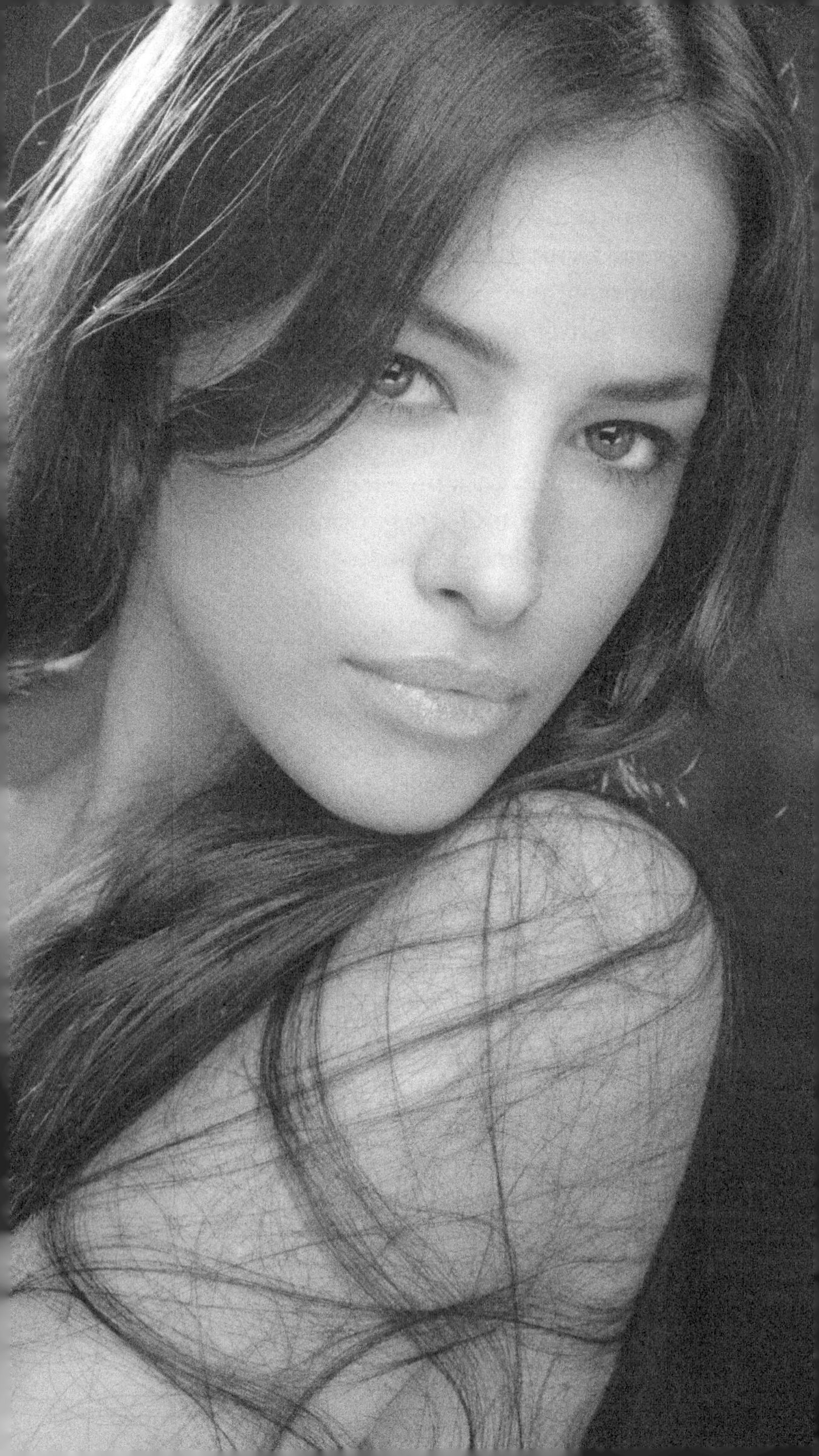

CHAPTER 18

Lucy

He knows, maybe not everything, but enough to piece it together. I slide the piece of paper with his number into my pocket and stand from the booth. He didn't stay, or push me, rather he left it in my hands to make a decision. Moving slowly, I pass by all my tables, ensuring that the patrons need nothing from me, before stepping behind the counter where Georgie is.

"What was that about?"

"He told me he wasn't mad at me. He knew I didn't know about his wife, and that her and his daughter died. Not anything more. Just that it's been hard for him. The ring was a way to keep a part of her with him." The sadness on Georgie's face tells me she already knew all this. It might have been nice if she had shared it with me.

"He's a good man, just been dealt a raw deal in life," Georgie says, before spinning in her spot and rushing off toward the kitchen, leaving me standing there with more questions.

Noah calls to me in a way I've never felt before, but I feel guilty. *I know I shouldn't.* I know my husband is scum. It's why I'm trying to get away. But until I do, I am still married, and I should respect that bond. *Shouldn't I?* But the way Noah treats me has me rethinking my situation.

The bell over the door rings as a group of teenage girls step inside and head to the booth that Noah normally sits in, pulling me back to work. Slowly, I head over to them, already pulling out my pen and notepad to take their order.

The rest of the day flies by and I feel more tired than ever. All this moving around has my body screaming at me even more. Just thinking about going to the club has me wanting to die. I've barely made it through the day here. How the hell am I supposed to dance on a pole tonight? Not to mention, I have to face Cal. My stomach is already tied up in knots just thinking about it.

As the end of my shift nears and most of my tables have cleared, I go about doing the side work for the next shift. Making sure all the silverware is rolled, the condiments on the table are filled, and then sweep under the tables. Every movement kills me.

While I'm doing all this, I begin to plan. If I were to just take the money I have and leave, how far could I get? Would there be a women's shelter I could stay in? Would I feel comfortable on the streets? But the most important thing I worry about is would Scott come looking for me or just move on.

Cindy waves as she passes me. She looks happy, and it makes me smile that someone is. She swapped shifts with one of the night girls, so she could come in later, since she went out of town to be with her sister who just had her baby.

She's back out before I know it, sidling up next to me to give me a hip check that has me flinching in pain. "Want to see my niece? She's so stinking cute, I could eat her up."

Biting back the scream that wants to rip from my body, I smile and watch as she flips through all the pictures in her phone. Such a beautiful baby. Once I wanted kids. But there's no way in hell I'd bring them into the world, not while I'm with Scott. Thankfully, he doesn't want kids, so when we do have sex, he makes sure to wear a condom. I was on birth control, but then the cost for it went up at the health department and I couldn't afford them anymore.

"She's beautiful." My eyes tear up. "Well, I'm going to head out of here. It's been pretty steady today. I overheard a couple of girls talking about some of the kids meeting here later before heading to some party, so it may pick up even more."

"Great, just what I want, smart ass teenagers," Cindy says with a laugh, as she puts her phone in the pocket of her apron.

I head to the back, pulling the cash from my pocket and count my tips. I'd love to be able to give some more to Georgie to save for me, but I didn't make enough. I debate saying fuck it and pulling about forty from the hundred I made and risk the beating I know keeping it would cause from Scott. Holding it in my hand, I go back and forth before sliding the full hundred into my pocket.

Reaching back, I untie the apron and pull my coat from the hook it's on, putting it on. I stop by the phone long enough to call the number for the cab service, then head out front to wait. The wind is blowing with such force I have to take a couple of steps a few times to stay upright.

It's not long before I see the yellow cab pull into the parking lot. Opening the door, I step inside and keep my head down, not wanting to make small talk today. I just don't have the energy to do it, nor the desire. Much to my relief, the driver doesn't want to chit-chat. Hopefully, the rest of the night proves to go as well.

As we pull up to the club, I take the money for the fare and a small tip and hold it in my hand. As I sit and count it, it hits me. It was a good thing I didn't pull the forty and give it to Georgie. After I pay for this ride and then the ride home, I'm only going to have about fifty dollars left to give Scott. He's going to think I kept money, not caring that I had to pay for the rides tonight.

In fact, he hasn't even asked for any of the money he expects me to make from the club, which leads me to wonder if he knew Cal was going to keep every dime I make. Jazmin and Candi had tried to convince me to keep some of the money from the tips I make and stash them away in my locker. Or give them some to hide for me, before I had to hand what I made over to Cal. Now it hits me how stupid it was of me not to do it.

Sucking it up, I hand the money to the driver when he stops the car, then I head inside, dreading the night to come.

"You've put it off long enough. It's time to get your ass on the stage," Cal barks at me from the doorway where he's standing. I managed to stay off his radar and just went about waiting on the tables. Jazmin and Candi helped me come up with an outfit that covers the bruises and welts on my body. They did the best they could after applying makeup.

"Cal—"

"What the hell are you wearing, anyway? This is a fucking strip joint. The men out there want to see skin, not you covered up. Take those fucking tight things off and dress in something else. Something that will easily come off while you're up there on the damn stage and make it quick," he barks, before turning and leaving the room.

My body shakes as I sit there. Terror courses through my body. I've got to get on stage and show them my body. How the hell am I ever going to do this? I slip off the shoes, knowing I need to dress the way Cal wants me to. Maybe if I show him how I look, he'll tell me to wait until my body has healed. He's an ass, but I'm sure he doesn't want any dancers on his stage that look like she's beaten the fuck-up. Which technically I do at the moment because I was.

I pull down the black tight-looking leggings that disappear under the tiny skirt I'm wearing and connect to the underwear by the garter belt. Ugly black and blue marks cover areas of my legs and I frown at the sight. Next, I pull off the sheer cover up top, leaving me in just a bra. Putting the shoes back on, I head out to the front to find Cal.

The club is packed, more so than when I slipped into the back. Looking through the crowd, I spot Cal talking to some overweight, balding guy at the bar and head his way. I offer up a prayer that he'll see reason and I can come out of tonight without having to take off my clothes.

He's talking, but I can't make out what he's saying to the guy. Cal doesn't even acknowledge me when I step up beside him, not even when I clear my throat. The man he's talking to does, though, letting his eyes trail up my body, stopping on my chest. He sees the bruising but doesn't say a word, like it was some kind of common occurrence for him.

"Who's this, Cal? You've been holding out on me?" The slimeball asks as he reaches out, taking hold of my hair and giving it a tug, pulling me closer to him, before letting go and wrapping his arm around my waist, holding tight. I go to resist, but Cal gives me a stern look, letting me know if I resist, there would be trouble.

"She's my new girl, John. Her old man got in deep with me and couldn't pay off his debt. Sent his woman to work it off for him. She's a bit frigid, but I plan to work that bitchiness out of her."

The both of them laugh, one that has the hairs on my skin standing on end like a frightened cat. "Looks like someone else has already taught her one." He grips me tighter, and I can feel the tips of his fingers digging into my body. I imagine he's already left his own marks, ones that I'm sure Scott will notice right away and question. "I love it when they're broken and weak. Makes the tears they shed when I fuck them even more delicious."

"What is it you want, Siren? You should be getting ready to go on stage," Cal demands as he glares at me.

"I...I..." I stammer, but it only makes him more pissed.

"Spit it out bitch, I ain't got all night and neither do you."

"Shouldn't I wait until my bruises heal?" I ask in more of a plea.

"Who the hell cares? They want to see your damn tits and that pretty pink pussy of yours. No one here cares if the package has some dents, as long as they get the flesh."

I stand there wide-eyed in disbelief. His words, so vulgar and cruel. Cal is truly just as heartless as Scott. Knowing I will never win, I turn and make my way to the stage with my head dipped low. I've got to find a way to make it through this, at least tonight. Then I need to talk to Scott and tell him there's no way I can do this. He'll have to find another way to repay his debt.

Candi is on the stage, finishing her dance as I slowly make my way up the steps to the stage platform, waiting to be announced. Candi does her ending move on the pole before picking up the cash on the stage and her discarded clothing and heads my way. She stops in front of me and leans in, whispering in my ear.

"You got this. Just get out there and move. They'll like it no matter what, just show your skin. Pretend they're not there and the room is empty, and before you know it, the song will be over, and you'll be done. The first time is always the hardest."

The emcee announces me, and I step out onto the stage and do just as Candi told me to. I pretend the room is empty and move to the beat of the music, allowing it to take over me and guide my movements as I slowly remove my clothes until I'm just in my thong. I know Cal said to strip nude, but none of the other girls do, so I don't either. Once the music ends, I snatch up my clothing and the cash and rush off the stage, straight to the back, ignoring all the cat calls.

Only when I'm back in the dressing room, do I let out a sigh of relief. I did it.

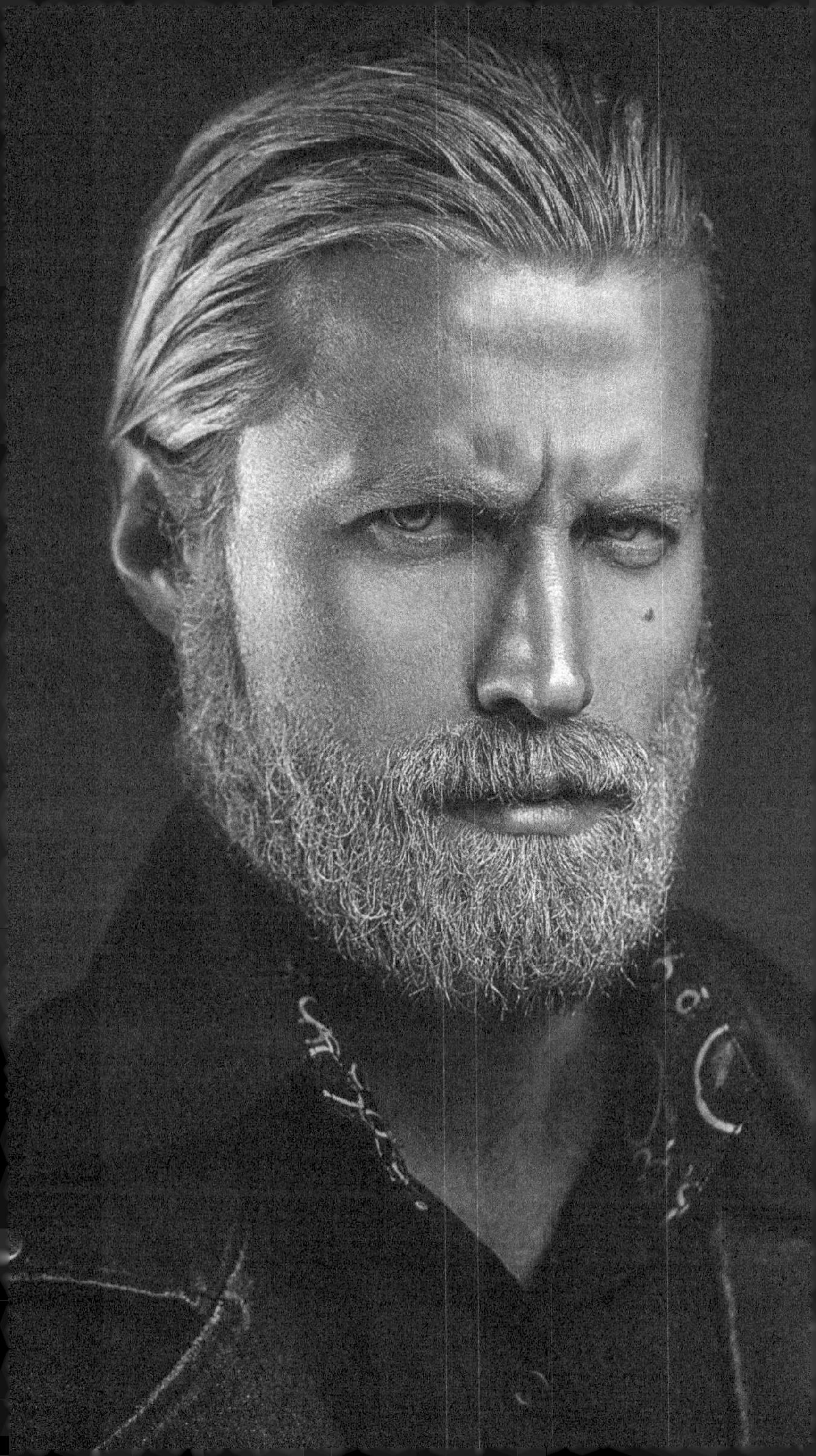

CHAPTER 19

Preacher

This place is a fucking dump. Of course, this would be where they would have their shady ass deal take place. With all the people in here, it's also going to make it harder to pick out our mark. We need to be on top of our game, our eyes scan and check every fucking person out. Cyrus and I are going in tonight without our cuts on, so we don't alert anyone we're part of the Merciless Few.

We both head straight to a table that gives us a perfect view of where he suspects the mark will be sitting tonight. Currently, no one is there, but it's only nine and the meeting is set to take place at ten.

"Can I get you boys something to drink?" a sultry voice says from beside me. Looking over, I see a brunette, with far too much makeup on and nothing left to the imagination with what she's wearing. She's not someone who interests me. There's one woman who feeds my mind right now, and if I need to get my dick wet, then I can get that at the clubhouse.

"Yeah doll, give us two Budweisers," Cyrus says for us, already sensing my annoyance.

"Come on, man, she was fuckin' cute. You can't tell me your dick didn't notice." He grins at me as he lets his eyes scan the room, never moving his head.

"She ain't my type, besides—"

"Brother, we all know you got it bad for the hot little waitress. You really think JD hasn't gossiped about it like a fuckin' girl? We all know about it, the rides and the coat you got for her."

"I'm gonna murder his ass. I don't care if he is related to Hawke." I clench my hands, an overwhelming urge to punch something taking over me.

"Nah, don't do that. Seriously, man, we're all happy for you. You deserve to find a good one, but you should probably let her know how you feel. Hold on, check it out. I think our mark is here."

We both watch as a guy about five foot eight, a hundred and eighty-five pounds with dark brown hair slides into the booth. He taps his fingertips on the counter as he looks around before calling a waitress over to him. The man slides his arm around the waitress as she steps up to him, planting the palm of his hand on her ass as he gropes her. We see her try to pull away, but he keeps a firm grip on her.

Scum. Another man comes from the left, over by the bar, and the scum drops his arm, allowing her to scurry away as the other man slides in on the opposite side of the booth with him.

"Think they're who we're waiting for?" Cyrus leans in, asking me.

"Possible. Let's keep our eyes on them."

They speak back and forth, both of them seeming to become more heated with every word before the other guy stands and makes his way back to the bar.

"That's fuckin' weird," Cyrus whispers, just as the girl with our beers appears in front of us, setting them down on the table. Pulling out my wallet, I take out a twenty, when I have an idea. I pull out another one and flash them to her.

"So, I got the change and an extra twenty for you if ya can answer a couple of questions."

"Okay, anything, baby." She sidles up between Cyrus and me and bends down closer to us.

I gesture in the direction of the man at the bar first. "Who's that?"

She stands and looks over that way. "Cal. He owns this place."

"And the guy over there?"

"Oh, that jerk. He owes Cal some money. The asshole even sent his girl here to work to pay off his debt. I don't know his name; I tend to stay away from him since he's bad news."

"Thanks, you can go," I tell her after handing her the money.

"That's some low-down shit man." Cyrus picks up his beer and takes a long swallow, his eyes never leaving the fucker in the booth.

The emcee announces another dancer, Jazmin, making her way onto the stage. Cyrus' eyes immediately perk up when he sees her. "They got some fuckin' hot women workin' here."

"I guess," I reply, just as I see the fucker stand and rush across the room, grabbing someone by the arm. I can tell it's a female, but her face is blocked from my view, before totally disappearing as he drags her down the hallway. Cal, the one the little girl called the owner, must catch what happens and storms off in their direction. Guess the asshole got handsy with one of his dancers.

"Guess he wasn't our guy, just happened to sit in the seat we expected," Cyrus announces.

"Yeah, let's keep our eyes open and that means you need to keep yours off the fuckin' women."

"Yeah, yeah, okay, Dad," he scoffs, as he waves his hands at me.

"You heard what I said"—then to drive the point home—"Son!" He barks out a laugh at my words.

"Hold on, we got incomin'." He bumps my hand as he shoots a low-key finger gesture in the direction of the table.

Stepping up to the table and looking skeezy as hell is a younger guy, with sleeves on both arms, dressed in tight jeans and a black t-shirt. He stops in his tracks when he sees the table empty, but sits down on the side facing the door, giving us a perfect view of his face. We watch as he reaches up, pulling his long black hair in his hands, and pulls it into a man bun on the top of his head with a hair tie he slips off of his wrist.

"Looks promisin'," I lean into Cyrus, whispering.

"Yeah, he's checkin' out the joint." Cyrus lifts his phone, making sure the flash is off and takes a picture, immediately sending it to the guys in our group text.

Gunner: Got it. Saw him go in. Fucker parked in the back, out of sight.

Me: Jenner, keep watch on the email cause this fucker looks cagey. We need to make sure he

doesn't message someone and let them in on shit not bein' right.

Jenner: Guys, really, so little faith. Already workin' on it.

Cyrus: That's right, the tech genius is here to save the day. Bet he can make a woman too, like in that 80s movie.

Jenner: Fuck you. Least I got skills.

Gunner: Both of you cut the shit. What's this plan, Jenner?

Jenner: Gonna send him an email. Bet the fucker has his phone on him. Give him some bullshit about runnin' late or shit and bein' sick and have him meet me out back.

Me: Good plan, but what if they don't know what the other drives? They could just meet inside every time.

Jenner: Preach, seriously, you should have more faith. That's why I didn't mention the car. Out back puts them out of sight of people seein' what's goin' on and lets us grab him up without pryin' eyes.

Gunner: Do it.

We watch as the guy keeps his eyes focused on the door, blowing off the dancer who stops by his booth and tries to talk to him. Making it even more likely this is our guy. A few moments later, he pulls his phone from his back pocket and then pushes some buttons. He appears to be reading something before he types out a reply.

Jenner: Worked. He'll be headin' out in about five minutes. Be ready to follow.

Cyrus and I wait, perched on the edge of our seats, for him to make his move. We're going to stay back far enough so that he doesn't see us. Once he rounds the building, the others will be there to get him. We'll be the backup in case he slips away from them, which is highly unlikely, but hey, there's always a chance.

When the fucker stands, we know it's time. We give him a small head start, not wanting him to catch on that he's being watched. Just as I go to stand, the emcee comes on announcing the next dancer. Siren. I don't know why I turn to look, but I do, and I see red. There on the stage is Lucy, and she looks like fuckin' hell.

"Come on, Preach, we got to go, man, and you were the one goin' on about me keepin' my head in the game." He's right. I fucking hate it, but he is. We got club business to handle, so this will have to wait. But you better fucking believe me and Lucy are having a talk.

I fight off the urge to rush onto the stage and throw her over my shoulder, and step in behind Cyrus as we follow the fucker out the front door. We hold on a moment when we step outside, giving him a chance to round the building. We know our men are in place and waiting.

Once he's disappeared around the side of the building, we move with speed, chasing behind him. Turning the corner, we see him there in a standoff with Jenner.

"Who the fuck are you? Get out of my way!" the mark shouts at him angrily.

"But I'm who you're waitin' for?"

"No, the hell you aren't," he barks back as he goes to shove Jenner out of his way, but Jenner is faster and takes hold of his arm, spins and twists it behind the guy's back, causing him to fall to the ground. Once he's down, he pulls the gun from the back of his pants and clocks him over the back of his head, knocking the fucker out.

Jenner releases him, and the man drops to the ground. "Thanks for the help, assholes."

"You had it under control. We just wanted to see what the tech genius could do," comes from Cyrus, before he steps up to the guy. He uses his foot to flip him on his side and then kicks him right in the gut. "Let's get him in the van and get the hell out of here."

Gunner and Sundance step out of the shadows, picking the limp body up and tossing him in the back of the van, where we have duct tape and rope waiting. Sundance climbs in the back and begins securing him, just in case he wakes up.

"Let's get out of here and get to the warehouse so Preach can do his thing," Gunner orders. Cyrus and I turn and head to our bikes as the rest climb into the van. As I reach my bike, my feet want to keep moving like they have a mind of their own and they want to head straight inside the club. If I'm honest, my heart wants to head there too. The thought of all those men in there looking at what's *mine* makes me want to go on a murderous rampage.

"Come on, Preach, what the fuck's goin' on with you, man? Let's go. It's time for the fun to begin," Cyrus calls out over the rumble from his bike. He backs his bike up slowly while I climb on mine and start it up. Tomorrow. I can wait until tomorrow, then I'm going to claim what's mine. Fuck everyone, I don't give a shit if she's married. Lucy Davis will be *mine*.

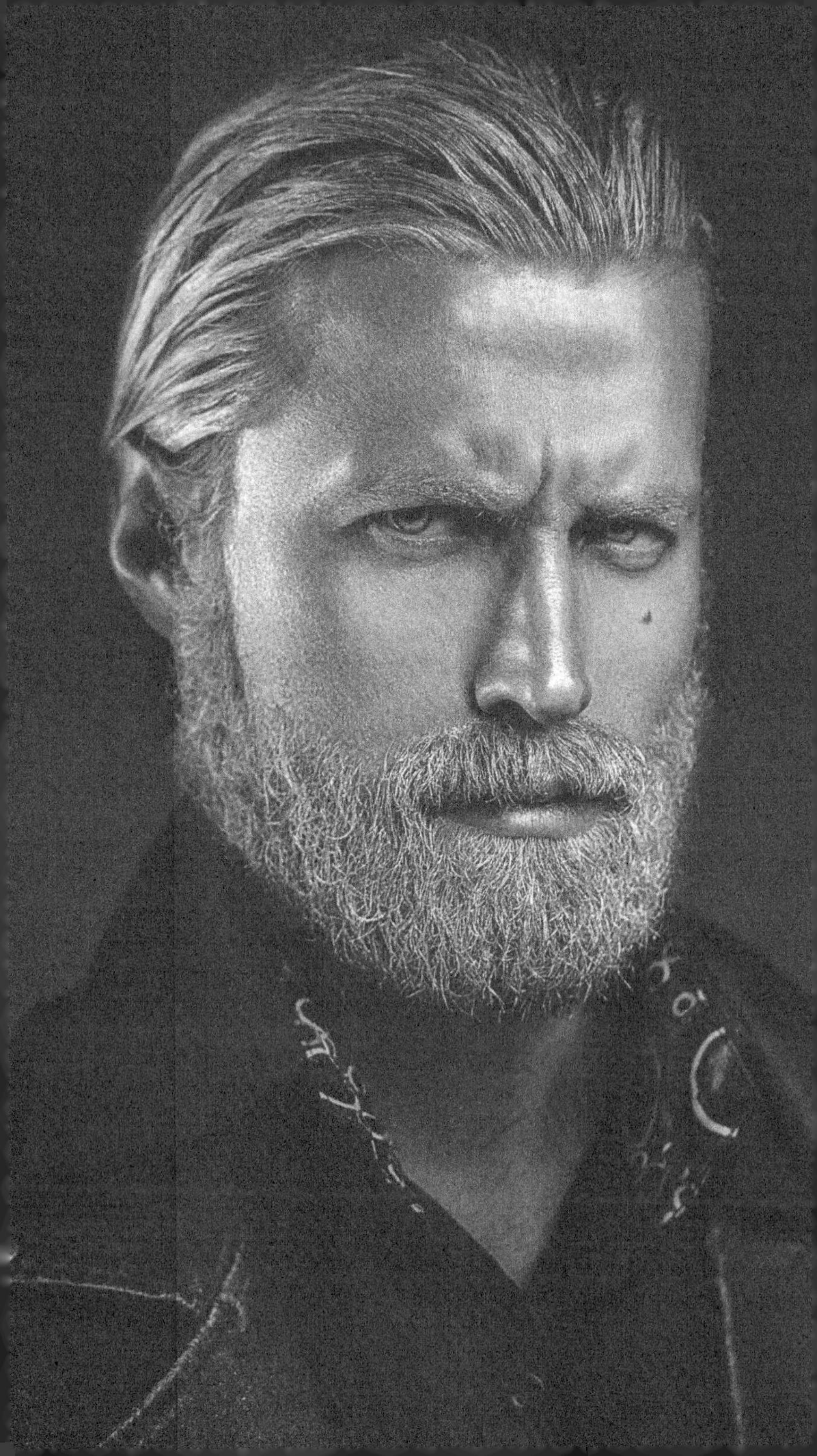

CHAPTER 20

Preacher

I pull my bike inside the warehouse, parking it next to Cyrus. Once we dismount, we both move over to the bay doors and close them, shutting the world out and leaving us to have fun in our playroom with our shiny new toy.

Gunner and Sundance pull him out of the van and then drag him over to the metal chair that's bolted to the floor in the middle of the room. They tie him up all nice, like a Christmas present. Stepping over to my worktable, I pick up my brass knuckles and slip them on each hand. Closing my eyes, I clear my head so I can prepare for what I need to do. Letting the calm pass over me, I do my routine. I pray to God, asking him to let this be the scum that gives me closure for my wife and daughter's murder. It's not the typical prayer I know, but it's only said before I use my brand of torture to get the answers the club needs.

The closure never comes, though. I don't expect it to. Years of service to the Lord taught me that it's not His way nor does He answer this particular type of prayer.

"Wake him up!" I shout, not caring who does it.

Turning around, I see Sundance pouring water on top of his head. Once the icy cold hits him, he's tries to jump up, confused about where he is.

"Well, hello douche bag. It's time for some answers. It can be the easy way or the hard way, depending on how you want it." Then the asshole does it; he spits at me, hitting me right in the face. Before I even know it, my fist is connecting against the right side of his face, sending his head flying back as blood gushes from the cut.

"Fuck you," he bites back as he glares at me.

"Do you know who we are?" My voice is cold as I speak, firmly in enforcer mode now.

"Like I fucking care?"

"Seems you and whoever you work for thought it would be cute to steal money from us." It's then that I see the light click on in his head.

"Where's James?" he asks, panic showing on his face.

"Where no one can find him. Seems he didn't want to give me the information I wanted. But now you have the chance to, or you can join him." My fists swing, taking turns hitting him in the head, then aiming down, I catch his gut. He's dazed, unable to focus, as blood drips out of his mouth.

He lets out a string of words, mumbled and unintelligible.

"Wondering how we found you? Well, interesting story. James wasn't good at coverin' his tracks. Now, who are you workin' for?"

"Fuck you, biker scum!" he spews with hatred.

I keep my cool, casually walking over to the worktable and pick up a knife. Twirling it around my fingers, I move back over to him. "Man, I really thought you were going to be more cooperative. Guess I was wrong." Moving behind him, I lift the knife, bringing it down hard, right into the front of his shoulder, stabbing right into the joint, under the clavicle. From my anatomy classes, I know that's where all the nerves that branch out into the arm are located. He lets out a guttural scream as we all laugh, taking joy in his agony.

"I ain't telling you fucking shit."

Oh, this one is going to give us a fight, too. Gunner, Sundance, and Cyrus step over to me. "We're out. Call us when he's ready to talk. We're goin' to check out his house, while Jenner stays here with you."

I just nod, too deep in the torture zone. It's about time for me to up my game. Looking over at the desk in the corner, I see Jenner's already set up shop. His fingers are busy flying over the keyboard of the laptop he has set up. That man is brilliant, and I wish I just had a smidge of his intellect.

Picking up another knife, I head back over to the asshole. "You know, I've had something eatin' away at me and it came to a head tonight. Since I can't take it out on the person I want to, you are a suitable replacement."

Stepping behind him, I lay my hand on the shoulder with the knife in it. "You know, people used to hang on to my words. Listening to everything I said, even sought me out for council. Then one day, one stupid punk took it all from me. Ripped my world apart. Then wouldn't you know it, a ray of light appeared, but I tried to push it away. The need to protect outweighed everything, and I failed. Now I'm goin' to give you all that rage until you crack."

"You don't sca—" He doesn't get to finish before he screams out again, the pain from the knife I just stabbed into the matching spot in his left shoulder.

"I don't scare you. Really, then what scares you?" I ask as he slumps his head down, the shock from the pain taking over as he passes out momentarily.

"Oh look, he matches now!" Jenner pops up with a joke.

"Yeah, we can have a game of ring toss if we get bored. First one to get four on the knife gets to chop off the first body part. We just need to find something to use as rings." Funny thing is, I'm not joking. Jenner immediately jumps up and rushes over to the lockers and begins plundering through them. I knew he would jump to the challenge; he's very competitive.

He shouts a 'hell yeah' before he turns back to me, holding a pack of zip ties in his hand. "Give me like ten minutes to make them and then you're goin' down, Preacher Man."

I turn back to the fucker who's still passed the fuck out and I step up, taking hold of the knives and twist them, digging them into his shoulder even more.

💀 💀 💀

The fucker still hasn't talked, and we've already removed a foot and two hands. What the fuck is this? Even stronger men have broken before getting this far.

"This could be over with; all you have to do is tell us." He's strapped down on a table now, moved him over about three in the morning, to make it easier to move pieces of his body.

"Fuck you," he gasps, his breathing labored, while sweat beads on his forehead. The fucker's in agony and I'd quickly end it for him, but only if he speaks.

"Nah man, I like pussy. But once I run out of shit to cut off, I can always make it, so you don't have to worry about fuckin' anyone anymore." His eyes go wide as he clenches his jaw, right as I swing the butcher knife down, removing his hand. Jenner steps over with the blowtorch, ready to cauterize it. Can't have him bleeding out too early.

He screams, and it's music to my ears. My very own concert, playing all the songs I want to hear, those of anguish and pain. His eyes roll back in his head and he's out again.

"Man, this guy has some balls. Who the hell could they be workin' for that he'd take all this instead of just handin' them over?" Jenner asks as he puts the torch away and hops onto the worktable. He's a good kid. Hell, I call him that, but he's a man, twenty-five. Older than the girl I'm obsessing over.

Fuck! It hits me then as I look at my watch.

Six-thirty.

I'm late, she's probably already left and I don't have any fucking way to get a hold of her other than to call the diner. Pulling out my phone, I search the web for it and then hit dial.

A sassy feminine voice answers on the third ring, *"JD's, how can I help ya?"*

"Can I speak with JD or Georgie?"

"You got her."

"Hey, this is Preacher. Lucy may be late this morning. I got tied up and missed going to pick her up. Can you let her know I'll be stopping by later?"

"Sure can, hon." I end the call, not even bothering to say goodbye. Guess I'll be needing to apologize to Georgie, too. I need to get this shit wrapped up.

Stepping up to the table, I slap the fucker across the face, shocking him awake.

"Look here, you're keepin' me from something important. I'm tired of playin' around with you. Either give me the information I need or I'm just goin' to end this shit. I'm sure no one will miss a worthless piece of crap like you." I take hold of the fishhook on the table and hold it in my hands for him to see.

"I can't tell you shit when I don't know. I got in debt and making these pickups is how I'm paying it off," he finally spills, his eyes wide in shock, most likely wondering what I plan to do with the toy in my hand.

"That's a good start, but I need more. How do they contact you? Once you met with James, what was next?"

"Everything is by email or texts on a burner phone that was delivered to my house." He's crying now, even wet his pants, and by the stench wafting off of him, I'd say he shit himself as well.

"What were you supposed to do after tonight's meetin' with James?" I shift the hook from hand-to-hand, making sure it stays in his eyesight.

"Take the bag with me, wait for a message to come to the burner phone, then follow the instructions. Honestly, that's it. I don't know anything more. Get me to the hospital. I promise not to tell them anything about you, and then I'll disappear."

"And where is this burner phone?"

"It's at my house, under my bed. There's a loose floorboard. I keep it in there with the cash while I wait to hear from them. They always contact me to meet the next day after I meet with James and the drop-off is always the next day after that. It's always at a different location. Same guy but different spot. I don't know his name. He always has a hat and face mask on, so I can't tell who he is other than that. Come on, I need to go to the hospital."

Pulling out my phone, I make a call to Gunner. He picks up right away. *"Did you find anything at the house?"*

"Nah, man. We stayed there until about three this mornin'. Sent the other guys home. I'm keepin' watch outside to see if anyone shows up. Did he finally talk, or did you kill him already?"

"Nah, he held strong, but he's breathin'. He didn't like the looks of my fishhook, though, so he spilled. Said there's a loose floorboard under his bed and has a burner phone hidden beneath it. That's how they plan to contact him, well today, for the drop off tomorrow."

"Hold fast. I'm goin' to go check and I'll call ya back." Gunner ends the call before I have a chance and I look over at my prey on the table.

"Hope you're telling the truth."

About ten minutes later, I get a message.

Gunner: Got it. End him.

"Well, looks like you told the truth." I set the fishhook back on the table, and I see a sense of relief come over the asshole's face. "But I think we all know you weren't walking out of here. Since you finally told the truth, I'm gonna make this quick for you." Reaching back, I pull the gun from off the table, point it right at him and shoot him between the eyes, twice. Blood and brain matter splatter everywhere.

"Shit, that's a damn mess," Jenner says as he not only looks at the body on the table, but at the state of the room, covered in blood.

"Yeah, that's what prospects are for. Go ahead and get their asses over here to clean this up. I'm going to the back to shower, then I'm out of here." Heading to the back of the warehouse, where we have an office that has an adjoining bathroom with a shower. I always keep a change of clothes here, for instances just like tonight.

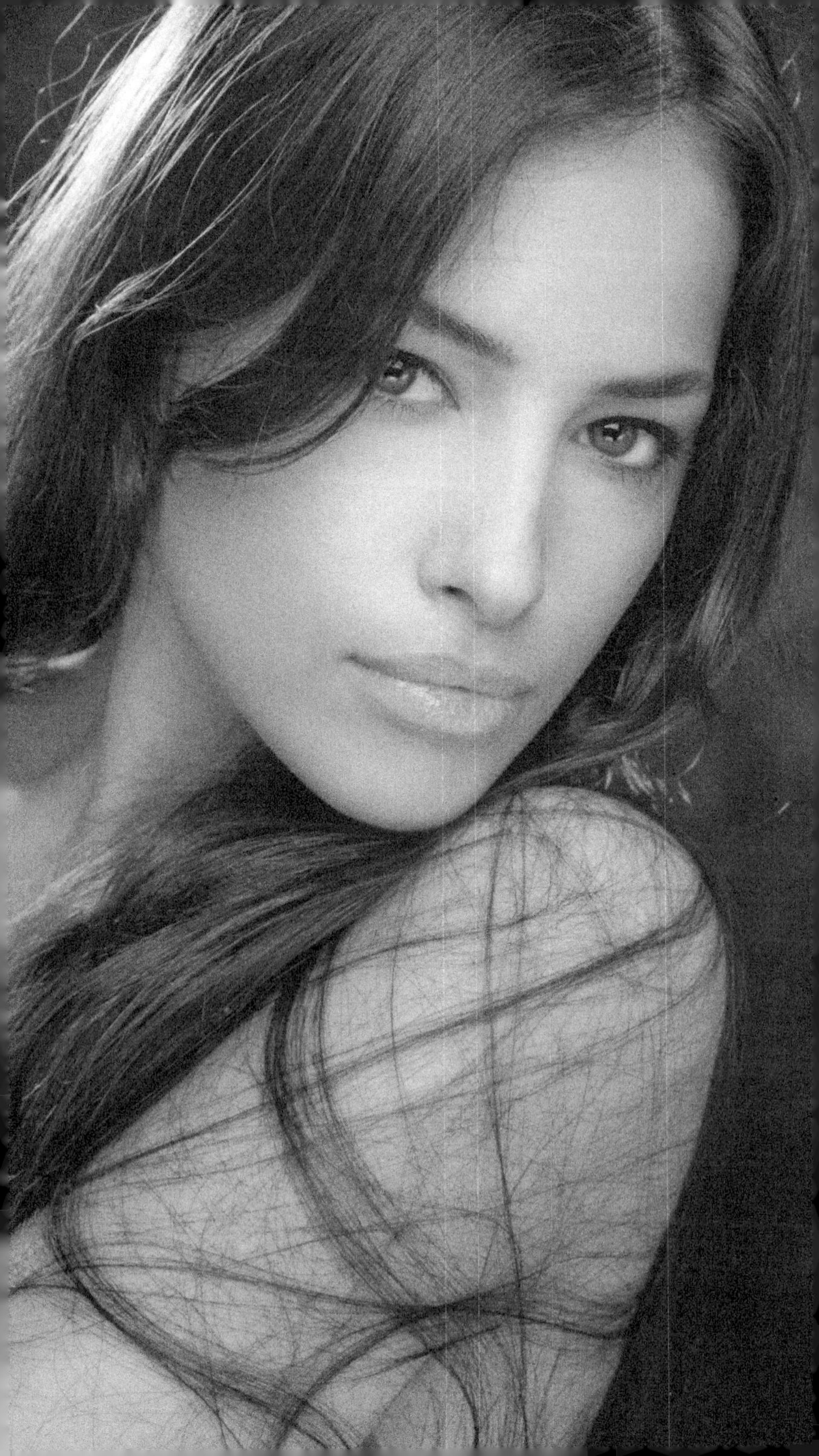

CHAPTER 21

Lucy

Scott showing up at the club tonight wasn't something I'd expected. Him being pissed about me dancing was mind-blowing, when he's the one that sent me there to work to pay off his debt. He'd dragged me to the back and was getting ready to punch me in the face when Cal showed up.

Cal took him, told me to get cleaned up and on the stage, then mumbled something under his breath about next time he'll take the cash and not entertain an idea like this again. I rushed away, holding on to my wrist that had the ugly imprint of a hand wrapped around it. All tonight had done was make it abundantly clear to me that I have to get out of here. I just need to save a little more money.

By the time I got off the stage, Scott was gone, and I prayed he'd be asleep when I got home.

My prayer went unanswered as he'd sat up waiting for me and drunk. A deadly combination.

"What the hell do you think you're doing taking off your clothes? I told you that you were too fat," he bellowed as he threw the bottle he was holding across the room at me. I'd barely ducked in time for it to miss me as it crashed against the wall.

"I had to. Cal made me cover the drinks I spilled on top of what I'm paying off for you," I bit back, a little harsher than I normally would.

"Bitch, you think you can talk to me like that?" He jumped up from the chair, made it across the room to me in a blink of an eye, and punched me dead in the face. It threw me off balance and I ended up falling backward, into the broken glass from the bottle.

"Don't ever talk to me like that again. You're paying off what you owe, not me. Any debt occurred on my behalf was for you, so remember that next time. What's owed to Cal is yours alone. Show that fat ass of yours off again and I'll beat you so bad no one will want to look at your ugly ass. Now clean this shit up." He picked up his keys and headed out of the room toward the kitchen. I heard the door slam, and a couple minutes later his car roared to life and lights shone into the house.

Just glad that he was gone, I slowly stood and headed to the bathroom to remove the glass embedded in my skin. There was some in my arm and hand and one large chunk in my leg. I undressed, quickly got in the shower, washed, and jumped right back out to cover the cuts. My face was a different story. Not much I could do about that; it'd look like shit no matter what.

Once I'd taken care of the cuts, then dressed, I headed out to the living room to clean up the mess. If I didn't then, when Scott came home and saw it, there'd be no telling what he'd do. Finally, at four, I'd crawled into bed, hoping to get a couple hours of sleep. Working at the diner and then the club was going to kill me. Thankfully, I'd be off the day after tomorrow, no, tomorrow, from the diner. I'd climbed into the bed, pulled the comforter up to my chin, and rolled to my side. I did a double take just to make sure the light was on the clock, telling me I'd set the alarm, and closed my eyes.

An annoying buzzing sounds in my ear. As I roll over, I pull the pillow over it to cut out the sound. But it doesn't stop, just keeps going. Finally, it hits me, work. I instantly, and painfully, sit up and shut off the alarm as I brace myself for Scott. But nothing happens. Looking over my shoulder, I see his side of the bed is empty. He must not have come home. While most would feel upset, I, on the other hand, am jumping for joy on the inside.

Getting up slowly, I dress for work, knowing that Noah will be waiting for me. I save the bathroom for last, realizing I'll need extra time to take care of my face. It already aches and feels tight, so I don't doubt it's swollen.

Sure enough, when I look in the mirror, I see all of my assumptions are correct. Reaching under the sink, I pull out the small pouch that holds my makeup. Taking out the concealer and foundation, I begin to try to cover the bruises. Twenty minutes later, I still look like shit, but they aren't as noticeable. It's also six-fifteen and I know Noah is already there waiting. Will he be pissed? Act like Scott when he's angry?

Hurrying out of the house, I make my way toward our meeting spot, only to come to a screeching halt when I see he's not there. My heart drops, and a pang of sadness takes over. I thought for sure he'd be there, even if I was late. He seemed like the kind of guy who would wait, even with that gruff exterior.

Shit, I need to move; I don't have time to linger on this or try to come up with some reason why he's not here. Increasing my speed, I make my way to work, already aware there's no way in hell I'm going to be there on time for my shift, and I can't even call Georgie to let her know.

It's seven-thirty when I step inside the diner, fully prepared to be fired on the spot. But I'm not. Instead, Georgie smiles at me. Did I fall asleep and wake up in some alternate universe? Or even better, did I die, and this is some crazy afterlife where I'm still me, but there's no Scott? If it is, then sign me up. I'm one hundred percent on board.

I head to the back first, hanging up my coat and putting on my apron. If I'm ready to work, maybe Georgie won't fire me, not today at least, and I can still make a little money. She's always been nice to me, but business is business and I can't help but let my anxiety take over. I need this job; if I lose it Scott will be furious. Taking a deep breath, I know I need to get this over with and face the music, so I make my way to talk to Georgie and plead with her to keep my job. Cindy is helping a table that just sat down, and as I look around, I see the place isn't too busy and everyone appears to be eating or have drinks and waiting on their food.

"I'm so sorry, Georgie. I overslept, and by the time I was ready, Noah was gone and I had to walk and had no way to call you." Wait, she's smiling. That doesn't seem right.

"It's okay. Noah called and explained. He got tied up and didn't make it. He knew you'd be late and maybe upset with him, so he called me. Wanted me to know and also to tell you he'd be in later to see you and explain." Did I just hear that right?

"Noah called you?" My voice cracks as I speak.

"He did. Now get to work." She shoos me off and as I walk away, I keep looking back over my shoulder, still trying to process everything.

"Hey girl, I got table four and five's order in. Once it's ready, if you can bring it out, that'll be great. Georgie has you in section A today." Cindy stops long enough to tell me.

"No problem. I'll go check in with JD and see how it's coming. Cindy..."

"Yeah?" she answers.

"Thank you."

"No problem, doll. You've helped me out before and besides, it wasn't even that busy and you're not that late."

All I can do is smile. When I leave, I'm going to miss this place and the people here. Shaking it off, I head to the kitchen to check on the order, just as JD calls order up. Not sure who ordered what at the table, I make sure to check what's on the plates so I can at least ask and not look like a total fool.

The morning passes quickly and each time the bell over the door sounds; I look up anxiously, expecting it to be Noah, but each time I'm left with disappointment. It's almost time for my shift to be over when I hear the jingle of the bell. I don't look up, it's just another customer.

My back is to the door, but I smell the pine scent of his cologne when he steps up behind me. *Noah.*

"Lucy." His honey voice fills me with so much warmth.

Turning around slowly, we're chest to chest and I can feel my nipples pebbling. The hardened peaks scrape along the material of my bra, as heat pools in my core. I'm on fire. Just as I am every time I'm near him, except this time it's somehow different. Could it be because I've finally accepted the farce of a marriage I'm in is one hundred percent over? That I'm ready to leave, damn the consequences or the fallout that comes from it?

"Is your shift almost over?" He doesn't move away; does he feel the same as I do?

"Yeah, in like twenty minutes," I tell him, as I swallow down the lump that's formed in my throat.

"Order us some burgers and fries for when you're done. We need to talk."

I nod my head, unable to even get any words out. He turns away from me, his hand grazing along mine as he does, and I feel a shock of electricity. He heads straight for our booth and sits in the same spot he always does so he can look out at the diner.

My anxiety is amped up the whole time. Each time I glimpse his way, he's staring at me. Watching my every movement like he's trying to figure something out. No, that's not it. Wait, is he actually looking at me? Each time I move and a spasm of pain hits me, I grimace, and his face tightens as his fist clenches.

Shit, if he's monitoring me this closely, then this pathetic job I did on my face this morning, which I've practically sweated off, is hiding nothing from him. He's going to have questions, and I'm afraid of how he'll react to the answer.

As the time on the clock on the wall ticks over to three, I know the wait is over. Heading to the back, I take off my apron and put on my jacket, assuming whatever he has to talk to me about probably won't happen inside the diner. Making my way over to JD, I pick up the bag with our food in it and give a small wave goodbye.

My steps are slow as I make my way over to him. Each step so small, you'd think I was walking on a tightrope in a carnival. Slow and steady.

He's standing before I get to his table, reaching out his hand and taking the bag from me. "Glad you made it to go. I'd rather talk to you in private." He takes my hand in his and leads me out of the diner, only letting go of it long enough to open the door for me.

"Okay, but we have to be quick. I have to be at my second job by five." I hope to God he doesn't ask me where it is or offer to drive me. Visions of the disapproval on his face fill my mind and there's no way I want to see it in person.

"That's one of the things we need to talk about." I can't help but notice how tense his voice is.

Making our way over to his truck, he opens the door, helps me inside, then hands me the bag before shutting the door.

Shit, this isn't going to be good.

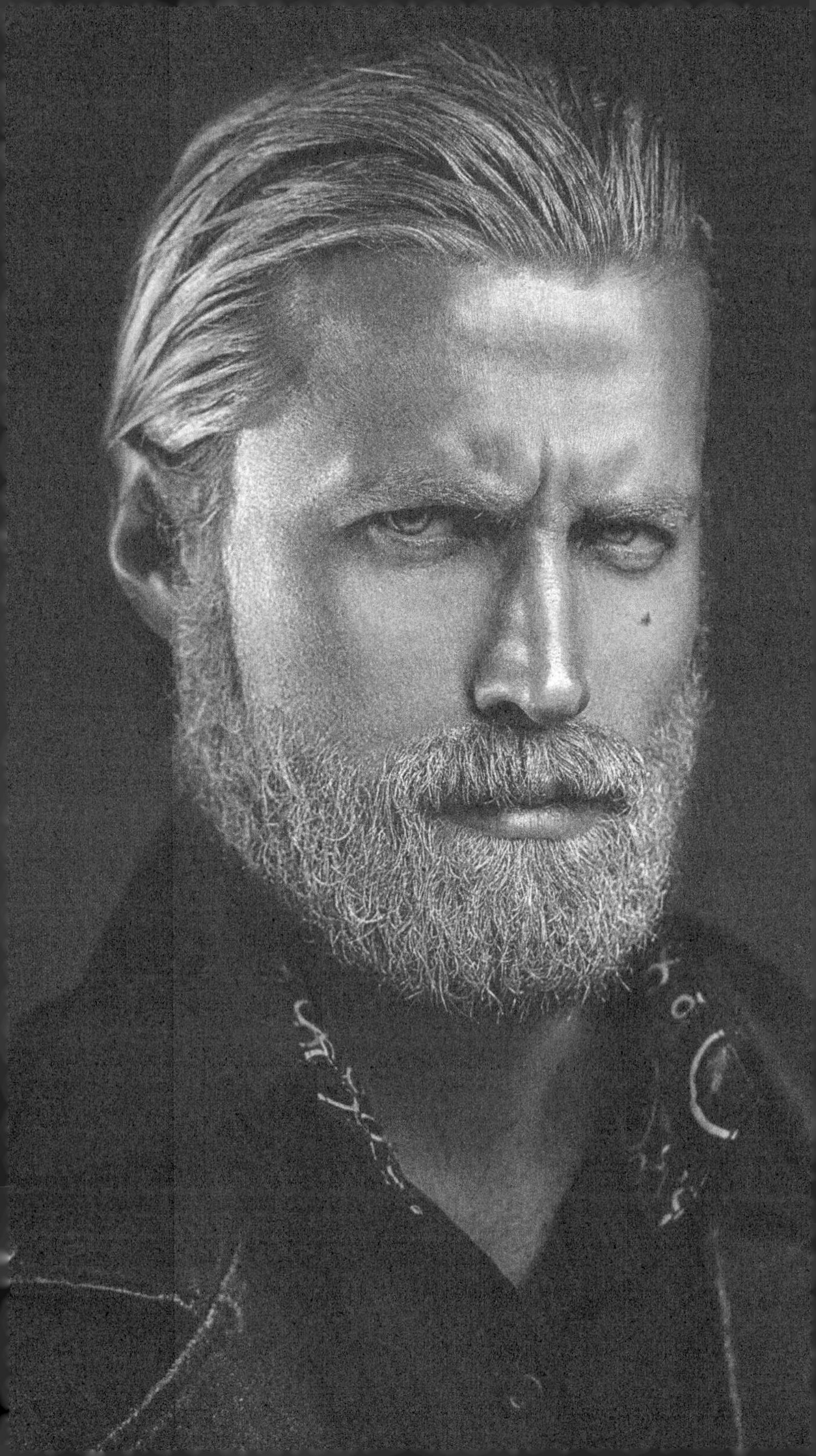

CHAPTER 22

Preacher

I need to talk to her in private, but where the fuck do we go? Do I park somewhere, and we just eat in the truck? Do I take her back to the clubhouse? Shit, I should have thought this through, but I didn't. I drive around, stealing glances at her before finally sucking it up.

"So, I'm gonna take us to the clubhouse so we can talk. It's too cold to sit in the car. You may see some things, just don't let them bother you."

"What do you mean, see some stuff?" Okay, not what I was expecting her to say. I thought for sure she was going to fight me about going there, but she didn't. I haven't mention anything yet about things she may see.

"We're not goin' to hang out in the common area. I'm gonna take you to my room. But we have women that hang around, and well, they, umm... so sometimes they have sex with the club brothers, and not always in the privacy of a bedroom."

I grip the steering wheel tight, as I wait to hear her objections. But nothing. She just sits there. Looking over at her out of the side of my eye, I notice her biting on her lip. She's thinking. I've watched her do it before at the diner.

"Umm, okay. Noah? Umm... do you sleep with them?" she asks quickly once she gets past being nervous.

Fuck me! If I answer truthfully, she's gonna be pissed before I ever get a chance to tell her how I feel. But if I lie, then she'll be even more pissed if she finds out. It's a double-edged sword and either way I go, I'll end up getting cut by it.

"Shit, here I wanted to talk to you about something and you're hittin' me with the tough as shit questions." I blow out a deep breath. "Have I? Yes. Even once after meetin' you, but something stopped me. So am I currently? No. Do I want to? No." She's quiet as I talk.

"Okay. Thank you for your honesty."

We drive the rest of the way to the clubhouse in silence. Pulling past the guard shack, I give the prospects a wave. The shocked look on their faces at my passenger doesn't go unnoticed.

Pulling up in front of the building, I park the truck and jump out, rushing to her side to open the door for her. She's still holding the bag nervously in her lap. Reaching out, I take it from her and help her down. We make our way to the door, but I stop her once again.

"Stay close to me," I whisper to her, wrapping my arm around her shoulder and gently pulling her to my side. She was limping more than normal today, so I know she's in pain and I want to know what that fucking asshole did to her.

Opening the door, I send up a little prayer that all the brothers in there have their dicks in their pants. Unfortunately, God is not on my side as one of the brothers, Wheels, has Cassie bent over the pool table, his pants bunched around his feet as he thrusts in her from behind. Nothing uncommon for the clubhouse, but not what I wanted to walk in on with Lucy.

I angle my body, hoping to shield her from seeing it, and head straight to my room, ignoring the brothers calling out to me, wanting to know who I have with me. Only when we're in my room, do I let out the breath I was holding.

"Sorry about that, Lucy. Wasn't expecting to walk in on it."

"You said it happens a lot, so why weren't you expecting it?" Her face is dead serious as she looks at me and I have no clue what to do. So, I stand there like a fucking idiot, before the corner of her lips curl up in a smile. "I'm just messing with you, Noah."

"Okay darlin', that's good. Have a seat on the bed. I'll be right back. I'm goin' to go get us something to drink."

As I leave, I see her sit on the edge of the bed as she lets her eyes roam around the room, soaking everything in. Shutting the door, I think twice and pop it back open.

"I'm just gonna lock it so no one can walk in," I tell her as I flip the lock on the inside of the door and shut it.

I need to get something to drink and go back to the bedroom. No one's in the kitchen when I walk in. Heading straight for the fridge, I open it and peer inside. Looking for anything that's not beer to get for us to drink.

"Was that who I think it is? You finally grew some balls?" Sundance questions as he steps inside, one of the club whores under his arm.

"Yeah, and fuck you." I don't want to tell him anything more.

"If you need any pointers, old man, just let me know. I'll be glad to give a demonstration and make sure she knows what she should be feelin'." He lets out a roaring laugh, but I'm fuming. If he even thinks he can touch what's *mine*, I'll kill his fucking ass, brother or not. No one talks about the woman who I'm going to make mine.

"Shit, Preach, I'm just kiddin'. I don't plan to end up on your table."

"Next time, keep your fuckin' mouth shut." I storm from the room, needing to be back with Lucy. We need to talk and she needs to know how I feel. She also needs to quickly learn she ain't going to the fucking House of Puss tonight. I already got plans for that place and the asshole who runs it, just need to wait for Hawke to get home.

Stepping up to my door, I pull out my keys and slip the key in the lock, opening the door. She's still sitting on the bed, only she's taken off her shoes and sitting cross-legged. On the bed in front of her is a towel with our food on it. She's made us our very own picnic, but inside.

"Got water and soda. Didn't know which one you'd prefer." Moving over to the bed, I sit down, placing the drinks beside me as I unlace my boots and take them off, then spin around to face her, mimicking how she's sitting.

"Noah, what did you want to talk about? I still need to be at my other job at five, so I don't have much time." It's cute how she still thinks she's going there, but I'll let her hold on to that thought for a little bit longer.

"Let's eat, then we'll talk." She shrugs her shoulders, picking up her burger with both of her hands and takes a huge bite.

"Can I ask a question?" Her words are barely distinguishable as she speaks around the food she's busy chewing on.

"Sure. But chew your food before you ask. Don't want you chokin' on me."

She nods, chewing her food quickly, only speaking again once she's swallowed. "Why do they call you Preacher?"

"Because I was one. Well, actually, I still am. I just don't practice anymore, not for a long time." I know I need to tell her about my past. She knows I had a wife and child and they passed away, but not how.

I eat quicker than her, a nervous twitch, or rather the need to do something with my mouth to keep from slamming my lips down on hers. Kissing her plump pink lips like I've wanted to from the first day I sat in her booth.

She takes her last bite and I know I can't put it off any longer, not with the way she keeps glancing at the small clock sitting on my dresser.

"Okay, Noah, spill it."

I take a deep breath and let it all out.

"Please listen and let me get it all out. Then, when I'm done, you can say or ask anything that you want. Can you promise me that?"

"Okay." It's not a yes, but I'll take it.

"My wife and daughter dying gutted me. This club saved me in ways that I'll share with you another time. I tell you that, so you know I've never sought out being with anyone. Even with the girls here, it felt as if I was cheatin' on my family. I loved my wife with every fiber of my bein'. She was it for me, and I never imagined havin' feelin's for anyone else again. Then I sat down in your section, and it was like a tidal wave rushin' to shore. I fought it. I'm older than you, not to mention you're married. But I saw it in you that first day. You were like a wounded bird, and I wanted to help you. I lied to myself, sayin' it was just one friend helpin' another. But it wasn't. I was fallin' hard for you."

I pause, debating if I tell her how I had Rizzo look into her. She may hate me, but I need her safe and to know the degree I would go to make it happen.

"One of the members of the club looked into you for me." She shifts back, and I know I need to hurry the fuck up and get to the point.

"I know you've been to the ER multiple times for injuries. I've seen them on you in the few days I've known you. Hell, I see them now and your attempt to cover them. Lucy, it's takin' everything in me not to go to your house and kill that fuckin' husband of yours."

"Noa—"

"No, baby, let me finish. I was in the club last night. I know you're working there to pay off his debt. Leave him for me, baby. Even if you don't want to be with me, don't stay with him. Don't go to that club, you're too good for it," I beg her. Reaching out, I take her hand in mine, happy when she doesn't pull away.

We sit there in silence with our hands entwined, for I don't know how long.

Then when I think she's never going to say anything, her sweet voice feels my ears.

"I could tell you that everything you've learned is a lie, but it's not. Scott's an abusive dick and I've wanted to leave for years but never had the courage. Mostly I didn't know how I would live, take care of myself and I knew he would hunt me down, and bring me back screaming. He's physically, verbally and emotionally abusive, and for the life of me, I don't know why he stays with me. I made my mind up to leave, even started giving Georgie money to save for me, so I can."

"Then do it," I tell her.

"I want to. I'm afraid that if I don't, then one day he's going to kill me. He owes the owner of that club money, and my working there is to pay it off. Then I spilled drinks and now I owe Cal money for that. I hate it there and since working at both places, I'm so fucking tired. All I want to do is sleep."

"Then let's sleep. Stay here. Stay with me."

"Noah, I'd love to. But I can't, not yet. I need to leave Scott and all my stuff is at the house." I can hear the desperation in her voice to be free from him.

"Fine, stay here, rest, then I'll drop you off at home. It'll be like you went to work. Then tomorrow I'll pick you up as usual and we'll make a plan to get your stuff."

"I don't work tomorrow," she tells me and that makes what I want to do even better.

"Fine. Then tomorrow you'll pack your stuff and I'll come get you, then we'll go file for a divorce and a restraining order. There ain't no judge who wouldn't look at you and grant it without hesitation. But I'm tellin' you now, Lucy, I want you as my Ol' Lady. I'll give you time to come to terms with everything, but you will be mine." Her eyes go wide, but she doesn't scream or run from the room, so I'm taking that as a positive sign.

Picking up the empty wrappers, I ball them up in my hand and stand. Taking the towel, I place it in the dirty clothes basket, then throw away the wrappers before turning back to her.

"What time do you get home from the club?"

"Between two thirty and three." Once I know how long we have, I pick up my alarm and set it. "Let's get some sleep." Moving over to the door, I lock it so no one can come in.

"Would you like something more comfortable to sleep in?" She nods her head again. I think I've broken my girl; she can't even speak. Moving over to the dresser, I pull out a shirt and a pair of boxers and hand them to her.

"Thank you," she whispers as she stands and disappears into the bathroom to change.

While she's gone, I pull down the sheets, thankful that they're clean, then empty my pants pockets, placing the contents on my nightstand.

When she steps back into the room in my clothes, my cock takes notice. "Do you mind if I sleep in my boxers? If you do, I can find some sweats to wear."

"Boxers are fine." She scurries across the room, climbing in on the right side of the bed. This is confirmation we were made for each other, because I sleep on the left. Undoing my pants, I take them off and lay them over the chair, thankful that my dick is cooperating and not at full mast.

Hitting the light switch, bathing the room in darkness, I climb into bed, the heat from her body already reaching me. She rolls on her left side and I scoot in behind her. "Can I hold you?"

It's barely audible, but she gives me the answer I desire. "Yes."

Reaching out, I wrap my arm over her, gently pulling her back into me so her back rests against my chest, and we both drift off to sleep.

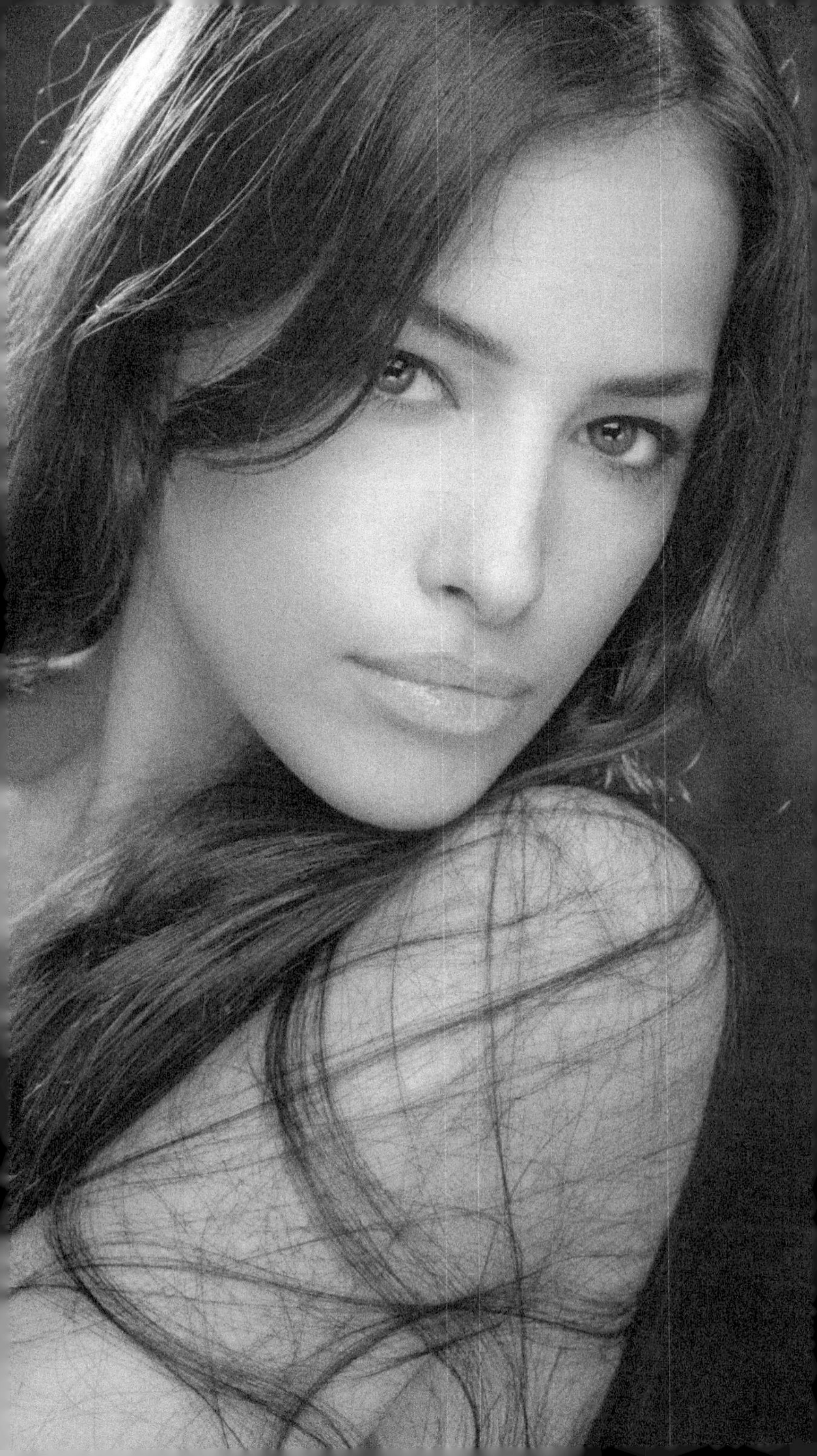

CHAPTER 23

Lucy

Waking up in Noah's arms was everything. Then when he dropped me off at the house, all I wanted to do was kiss him. His lips call to me in a way I never knew existed, and the first chance I get I'm taking it. But not yet. I need to leave Scott.

And that's the plan for today. Scott leaves every day at nine AM; where he goes, I have no clue, but he's always out by that time. Noah plans to show up at nine-thirty. I'm only taking what I want and to hell with the rest. Today is the day Lucy Davis will be free from Scott Davis.

The house is dark as I step inside, giving a wave to Noah as I shut the door behind me. I'm still on cloud nine as I take off my jacket and hang it up, inhaling deeply before I release it. It still smells of his woodsy cologne from the hug he gave me before I said goodbye.

Sliding off my shoes, I turn and begin to tiptoe across the room.

"You think you're slick, don't cha?" his deep, slurring voice echoes across the room.

Focusing my eyes, I squint, barely making out the outline of his body seated in the chair. He's awake, and he saw me come in. *Shit!* Did he see Noah? My mind races, formulating answers for any questions he may have.

"Hey hun, what are you doing up? I thought you'd be asleep." My voice cracks, as my nerves tear me up inside. I don't move closer, making sure to keep distance between us.

"I knew you were a stupid bitch, but I thought you had just a little bit of sense." His words are venomous, and when he flips on the lamp beside me, I see the dead look in his eyes. Something's wrong and I don't have a clue what I did.

I replay everything. A quick glance at the floor reveals no glass, and I'm pretty sure I cleaned it all up. I didn't eat anything, so I know there weren't any dishes left in the sink.

"What are you talking about?" I take a step back, my heart racing as fear courses through me.

He jumps from the chair, rushing toward me, taking hold of me by the arms and slamming me against the wall before I even have a chance to process anything.

"You fucking little slut. You think I don't know what you did? I saw you climb into that biker scum's truck when you got off work at the diner, the same fucking one that dropped you off tonight." His hand goes up around my throat, squeezing tightly as I struggle against his hold. My arms thrash out at him, catching his face as I scratch down the length of it.

"Think I don't know you didn't show up at the club tonight? Cal called me, thinking I was weaseling out on our deal and wanted his money. Even had the balls to tell me you were more trouble than you were worth."

I can't form words, barely getting enough air in my lungs to breathe as his grip around my throat tightens. I kick my legs out at him over and over before bringing my knee up and catching him in the balls. He releases me and drops to the ground, gasping for air.

I need to get out of here. My limbs slowly begin to move as I try to crawl for the door. But he's faster than me. The weight of his body comes crashing down on my back, slamming me to the floor, my head bouncing off of it.

He snatches me by the hair, as his knee digs into my back and leans down, the spit flying from his mouth as he speaks. "You want to spread your legs and whore yourself out, then you can start doing it for me."

His fist comes down and punches me in the head, before his weight lifts off of me and he flips me over. Kick after kick reigns down on my body, and I know he's going to kill me tonight. There's no way I'm going to live through this.

Suddenly, he releases me, storming out of the room, and a small sigh of relief leaves me.

Rolling over, I slowly come up on my knees, ready to crawl out of here, to take this fleeting moment to escape. My head screams at me, telling me what a fool I was to come home. I should have stayed with Noah. The only thing here were clothes, and I could've replaced them. Whatever happens to me tonight is my own damn fault. I've barely made it to the front door, my hand reaching upward to turn the knob, when searing pain shoots across my back, over and over, never in the same place twice. I curl into a ball the best I can, taking in each moment of it. Screams fill my ears, but why isn't anyone coming? Why hasn't someone called the police?

He picks me up and tosses me across the room, hurling me into the coffee table. As it crumbles beneath me, splintering pieces of wood embed my exposed skin. But once wasn't enough; he does it again. This time he sets me on my feet, then throws his fist, hitting me dead in the chest as I stumble back into the television. I drop down on my hands and knees just as the television flips forward onto my back before crashing onto the floor.

"See what you did? You fucking broke the TV, bitch. Another fucking mess you've made that I'll end up having to take care of."

Scott takes hold of my ankle and drags me across the floor, my fingers reaching out, trying to grip anything I can as I dig my nails into the ground. But it doesn't work. He takes me to the bedroom, flips me over, then begins raining punches down all over my body and face. All I can taste in my mouth is the coppery, metallic taste of blood. *My blood.*

"You're nothing but a bitch, a good-for-nothing whore. Why I settled for you when I could have had my pick, I'll never know."

"Why did you then? Why not just leave?" I moan out with the last bits of breath I have.

He doesn't like that. His hands once again go around my neck, squeezing so hard I feel as if my eyes are going to pop right out of their sockets.

I can't breathe, and as hard as I try, I can't get a sound out. Scott always made sure I knew if I made a peep, he'd kill me. So, I always endured his beatings in silence, swallowing my screams and burying them in the pit of my stomach.

The world begins to spin, patches of my vision going black, before total darkness overtakes me, and I make peace with the fact that my life ends here tonight. My only regret is not knowing where it could have gone with Noah and me. Pain that I'm leaving him this way, especially after all the sorrow and loss he's had in his life. Just as I slip away, a piercing pain takes over.

Peace. That's what I feel. Peace.

Preacher

I slept in this morning, since I didn't have to pick Lucy up for work. If it wasn't for the amazing rest I got before having to take her home, I'd be dead to the world right now. Waking with my arms around her was amazing. A feeling that I've missed. Not once have I actually slept in a bed with anyone since Bianca. Never intended to again. Then Lucy popped into my life, coming out of the blue like a tornado and spinning me into a web of chaos. One I eventually succumbed to and I'm glad I did.

I'm not meeting her at her house until nine-thirty, so I have a couple hours. I need to check with Jenner to see about the message from the phone, and now is as good a time as any. With the torturing, then getting Lucy, I'd forgotten to ask. But first I need coffee. Heading out of my room, I shut and lock the door behind me, then make my way down the hallway. Hopefully tonight, I'll have Lucy in my arms once again.

Not a soul is around, probably all sleeping off the events from the night before. There were still a few brothers up and partying when I took Lucy home early this morning, but now it's like a ghost town in here. All we're missing is the tumbleweeds.

I make two cups for me and Jenner and head toward his office. If I was a betting man, I would say he's in there. When I push open the door, he's seated behind his desk, fingers flying across his keyboard, giving me all the satisfaction I needed.

"Hey man, what's the news on the phone we recovered? Shouldn't the message about the meetup today have come in?"

"We got one late last night. It said to hold for another message today and another job that needs to be done. I've been watching it and James' emails, to make sure we don't miss anything from either of them, but they're both quiet. The day is just gettin' started, though, so it could still come. Saw you had Lucy here last night."

"Hopefully they haven't figured out we're on to them. And yeah, we had some stuff to talk about. I'm helpin' her pack some stuff and get a restraining order on her husband while we work on her divorce. Since I'm here, I need a phone for her, all the bells and whistles to include trackin'. I'll pay for it."

"So you claimin' her."

The corners of my lips turn up in a smile. "I am."

"Well, if it ain't about fuckin' time. I'm happy for you, brother. You need any help, let me know." He goes back to his keyboard, pounding away at the keys like a man on a mission.

"Wait, Jenner. Will you look for some houses? I don't think Lucy is goin' to want to live in the clubhouse, so we'll need a place to live. Somewhere close by, but still with privacy."

"I'm on it, brother. I'll let you know what I find. Once I hear something on the meetup, I'll let you know, too."

I shut the door behind me and head back to my room. Might as well clean up a little. Not being able to just pick up a phone and call or message Lucy kills me. She needs to be able to get a hold of me if she needs to, and vice versa. A problem that will be fully rectified today now that Jenner knows what I want.

Fuck, the time needs to hurry up. I want my woman here with me. Damn if that doesn't sound good. I pace the room, making and remaking the bed, moving my clothes around so that Lucy can have a drawer to put her things in. Shit, that reminds me, I need to let Hawke know we'll be staying here for a little bit until I can get us a place. Hell, I need to get Lucy a car. Until I do, she can drive my truck. She's not going to be walking or taking cabs anymore.

Pulling out my phone, I send Hawke the message.

Me: Got an ol lady now, gonna make it official soon. She's leavin' her scumbag husband today. Riz can fill you in on the details until I see you. She's gonna stay here with me until I get us a place.

He doesn't answer and the closer it gets to time for me to leave, a sense of dread overtakes me. A familiar feeling that something bad is coming. I race out of the clubhouse straight to the truck, needing to see Lucy to make sure she's okay.

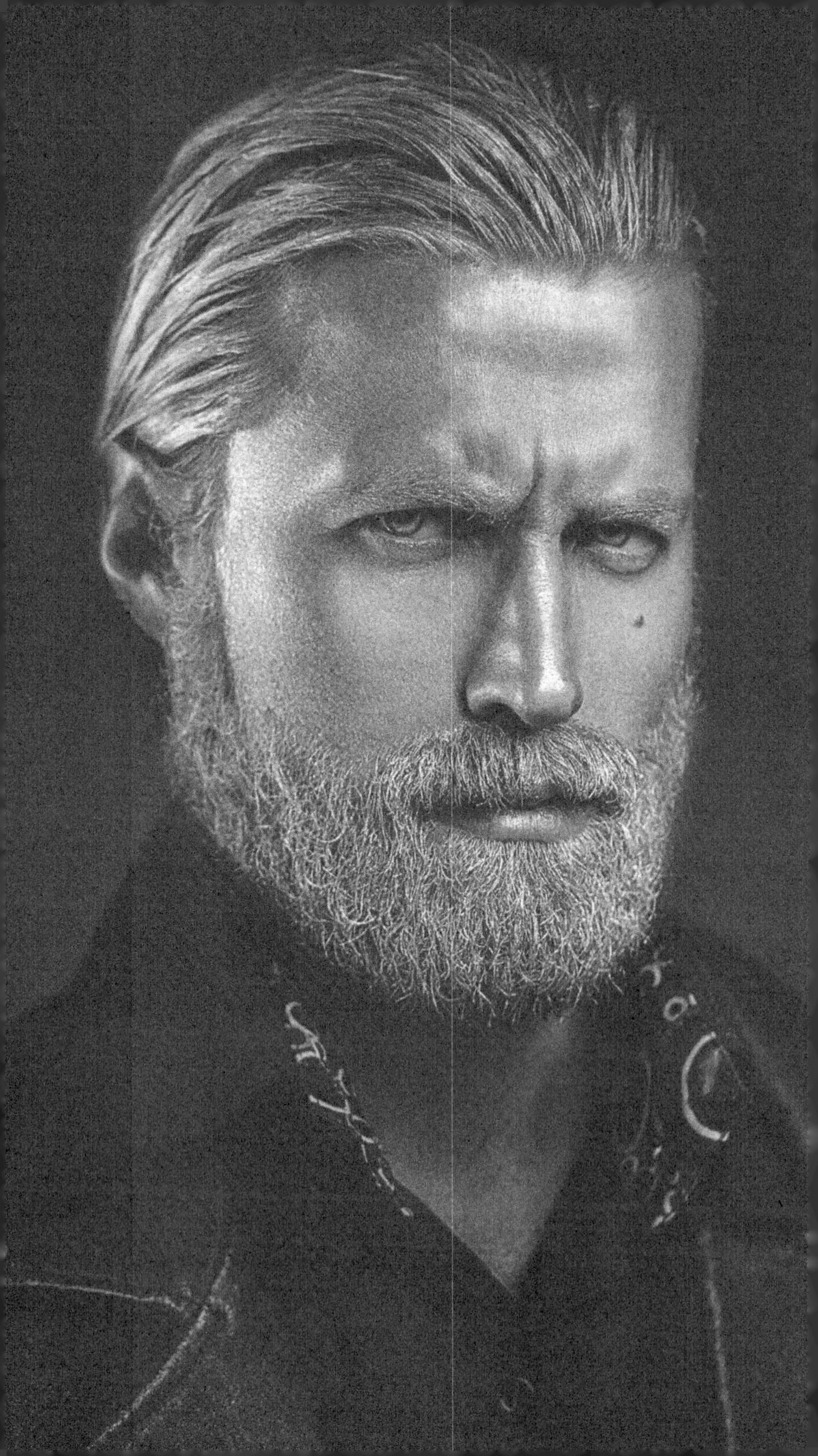

CHAPTER 24

Preacher

I make two passes by her house. The car is gone, but I want to be sure he's not going to pop back up. Slowly, I pull my truck over to the curb a few houses down and wait for the clock on my dash to click over to nine-thirty. I grip the steering wheel until my knuckles go white, watching her house, but there's no movement.

Once the clock hits the time, I'm pulling away from the curb and right into her driveway. I don't give a fuck who sees me. *Lucy Davis is mine.*

Turning off the truck, I get out and rush up the steps to her door. But something feels off. The plants on the top step have been knocked over like someone left in a rush and stumbled over them, not caring to pick them up.

Stepping onto the porch, I notice the inside door is ajar. Lifting my hand, I knock, but nothing. Not even a sound in the house. It's eerily quiet and has the hair standing up on the back of my neck. Knocking hard this time, I also call out, "Lucy! It's me, Noah!"

I wait.

Nothing.

Fuck this! Reaching back, I pull the gun from the back of my pants and turn the safety off before pulling out my phone, calling the one person I know is up.

"I'm at Lucy's. Something's not right. Get the brothers here now. I'm goin' in. Appleberry Lane."

"I know where she lives, will be there in twenty, ten if we speed and say fuck the cops," Jenner replies before disconnecting the call.

Holding the gun in position, ready to take out anyone in my path, I push the door open and take my first step inside. My heart drops into my stomach at the sight. The house looks like a bomb went off inside of it. Broken furniture, shattered glass, television busted, and then my eyes catch sight of the floor, blood and what the hell is that? Are those claw marks on the ground? Bending down, I pick up something embedded in the wood floor. Lifting it up, I see it's a fingernail.

"Lucy? Lucy, where are you?" I holler, desperation in my tone. When there's no answer, I continue moving further into the house, searching for her. Taking my time, I slowly make my way through the kitchen, bathroom, and spare bedroom until I reach the final door at the end of the hallway.

Panic floods my system as I step up and push it open. My eyes immediately drop to the floor where there's a body, one I know, curled up in a ball and not moving. Rushing over to her, I drop to my knees and carefully roll her over. Her face is bloody, swollen, and covered in bruises. If I didn't know it was her from her clothes, I wouldn't have been able to identify her. On the front of her shirt and underneath her is a pool of blood.

Please, baby, I need you to be alive.

Placing two fingers on her neck, I check for a pulse. It's faint, but there.

Pulling out my phone again, I call 911, providing all the information I have, as well as the possible suspect. They better hope they find him before I do, because I'm going to murder the fucker. Make him pay for every fucking thing he did to her. The old term an eye for an eye is going to be shown to Scott fucking Davis.

Sirens blare in the distance as I hold my girl in my lap, carefully brushing her hair back from her face. I shouldn't have moved her, but I couldn't help it. The rumble of engines intermix and I know my brothers must be arriving as well.

"Hello, paramedics!" is called out from the hallway.

"Back here, hurry," I yell back.

Footsteps pound down the hallway before two men step into the room, a gurney behind them as they head straight for us.

"What happened?" the younger of the two asks me as the other one begins checking her over.

"I don't know. I found her like this. She was leavin' her abusive husband this morning, and I was takin' her to the courthouse for a restraining order."

"Okay, step back. The cops will have some questions. What's her name?"

"Lucy Davis." I scoot back, standing up as I watch them work on her before placing her on the gurney and rushing out of the room.

I follow closely behind, coming face to face with four burly cops and my brothers all in a standoff in the yard, until Jerry pulls up.

"Stand down boys. That goes for you too, Gunner. Get your boys back, so I can talk to Noah." Jerry's forceful voice has everyone listening as I head for my truck, ready to follow the ambulance. Normally, the club would just blow off the cops, not caring to listen to them, but Jerry is different. He's bound to the club by family, being the son of the previous prez before Hawke came into power. Jerry chose a different path in life for himself, but always swore to look out for us the best he could within the confines of the law.

He makes his way over to me, but I don't have time for this bullshit. He must sense it, too. "Noah, stop."

I keep walking, ignoring him. I need to make sure that Lucy's okay. This is my fault, just like that day with Bianca and Carmen. I let them go, and look at what happened. Lucy should have stayed with me.

"NOAH!" he calls out more forcefully, stopping me in my tracks. Turning, I face Jerry, annoyed and pissed that he's keeping me from getting to where I need to go. The ambulance pulling away without me following adds to my emotions and all I want is to fucking kill someone. Rip them apart, tiny piece by piece, ensuring their agony goes on for hours and right now I don't give a shit who that person is.

"What!?" I bark back.

"Calm down. I need to know what happened and the club's part in it. If this is something to do with y'all, I need to know how to handle it."

"It wasn't anything to do with the club. That beautiful woman leaving in the ambulance, barely breathing after bein' beatin', is the victim of domestic violence. I was coming to help her leave her husband today and file for a restraining order. But I was too late. He must have found out and took his rage out on her last night. No one was here when I arrived but Lucy." I'm trying hard not to break down, to fall to the ground and scream at God for yet again forsaking me. Taking someone else I love from me.

"What's the husband's name?"

"Scott Davis. Can I go now? I need to get to the hospital and make sure Lucy is okay."

"Yeah. But when I call, pick up the phone."

I turn to walk away.

"And Noah, I don't want to catch word that you or the club are out seeking vengeance." He looks hard at me, waiting for my answer. One I won't give because I can't make that promise. If I find the asshole, he's dead as a doornail. His grave's already been dug; he's just not in it yet.

"Can't make a promise I won't keep." With that, I turn and climb inside my truck. I already know once night hits or the cops leave, my brothers are going to be inside that house looking for any clue as to where Scott disappeared to.

The entire ride to the hospital, I battle my emotions. Going over and over in mind why I didn't just make her stay. She was safe, unharmed, and heaven forbid this takes a wrong turn, alive. Just like that day with Bianca. I should have gone to the hospital later for my rounds. If I had been at the church, maybe I could've stopped the shooter. Saved the ones lost that day, or even better, joined them. But then I wouldn't have been here with Lucy. Lot of good I did her, since she's riding in the ambulance.

My mind keeps going over everything. I'm so distracted I don't realize I'm running red lights, not checking for cars as I turn a corner. This could've been because of me. What if he figured out what she was doing? That she was with me and not at the club last night.

Pulling into the parking lot of the ER, I whip my truck into the first available spot. The irony not even hitting me that it was marked for clergy. All I care about is finding out how she is. Pulling out my gun, I toss it in the glove box, knowing if I carried it in, I'd be arrested. Jumping out, I head straight for the door at the same time my brothers pull in. I don't have time to wait. They'll find me.

Heading straight to the check-in desk, I bypass the wannabe cop at the door. "I'm here for Lucy Davis. She was just brought in by ambulance," I tell the older woman sitting behind the desk. She busily begins pounding the keys on her keyboard.

"What is your relation to her?"

"I'm her friend." Then I add, "I'm also her pastor." She looks at me with a scowl, eyeing my cut, before her face immediately goes ghostly white. Guess she's heard of us, and unlike James, she's scared.

"I'm sorry, Sir, but I can only give out her information to the next of kin." Her voice is soft and shaky, and I feel the fear coming off of her in waves.

"Her fucking next of kin is the reason she's here," I bark out through clenched teeth as I grip the edge of the counter to keep from yanking her up by her neck.

"Sir, I need you to step back." A deep voice speaks from behind me. Glancing over my shoulder, I see it's the security guard that was manning the door when I came in. The one I blew past and didn't say a word to. Guess he grew some balls.

Turning back to the woman, I blow him off. "Can. I. See. Lucy. Davis." My words come out slower, choppier.

"I'm really sorry..." Her eyes go wide as she stops mid-sentence. Guess my brothers have entered the building.

"Why aren't you in the back with Lucy?" Gunner asks.

I don't even turn around. "Seems only the dickhead that put her here can go back with her."

"I'll handle it," he says, stepping to the side, pulling out his phone, and dialing a number. He then puts it to his ear and paces back and forth as he talks to whoever is on the other line. He's too far away and his voice is hushed, so I don't have a clue who it is. A couple minutes later, he slides the phone back into his pocket and turns to me with a smile, just as the phone at the desk rings.

Matilda, according to her name tag, looks at the phone for a minute as it rings, then finally picks it up. She repeats 'Yes, sir' and 'I will' before she hangs up.

Standing from her seat, she walks over to the triage door and opens it for me. "I'm sorry, sir. If you and two of the other gentlemen could follow me, please. We have been instructed that you will be in the room, and the other two will be guarding the door. No one but you and your"—she clears her throat—"associates, are permitted any information regarding Mrs. Davis."

I flash Gunner a smile as I fall into step behind Matilda, with Gunner and Jenner following. While seeing how they are the only ones here, the others must be guarding the house, waiting for a chance to slip inside.

Jenner takes that moment to speak up. "Matilda, sweetheart, one of my assistants will be stoppin' by with some things I need. If you could, please escort them back so they can deliver it to me. I'm sure you understand when it's confidential information, it can't be given to just anyone."

"Of course, Sir." She's like a timid mouse scared of the big bad cat.

"Sir, I like that. You boys need to start showing me that same respect."

Just as soon as Jenner finishes speaking, doctors and nurses go rushing past us, to a room on the left-hand side. Matilda gasps and I take off running. That's Lucy.

I skid to a stop outside her door, just as the doctor lays the paddles on her chest, shocking her as her chest rises up in the air.

Nothing.

He does it again.

Nothing

And again.

I drop to my knees on the floor, as my face crashes into my hands and I cry out.

Not Lucy. God no.

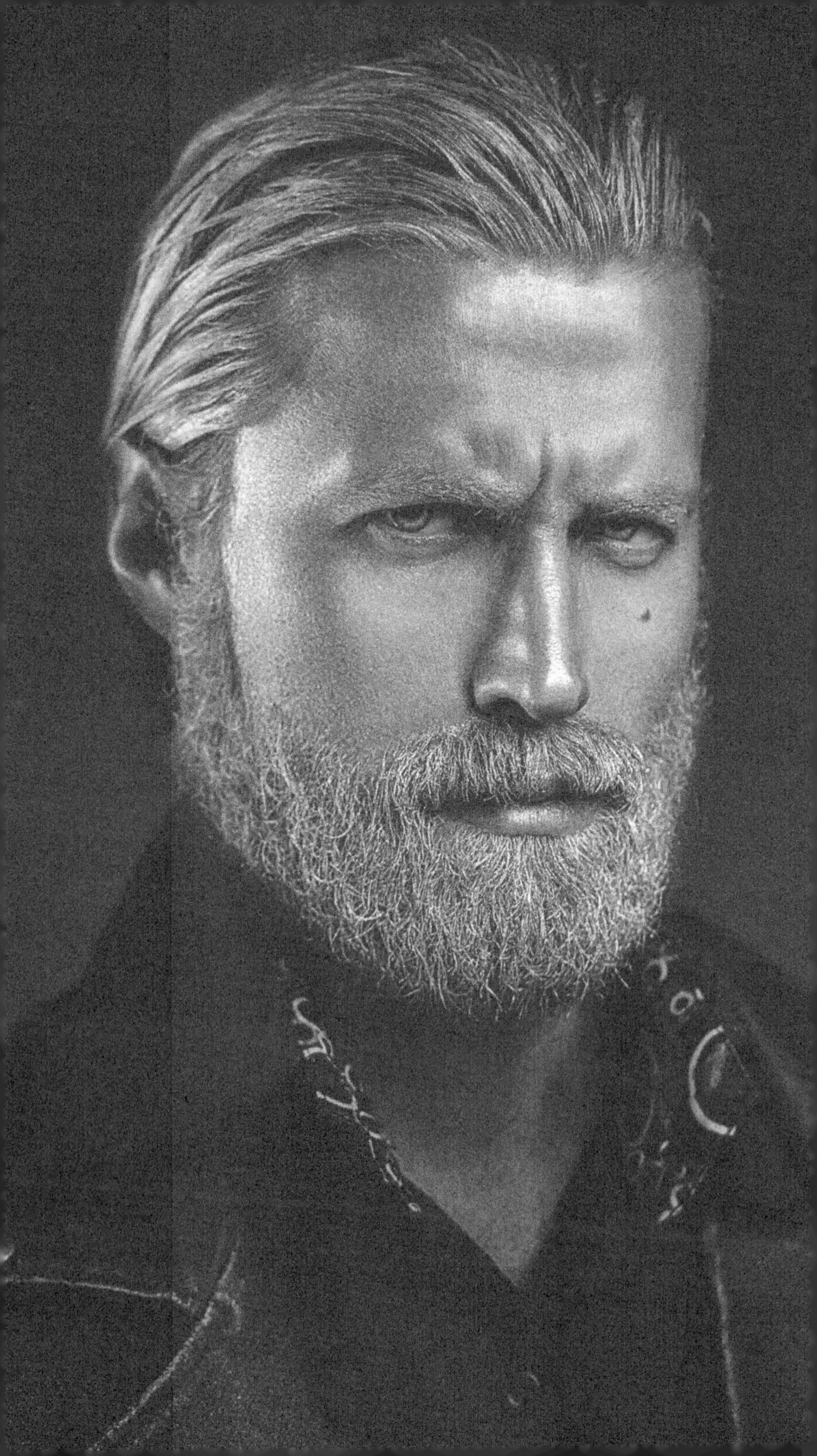

CHAPTER 25

Preacher

Two days later

Beep. Beep. Beep.

The sound echoes in the stillness of the room, but it's how I know she's alive. The machines are helping her breathe, but at least she is still here with me. I lost her, her heart stopped for three minutes, and we've yet to know what damage that time will cost. So we wait until she wakes and pray. Not that he's listening to any of my prayers lately, but I still try.

Jenner's in the corner, checking emails, and that damn phone. We never got another message, so we know they found out somehow that we were onto them. We're not sure how they did, but we plan to find out. Between that and trying to hack into the laptop we found hidden in the back of the closet at Lucy's, he's been busy. But knowing he's checking into everything gives me a sense of relief.

Scott hasn't shown his face, and there's been no activity on his account. His money's sitting there, except it's not in his account anymore. Jenner moved it all to another one with his name on the account. Once Lucy wakes up, he'll do what needs to be done to add her to it. She will wake up. I don't care what any of these fucking doctors say.

"I'm gonna go to the cafeteria and get some food. Want me to bring you back something?" Jenner asks as he stands from the chair pushed into the corner.

"No, I'm good."

"Okay, so meatloaf and potatoes if they have it, or a burger. The pasta here tastes like crap," Jenner says, ignoring what I just said. They all have, and it's been pissing me off. How am I supposed to eat with my woman like this?

"I said I was fuckin' good, asshole," I growl out as softly as I can. The last time I lost my temper, they had fucking security up here, thinking I was going to hurt someone. It was the damn doctor. He kept saying my girl may never wake.

"Okay, two servin's it is. See you in a bit." He runs from the room like the fucking coward he is.

I scoot my chair closer to the bed, taking Lucy's hand in mine. Reaching up, I move the hair from her face. She looks like a fucking angel. Some of the swelling has gone down, but her face is still an angry color.

"I'm so sorry, Lucy. I failed you, baby. I promised to be there for you and the moment when you needed me most, I wasn't. But you need to wake up. Come on, show me those beautiful eyes. Wake up, Lucy. You can hate me when you do. I can take it. What I can't take is losing you."

"She's not going to be mad at you," a familiar voice says from behind me. Glancing over my shoulder, I see Rizzo standing there. She's lost some color and there are dark bags under her eyes. She and Hawke returned the day after Lucy was taken to the hospital. I tried to talk to him about what happened, but he said it could wait a little longer. But seeing Rizzo today, he needs to hurry up. Something is wrong, and I need to find out what. Be there for them the best I can, like they have been for me.

Letting go of Lucy's hand, a piece of me dies, like I'm leaving her again. But I need to help Rizzo. She looks out of breath. "Where's Hawke?"

"He went with Jenner down to the cafeteria. And I came to see you. Good thing too, with the woe is me story you were laying on your girl." She just shakes her head as I reach out, wrapping my arm around her and leading her over to the chair Jenner was sitting in.

"Told the fucker I wasn't hungry," I mumble like a kid.

"You need to eat. They're getting something for all of us. We're going to have a family meal." She glances over at Lucy's still form on the bed.

"She really is beautiful. You did good, Noah. You're wrong, you know. She will never be mad at you, not when you were helping her. He did this to her. Not you. Not God. Scott Davis. And when he slips up and makes his presence known, you'll make him pay for every bit of it." Rizzo stares at Lucy, sadness in her eyes as she says the next part so softly, I almost don't catch it. "I just hope I'm here to see you do it."

I want to press, to find out what she means, but now is not the time.

"Go in the bathroom and take a shower. I'll watch over your girl."

"I can't." Moving back over, I sit back down in the chair by her bed. What if in that one moment I'm gone, she decides to open her eyes and I'm not here? I never want her to think she is alone, because she never will be as long as I'm alive. Even when she rejects me for letting this happen.

"Noah, shower now. I have her and if anything happens, you're only in the next room, not even three feet away. Besides, you smell like horse shit. I wouldn't want to wake up either if the man I love smelled like you. I'd hold out for one of these hot ass silver fox doctors." She lets out a laugh, but it's labored.

"Fine," I relent, standing and stepping over to where Jenner has a bag with some clothes in it for me. One I've only opened once, and it was to take a damn whore's bath standing at the sink, only after I had a nurse move Lucy's bed slightly to the left, so I could keep her in my eyesight. I would've done it, but I was so afraid of pulling loose one of the tubes that are keeping her breathing.

Stepping into the bathroom, I shut the door, but leave it cracked open. Not sure Hawke would be too keen on me showering with the door wide open and his sister in the other room.

Taking off my clothes, I drop them on the floor, then walk into the shower stall and turn the water on as hot as I can get it. The heat burns my skin, but it's my penance. A small price to pay for what Lucy had to endure.

I hurry, not wanting to be away for long. I've just turned off the shower when I hear Rizzo's soft voice and step closer to the door to eavesdrop as I dry off.

"Lucy, you've got to wake up. Noah has been through so much loss. I don't think he could take anymore. You're the first woman I've seen him act all growly and protective over in the five years I've known him. Now it's not for the lack of trying. All those skanks at the club try their damndest to get in his pants. It's okay, though. I'll show you how to handle them. They're scared of me. Rightfully so."

She takes a deep breath as she reaches out and rubs her hand along Lucy's arm, offering some comfort, but I'm unsure which of them is the one getting it.

"He thinks what happened to you is his fault, just like his wife and daughter, but we both know it's not. He's going to be hard-headed about it. But you need to set him straight. I can just tell you got some fire in you. Just promise me to love him and be patient. He's like a brother to me and he's going to need someone to be there for him, especially with what's to come. With you by his side, I know he can fight those demons that lurk deep within."

Stepping back away from the door, I dress quickly, then wipe the tears that slide down my face. She's right. If something happens to any more of my family, my demons will want to take over. I'm barely keeping them contained now as it is.

I clear my throat loudly, making a show of adding a cough to it, before opening the door. Rizzo was speaking to her in a moment of privacy and I never want her to feel like I violated that, even though I did.

"She's still asleep. I like her, Noah. You need to hurry up and make her your ol' lady."

"That's the plan. Well, that and her divorce. Jenner's already talkin' to a lawyer he knows about helpin' us speed the process up. We just have to wait for her to wake up."

"We got food!" Hawke announces as he steps into the room, with Jenner following close behind him.

"Let's eat. I'm starving. Can't you see I'm wasting away to nothing?" Nobody but her laughs. It's not slipped our notice that she's lost weight.

💀 💀 💀

A hair tickles my face from the gentle breeze caressing my skin. Reaching up, I push it out of my face and settle back down. Then it happens again, this time harder. Opening my heavy eyes, the room slowly comes into focus. The lights from the hallway, peeking through the open door, along with the illumination coming from the equipment.

My body jerks up as I push the call button for the nurse. Lucy is awake. She reaches out for me with one hand while the other comes up to the tube going into her mouth, breathing for her.

"No, don't touch that. The nurse is coming. It's helping you breathe, baby. I'm so sorry." She reaches out, gripping my hand in hers and holds it tightly.

The nurse comes running in and I step back, not wanting to be in the way, but unable to leave. Pulling out my phone, I shoot off a text in the group chat with the officers of the club.

Me: She's awake.

Two words, but they mean everything. Now I just need to know she's going to be okay and that she's going to forgive me.

The nurse and doctor step inside the room, checking her vitals. Once they've looked at everything, the doctor lets us know he will check first that she is able to breathe on her own. If she can, then they'll remove the tube.

They go through the process and once she shows she can, they announce they'll be removing it.

My heart races as they remove the breathing tube, telling her that her throat will be sore and to try not to talk. I'm going to make sure she does that even though I won't be able to hear her sweet melodic voice.

All I want them to do is leave, so I can be near her once again. To hold her soft hand in mine and tell her the words she couldn't hear before.

Another twenty minutes and the doctor is stepping out, providing the nurse with orders for tests to be completed in the morning.

She's still awake, but the doctor instructed she would be weak and most likely fall back to sleep. I start to panic, but he assures me it was perfectly normal and nothing to worry about.

Moving over to the bed, I pull the chair with me and sit down beside her.

"I'm so sorry, Lucy. I should never have taken you home. If I would've kept you with me, you'd be okay. I love you so much baby, and I know I haven't known you long, but I know what I feel." I'm a blubbering mess at this point and I don't give a fuck.

"No—"

"Baby, the doctor said no talking," I remind her, but she just shakes her head at me.

"No-t yoour fa-fa-fault. I lo-ve you," she manages to squeak out, and that's all it takes to send me over the edge.

"I love you, Lucy Davis. Now and forever."

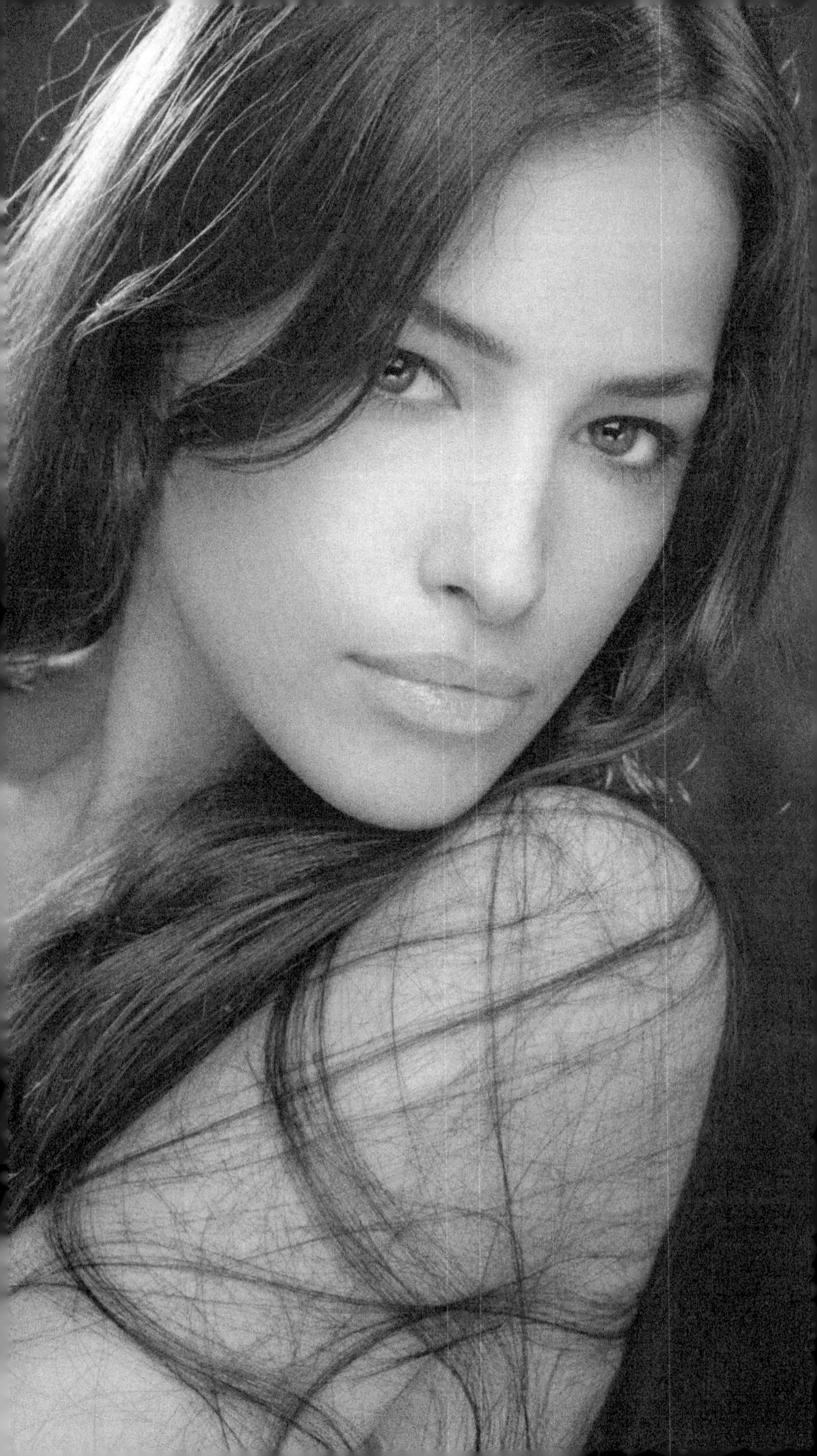

CHAPTER 26

Lucy

He loves me. He said the words, but it's been three weeks since then and he hasn't said them again. Instead, he's treating me like I'm some sort of fragile piece of china that he doesn't want to break. My body hurts, but I'm healed for the most part. I just want him.

We've been sleeping in the same bed since I've been released from the hospital, but he doesn't hold me like he did that night. The most he's done is hold my hand or put his arm around me as a shield when we enter or exit the clubhouse. He's afraid of the club members saying anything to me.

There's a knock at his bedroom door, and I go to answer. If he was here, he'd have a cow. It's soft, so I'm assuming it's a female and the only one who has been by to see me is Rizzo. At first, I was jealous until she told me who she was and assured me Noah was nothing more than a brother to her.

Opening the door, I'm happy to see it's her. "Come on, Luce, let's go to the kitchen and get something to eat before me and Hawke have to leave." This is their second trip since I woke up at the hospital that day. Last time they were gone for about a week. They never say what happens or where they go. At least not to me and from the bits and pieces I've overheard, not to Noah either. Speaking of him.

"I don't think Noah would want me to, with him not being here."

"If he says anything, I'll handle him. Now come on, I'm starved," she croons as she turns, taking my hand and pulls me behind her, barely giving me time to close the door.

As we make our way to the kitchen, I see she already has something warming in the microwave and three plates set out on the table. One of them is in front of Jenner and he's working on... Wait... is that what I think it is?

"Jenner." My voice trembles as I speak, unsure if I should even be questioning him.

He looks up at me, his dimples winking at me as he smiles.

"Is that Scott's laptop?"

"It is. We recovered it from the house and I thought there might be something on it to help us find him. Only thing is I can't for the life of me figure out how to get in it. He's got this thing set up good. It has a password, then a fingerprint that's required."

"Oh, he has a backup for that, too. It's a question you have to answer," I let him know, hoping he finds him. Not knowing where he is, and that he can pop up at any moment, has me on guard all the time. I'm planning to go back to work at the diner in three days and I'm scared of him showing up and kidnapping me.

"Yeah, don't take this the wrong way, but I didn't think your husband was very smart. But technical wise he is."

"Please stop referring to him as that. He shall forever be known as cunt ass prick."

"I got one more guess, and that's it. I have a feeling the warning about the hard drive being wiped is true," he tells me.

I take a seat in front of one of the plates as Rizzo brings over a bowl of pasta and a plate of bread and sets it down in the middle of the table.

Rizzo makes her plate, then Jenner's and goes to make mine, but I stop her. "I'm not an invalid. I can make my own plate. It would be nice if people started noticing that fact."

She drops the spoon, throwing her hands up in surrender, before picking up the container of parmesan cheese and sprinkling it on her food.

"What have you tried, Jenner?" I ask, trying to change the subject as I begin dishing out my own food.

"Let's see, I tried your name, his, then the make of his car and his birthdate the common ones. I wasn't expecting to only have five tries." He picks up his fork, twirling the spaghetti around it before stuffing it in his mouth, sucking up the noodles that are hanging from his lip.

"Scott is a fucking narcissist, so it would revolve around him and not me. He thinks he is god's gift to women. Hell, he even refers to himself as a god."

Jenner drops his fork mid-bite and turns to his laptop and begins to type. Rizzo and I both look at each other in confusion before he jumps up, whooping and hollering.

He places a hand on either side of my head, kissing me on the forehead.

"You, Lucy, are a freaking genius. I'm in. I've got to go see what I can find." He snatches up the laptop and a piece of garlic bread and runs from the room, leaving me and Rizzo alone.

"Rizzo, can I ask you a question?"

"Sure, anything."

"Well, I have a couple. One, what's wrong with you and don't tell me nothing, and second, what happened to Noah's family? He doesn't ever say, just that they're gone, and I know he blames himself."

She puts down her fork ever so gently, chewing her food slowly, as if she's trying to prolong it to keep from saying anything. I stare her down sternly, showing her I'm not going to let it go, which she must realize. She swallows her food and takes a drink of water.

"Okay. Yes, something is going on with me. But I'm not ready to share it yet. I will. I promise, in due time. It's just too fresh yet and I need to be sure. For Noah, his story is complicated. You know he was a preacher before, right? He did share that with you?"

"He did. Noah said that his wife and daughter died. But I don't know how."

"They were shot and killed at his church. He blames himself for not being there to save them. He was at the hospital visiting with one of the deacons of the church. It killed him. He turned to drinking. He was in a dark place when my brother found him and saved him. The rest is history."

"But that's not his fault. Even if he was there, it doesn't mean he could've saved them."

"I know that, and you know that, but Noah, well, he's a little slower at realizing that."

"Rizzo. When you're ready to share what's going on with you, just promise you'll come to me. Let me help you." Tears well in my eyes, knowing that whatever it is, it's not good.

She reaches across the table, placing her hand over mine, squeezing tightly. "I promise. Now eat."

And that's what we do until it's time for her to leave and she walks with me back to Noah's room.

💀 💀 💀

We're lying in bed, Noah on his side and me on mine, and I've had fucking enough. Sitting up, I let the sheet fall, just my thin sleep tank covering me, as I angle my body toward his.

"Noah, we need to talk."

He sits up, turning to face me, and I can see the hurt in his face and I don't know what I said to put it there.

"Okay. You're finally gonna tell me you hate me for lettin' this happen to you?" Then it clicks. He's been holding this inside of him, his guilt. It's been festering and eating away at him.

"No, I'm not. I've never blamed you for it. Scott is the only person to blame, just like the shooter is to blame for your wife and daughter." His eyes go wide as he looks at me, and I can feel the anger simmering underneath his skin.

"Who told you?" His teeth grit as he clenches his fist, and for a moment, I flinch and start shaking. Before I can recover, Noah notices.

"I'm so sorry, baby. I didn't think."

"It's okay, and it doesn't matter how I know, just that I do. Do you really think your wife would blame you? She knows just as well as I do that there's no guarantee you could've saved her or your daughter. I bet she's up there smiling down on you, happy that you get to go on living. I'm thankful because if you were there, you may not have lived. Then where would I be? You saved me in so many ways. You kept me warm when I was freezing. Reassured me there were honest, good men out there. Most importantly, you saved me when I needed it the most. When I was lying on the floor, slipping away from this world. There's something I want to tell you now."

"What?"

I already feel the tears falling, sliding down my cheeks as they fall onto my hand. I haven't told anyone this and now I'm afraid of how Noah will respond. I take a deep breath and look down at my hands.

"As I was laying there, ready to give up, I saw an angel. She was so bright, and I couldn't make out everything, but she had the darkest hair. I didn't understand it at first. But she told me how in her final moments, as she held onto her daughter, she thanked God. She thanked him for sparing her daughter's suffering, allowing her to die instantly, and for saving her husband. Knowing he wasn't there and would live made her happy and in those last few moments, she had peace as she slipped away to join her daughter, and her parents, who died before her. She knew his faith was so strong he could withstand any storm. She even laughed at how he lost his way and she set two men in his path. They were harsh looking on the outside, but their hearts were made of gold. She told me she knew her husband would fit in with them and that he had a bigger job, someone else to save. She told me it was me."

His eyes go wide as he just stares at me until finally his lips part. "Bianca came to you?"

I nod. "She did. At first, it was a hazy memory, then it came back. But at the time, I wasn't sure how to tell you. I know now was the time. Noah, I love you, but if you can't reciprocate it or feel the need to keep up with this guilt trip, then it's time for me to leave. I can't sit here and watch you suffer any longer. So you need to decide now, is there an us? Because if there isn't, I need to go. Each day that there's this distance between us, my heart breaks more and more."

"Lucy—"

"No, there's no Lucy. Do you love me and want to be with me, Noah? It's a simple answer. Yes or no."

And I sit there waiting for him to respond. When he doesn't, I turn away from him and stand up, fighting back the tears.

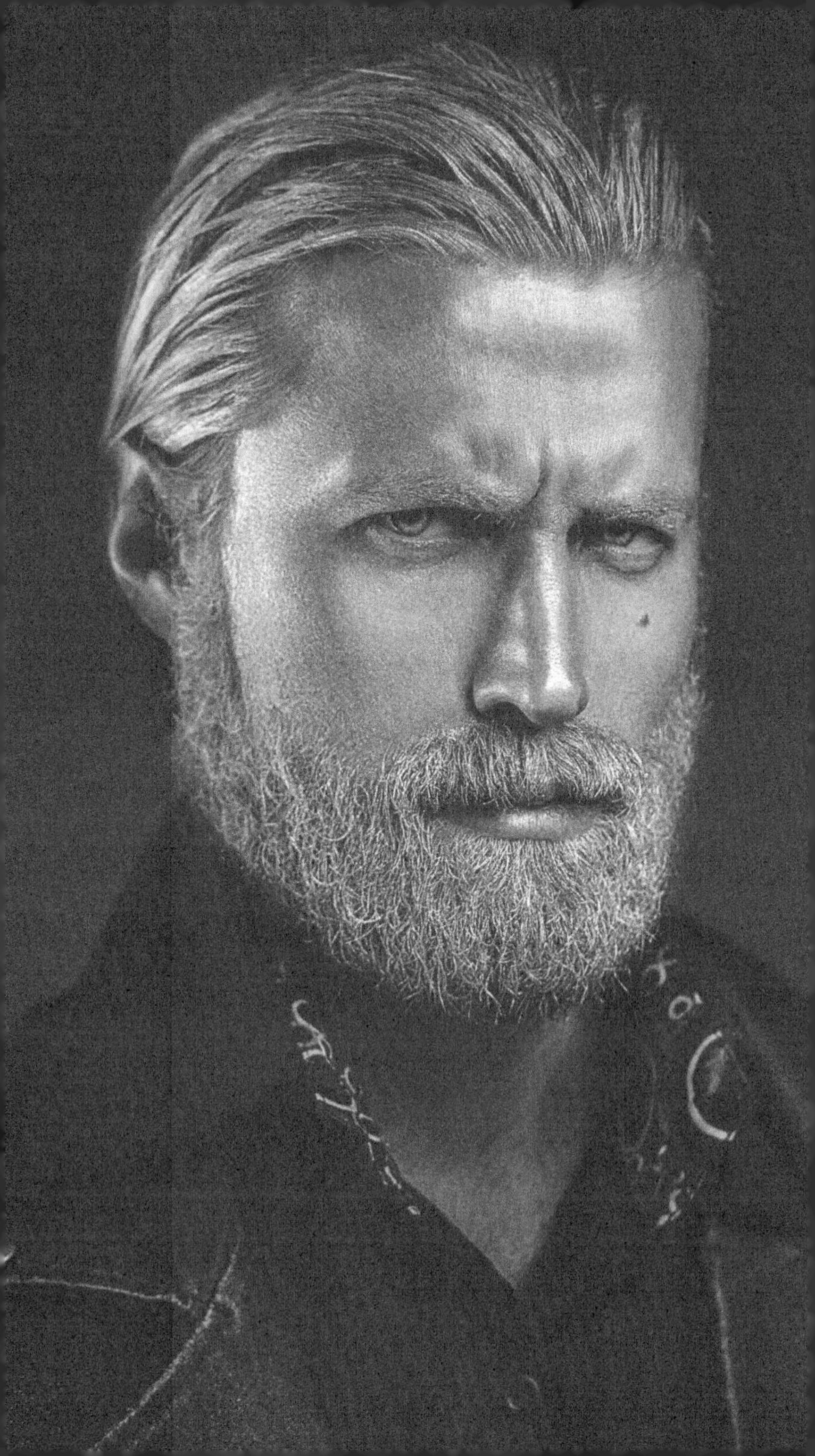

CHAPTER 27

Preacher

She stops at the door, looking back over her shoulder at me. I can see the hurt in her eyes and know I'm the cause of it. She just stares, waiting for me to say something. But I don't.

"Nothing? You really have nothing to say? Everything you did for me. You convinced me you were going to help me. Be there for me and now you're as absent as my parents are in my life. You said you loved me, Noah. Was it all just a lie?"

In my head, I'm screaming no. I do love her. But look what loving her did. Nothing. Just like with Bianca and Carmen.

"I don't know what more to say to you. Your wife and kid dying, Scott beating the shit out of me; yes, these were terrible things. But they would have happened, regardless. You can't control everything in life, Noah. Bad shit happens, but you're letting it control you, consume you. You need to let yourself heal. The past is the past and none of it is your fault." She takes hold of the door handle and storms from the room.

She left me.

What the hell is wrong with me? I'm about to let the woman I love just walk away from me. I'd be an idiot to do that. Jumping from the bed, I run from the room straight through the door she didn't even close behind her. She's moving so fast, by the time I catch up with her, she's in the common room, heading straight for the front door.

"LUCY!" I scream out across the room, over the music and raucous taking place.

She stops, turning to look back at me, tears streaming down her face.

"What, Noah? What could you possibly have to say now that you couldn't a few minutes ago?"

Stepping up in front of her, I take her hand in mine while I reach up and wipe the tears from her cheeks with the pad of my thumb.

"Lucy Davis, I'm a fuckin' idiot. It killed me, knowin' that I almost lost you because I let you go home, knowin' the hell you lived in."

"But you didn't let me. That's the point, Noah. I went home willingly. I knew what I was doing. Scott knowing I was with you, that I didn't go to work, didn't fit into our plan. He threw a wrench in it, but we still came out on the other side. I'm here. You're here."

"I know that, babe. It just brought up all the memories of Bianca and Carmen and how I couldn't save them. Their loss devastated me, and I couldn't go through it again. It was easier to push you away than to deal with my feelin's."

"And now? What are your plans now? Because I love you and I won't sit by while you push me away and treat me like I'm fragile. If that's what you plan to do, then step back and let me go. Don't contact me again. Your heart may be fragile, but so the fuck is mine."

"Lucy, I love you. I can't promise I won't do something stupid like I almost did by lettin' you walk away. But I will always love you. Just give me a good swift kick in the ass when I start actin' like that."

I wrap my arms around her, pulling her body in tight to mine and crash my lips down on hers. She parts them just like Moses and the Red Sea, allowing my tongue to slip inside her sweet mouth as I capture her sweet moans.

The brothers all start shouting varying versions of congratulations around us; "Bout damn time," "Get a room," before I finally release her mouth. Scooping her up bridal style in my arms, I carry her to my room. I skipped throwing her over my arm like a caveman, not wanting to hurt her.

Once we're back inside our room, I kick the door shut with my foot and juggle her in my arms while I lock it. There's no way I'm going to let anyone interrupt what I'm about to do. My woman made it clear I've been ignoring her, it's time I changed that.

I carry her to the bed, laying her down on it before lying down beside her.

"Lucy, I'm sorry for ever makin' you feel as if I didn't want you. Shit, I've wanted you from that first day in the diner. I fought it for the longest time, being so much older than you are."

She reaches up, stroking her fingers down the side of my face, and my cock twitches in my pants. "Noah Adler, I've never cared how old you were. I wasn't happy in my marriage and dreamed daily of leaving Scott. You gave me the courage and the power to do it."

Leaning my head down, I capture her lips again, kissing her with a passion I haven't felt in years. It's a familiar feeling, but different. And in this moment, I feel warmth and calm. There's no guilt or betrayal coursing through me, only love.

Pulling away from her, we're both gasping for breath. "I want you, Lucy. I need you so much, baby!" I grind out. Placing my hands on her stomach, I let them drift upward, over her heaving breasts, cupping one of them in the palm of my hand as I squeeze gently, eliciting a soft mewl from her.

"I want you too, Noah."

I sit up and take hold of the bottom of my shirt, pulling it over my head and tossing it on the floor. Standing up, I move to the end of the bed, where her feet are, slipping off her shoes and taking hold of her leggings, pulling them down her smooth legs. I'd seen her naked, both in the hospital and since she's come home with me to the clubhouse, but we haven't done anything. I never got to gaze upon her pretty pink pussy until now, and my cock likes what I'm seeing. She's already glistening, her juices making her folds slick as I climb between her legs, ready for my first taste of her sweetness.

Taking hold of her thighs, I push them farther apart. "Fuck baby, your pussy is gorgeous, and it's all mine," I growl.

"All yours," she cries out as I let my fingers slide through her folds, from the back, up to her tiny little nub as I move the pad of my thumb around in circular motions, reveling in how she's squirming underneath me.

"Oh god, Noah, that feels so good."

I lean down, blowing a breath of warm air against her pussy. Taking my hands, I spread her lips apart and lick up and down her slit. I make sure to stop and nibble on her clit, while I slide one, then two fingers inside her tight hole and pump them in and out. Each time, I make sure to curve the tip of my finger, so I can hit her G-spot.

Lucy's enjoying every minute of it, arching her back up off of the bed, before she screams out as her orgasm hits her. But I'm not done yet. I still need her, to be inside of her, and feel her pussy clamp down on my cock as I fuck her.

Standing up once she's ridden out her orgasm, I undo my pants, her eyes taking me as I slide the jeans down my legs. My rock-hard cock springs free as it slaps up against my stomach.

Reaching down, I grip it, sliding my hand up and down its length as I look down on her, and thank God for bringing her into my life, even when I abandoned him.

"Fuck me, Noah Adler. I need your cock inside of me," she cries out in need as she rubs her legs together to ease the ache.

Then it hits me, and I want to slap myself. "Shit, babe, I don't have a condom. Let me get dressed and I can go run and get some from the guys."

"No, you won't. I'm clean. Scott never fucked me without one and he hadn't slept with me in months before you saved me that day. I trust you're clean."

"But what if you get pregnant? I can pull out, but you know that's not foolproof." *Fuck me, she's perfect.*

"Would being pregnant with your baby be so bad?"

"If you're asking me if I care if you're pregnant, the answer is no. There's nothing I'd want more than to see your belly swollen with our kid."

"Then what are you waiting for?"

A growl works its way out of my throat as I crawl between her legs. I rub my cock through her slick folds before lining up at her tight little hole and pushing inside. Shit, the way her walls clench around my dick, I don't know how long I'm going to last. I place a hand down on the side of her body, pulling her top up so her glorious tits pop free. Leaning down, I suck one of her dusty pink buds in my mouth, gently at first, then harder.

Lucy doesn't know it yet, but she's going to get an ear full about how she was dressed when she left this room, but that's for later.

I reach down, take hold of her leg, and lift it over my shoulder, giving me a better angle as I pound in and out of her. When I release my seed inside of her, I hope one of those lucky little swimmers makes her pregnant.

"Fuck, baby, I'm not going to last much longer. I need you to come one more time for me."

She cries out as I place the pad of my thumb over her clit, rubbing in a circular motion, watching as she chases her orgasm. I pinch it a little and she explodes around me. The punishing grip her pussy has on me pushes me over the edge. I thrust one more time and still, filling her up with hot ropes of cum. My cock continues to twitch, emptying everything, before I collapse down on her, being careful not to hurt her.

Pulling out of her after we both catch our breath, I instantly miss being inside of her. I step inside my bathroom and wet a washcloth, cleaning myself before heading back out. Lucy looks like a fucking angel in my bed, skin all flush as her hair fans out around her head like a crown.

I run the washcloth between her legs, cleaning her up, before tossing it on the floor and lying down beside her. Propping myself up on my forearm, I trail my right hand along the scar on her stomach, before laying it flat, imagining what she would look like with a baby bump.

"I love you, Lucy. Will you be my ol' lady? Not just by club standards, but when your divorce is final. Will you marry me? Have my babies?"

Her eyes go wide as she looks at me, and I wait for her answer. Sweat pebbles on my forehead, nervous about what she will say.

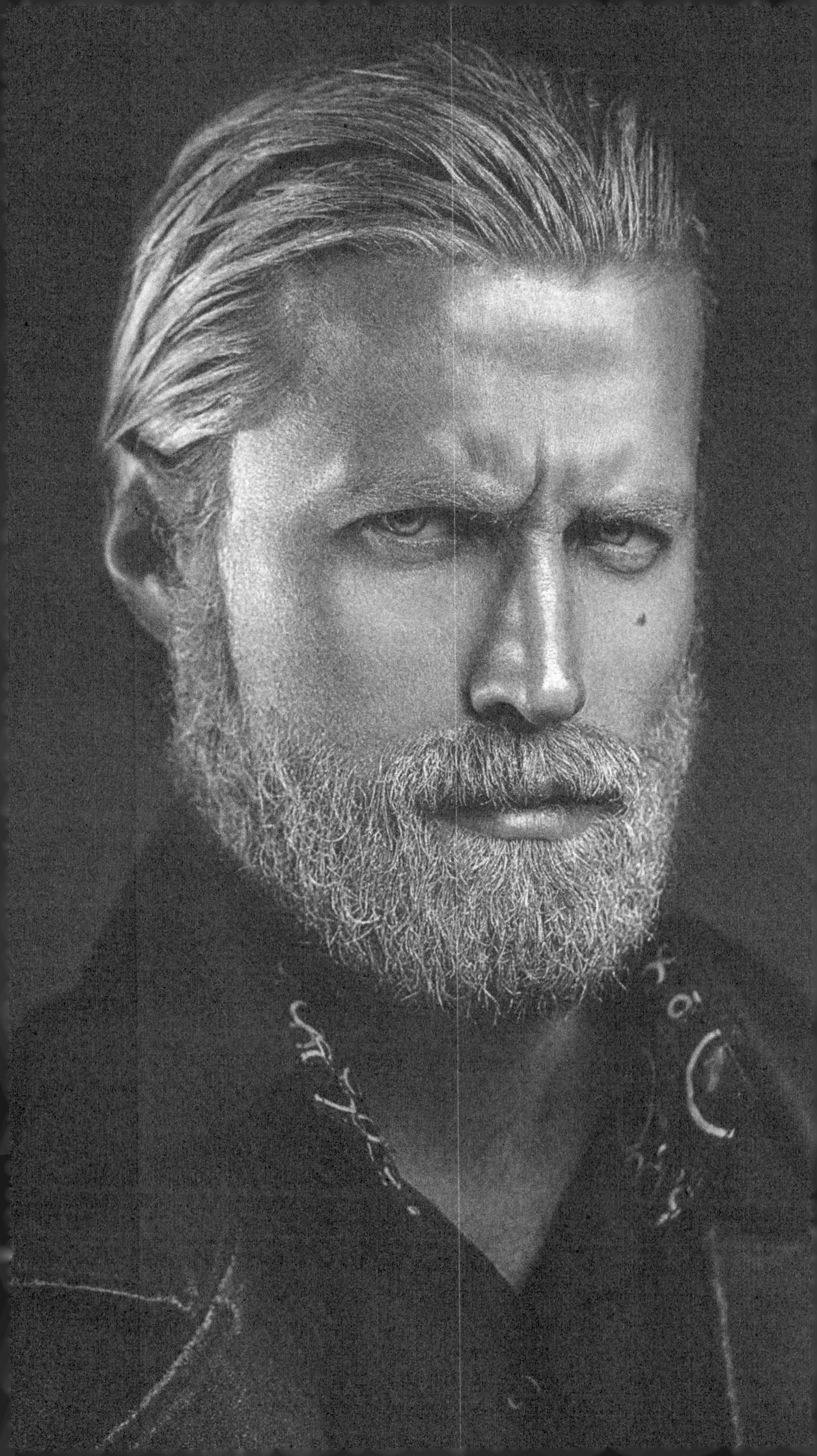

CHAPTER 28

Preacher

Lucy had three more orgasms before we both passed out from exhaustion. Having her in my bed and finally feeling complete was amazing. I don't know what happened during the night while we slept, but when my eyes opened this morning, there was no guilt. Bianca and Carmen would always be a part of my life and hold their own portion of my heart, but there is room for Lucy, for the children we would bring into this world together. Could it have been her story of seeing Bianca as she teetered at the boundary of life and death? Possibly, but I'll never know, and I don't want to question it.

Turning on my side, propped on my forearm, I gaze down at Lucy as she sleeps. A restful one, which I'm thankful for. She needs the rest to recover fully from the ordeal she's been through. Reaching out, I gingerly move the strands of hair that cover her face. She's lying on her back, one arm to her side and the other bent up, the tips of her fingers disappearing under the side of her face.

Her pert breasts are bare, from where the sheet is bunched around her waist. Her shirt disappeared during our second round of sex, when my need to see my woman completely nude took over. I let the tips of my fingers trail along her skin, starting at her clavicle, moving between her tits, fighting the urge to trace them over her nipples. I scoot closer and suck on one of them, nipping them with my teeth as she squirms underneath me.

My fingers continue their dance along her skin until I come to the sheet. I take hold of it and pull it down, exposing her lower half to me. Gripping her thigh, I carefully pull her leg up, placing it over mine, giving me access to the beautiful view of her body.

My fingers slide down her creamy thigh, straight to the apex where it meets with her sweet shaven pussy, dragging through her folds before coming to a stop on her clit as I rub tiny little circles. She begins to roll her hips in sync as her hand moves up, caressing her tit, squeezing it as soft moans fill the room.

Fuck! I get to live the rest of my life listening to that sound. My cock stirs, craving to be buried deep within her. My fingers move more forcefully over her clit before sliding through her folds, straight to her tight hole. I slip one in, then two as I pump them in out of her, reveling in the pleasure I'm able to make her feel.

Her eyes pop open, realizing she's not in a dream and I can't help the seductive grin I give her.

"Good mornin' baby. I couldn't help it. You just looked too damn temptin' beside me."

"Oh god, Noah, you're gonna make me come," she cries, her hips thrusting in sync with mine. I know she's close, and I can't wait to see the look of pure bliss on her face when it happens.

"That's the point, baby. Reach down and play with your clit. I want you to come, to soak my fingers with your juices, so I can lick it off."

She does exactly as I say, and within moments, she cries out. The walls of her pussy clamp down on my fingers, squeezing them tightly, soaking them with her sweetness as her body quivers.

Her eyes stare lovingly at me. "I could wake up like that every morning."

"I'll do my fuckin' hardest to make sure you do." I grin as I pull my fingers out and lick them clean, moaning as her essence hits my taste buds. Fuck if she isn't the sweetest dessert.

"Fuck me, Noah," she orders, and hell if I'm not going to obey.

Moving her leg off of me, I quickly slide between them, taking my already hard cock in my hand and running the head of it through her slick folds. I've just lined it up with her hole when someone beats on my door, pissing me off.

"Preach, get up, man. We got a lead. Gunner wants you out front now. Lucy too. You can finish what you're doin' later," Jenner hollers from the other side, laughing.

Lucy's face reddens, and I lean down, kissing her sweet lips.

"He's just bein' a jerk. But we will finish this later." Standing from the bed, I take her hand and help her up.

"I'm just going to get cleaned up."

"No problem, baby. They can wait. Do what you need to."

She rushes off to the bathroom and I can't take my eyes off of her. Her hips are giving the right amount of sway that matches perfectly with the jiggle of her ass.

Walking over to where I dropped my clothes, I pick up my jeans and pull them on, tucking my dick inside before zipping them up. I grab my shirt and slip it on before pulling out some socks from my dresser. I've just sat down when Lucy steps out of the bathroom and hurriedly dresses in some leggings and an oversized shirt. I nod in approval, happy she is wearing a bra without me having to remind her. Those tits are mine and mine alone. None of those fuckers out there need to see when her nipples get hard.

"Okay, let's go," I tell her as she slides on her sneakers.

We head straight for Gunner's office, knowing that's where everyone will be, gripping her hand in mine.

Stepping up to the door, the others are already inside. The only person missing is Hawke, but his voice drifts through the room on speakerphone.

"Okay, they're here, so we're going to get started. Preach, shut the door behind you." Gunner's voice is calm but forceful and his face is giving nothing away about what's going on.

Hawke's voice speaks again through the line. "Lucy, I wish I was there for this, but matters called me elsewhere. Whatever you hear today must stay with you and cannot be shared with anyone. Normally you wouldn't even be privy to it, but with the connection to you, we're including you. Don't make me regret it. Gunner, Jenner, fill them in." Hawke goes quiet, not a sound coming from his end, so he must have muted his phone.

"Okay, so I'm gonna keep this vague. We've had some club issues, and we've been tryin' to find the source. We managed to follow the trail to yet another middleman, but the lead went cold there. Somehow, we think they found out we knew about them, but couldn't figure out how they were tipped off. But then you dropped in our laps, Lucy, and that led us to finding a new trail unknowingly."

"I'm sorry. What could I have led you to?" Lucy asks softly, her hand shaking in mine, being surrounded by all these alpha males.

"Your husband. Did he know about your connection to us? About Noah?" Gunnar asks, moving his gaze between the two of us.

Lucy's face goes white, her breathing increasing as she nods her head.

"Apparently he did. Lucy explained how he saw us together, and when she didn't go to work, he knew she was still with me. It's why he beat her like he did." I answer for Lucy, not wanting her to rehash the story.

I give Lucy's hand a squeeze, reassuring her I'm here for her.

"What does he have to do with anything?" I turn back to my brothers, needing to know.

Jenner decides at that moment to speak up. "Lucy here helped me crack into his laptop. Once I did, I could see everything and found something interesting. He had the contact information for both the"—he clears his throat—"parties we knew about. We also found an email sent from Scott to a no longer active email address, alerting whoever it belonged to that the person he was supposed to meet at the club never showed. Guess things were going to go down differently that night and our boy didn't know. Then on the day of what happened to you, there was a message that our MC was sniffin' around his woman."

"Wait, her soon-to-be ex was involved in all this all along and we didn't know?" I ask as Lucy stands there, confused.

"So, what does this all mean?" her soft voice asks.

"It means he's an even bigger jerk than we thought, and we need to find him pronto. Not only to make sure that he never touches you again, but because of what he knows about our club. I'm sorry we can't tell you more, babe, but it's club business."

"Okay, I understand. Do you know where he is?" Lucy asks.

"No, but we think we have a closer lead on where he may be. We also found an account in his name only, and we're watching it. If he doesn't have any money on him, then he's going to need some soon. I'm sure he's going to think he's okay to try to access the funds. He'll have a nice surprise when he finds out there's nothing there." Jenner laughs.

"Yeah, he's a cocky ass. Thinks he knows more than anyone else," Lucy says, rolling her eyes, and we all chuckle.

"Okay, so we're watchin' where we think he may be. When you find him, you know what to do. Keep me posted. I've gotta go," Hawke says before disconnecting the call.

"Okay, that's it. Jenner will alert us when he finds something more. Until then, it's business as usual." We all leave the room. Lucy and I walk out first, and I guide her back to our bedroom, wanting nothing more than to finish what we started.

"Hey, Preach," Jenner calls out and we stop, turning around to see what he wants.

He scoots past Cyrus, stopping in front of us. "I just sent you an email about some houses you wanted me to check on for you. You have an appointment with the realtor in an hour to look at them. Her address and contact information are in the email."

"Thanks," I tell him, a small smile creeping up on my face. Lucy and I are about to have our own home. Turning to Lucy, she's looking at me curiously. "Want to go get something to eat before we see our future home?"

"Home? You're getting us a home?" she asks.

"Well, we can't keep living in the clubhouse. And what if I want to fuck you over the kitchen table? Can't do that here." I wink at her.

Her eyes glisten as she looks back at me, the smile she's wearing full of emotions; happiness, her love for me, and a small trace of fear. I know this is a big step for her, especially with the threat of Scott still out there, not to mention she's still married to him. She doesn't know I've already started taking some steps. Her filing the restraining order was the first. But I also took the liberty of posting an ad about the divorce as a method of trying to contact him and had the papers delivered to his parents. We needed to show proof to the judge that we attempted to serve him.

"No, we can't. Not unless we want everyone to see," she whispers, raising up on her tip-toes and wrapping her arms around my neck, pressing her lips to mine.

All the guys catcall behind us, but I don't give a fuck. Having my woman in my arms is the best feeling ever.

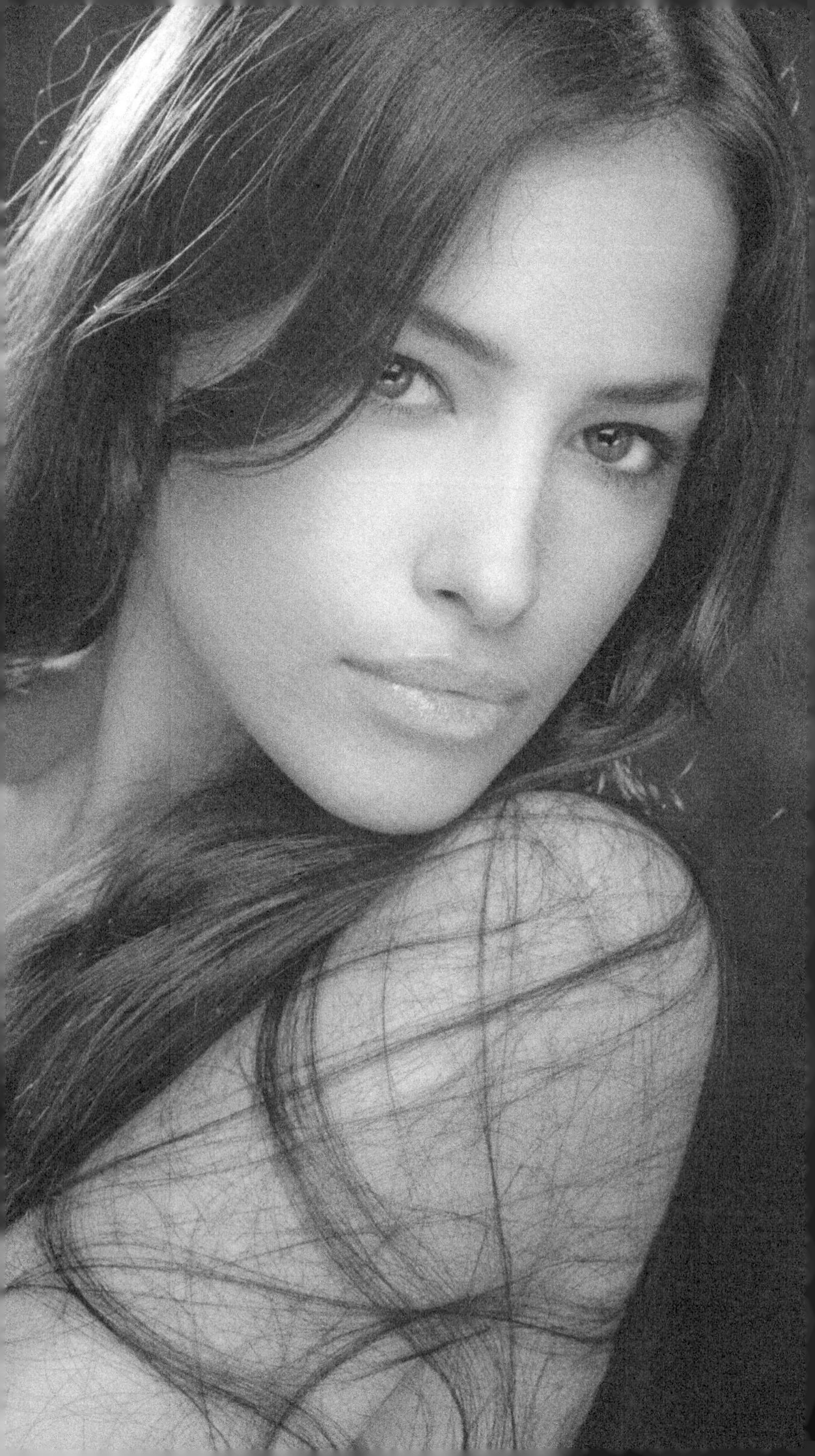

CHAPTER 29

Lucy

We're in the last house and it's everything I've ever wanted. It has a white picket fence with a wrap-around porch. I can already picture Noah and myself sitting on the porch as we drink our coffee. It's two stories, with four bedrooms and a huge family room. The best part is the kitchen with the bay window and island counter. It also doesn't hurt that someone had one room turned into their very own library. There's floor to ceiling shelves that I can already see filled with romance books of every genre. In the backyard, there's a tire swing hanging from the huge oak tree that also has an old treehouse. Visions of children playing fill my mind. This house is perfect.

"So, what do you think, babe?" Noah whispers as he pulls me into the other room, away from the agent. She's been wonderful, but he said not to let her know if I got excited about any of the homes. I thought it was odd since it was a rental. Normally, that would be something you wouldn't want to do if you were trying to purchase it.

"I love it."

"I do too. Okay, I'm going to have Jenner put in an offer."

He goes to walk away, but I grab him by the arm, pulling him back. "What do you mean, an offer? I thought we were looking at rental homes?"

"We were, well, the first few were. But the last four? They were for sale. I saved the one I loved the most for last, hoping you'd feel the same way." He quickly kisses me and then takes off to the other room, where the realtor is.

Stepping over to the window, I look out into the backyard, already planning how I want to decorate. Imagine the amazing future I know Noah and I can have here.

As I stare at the swing, it looks familiar, reminding me of another yard with a tire swing in it. And then it hits me. *I know where Scott is!*

I know I need to tell Noah, but I have to wait until he's done and we're alone. There's not a doubt in my mind that as soon as I tell him, he's going to find him. And honestly, I don't care. I've heard the rumors about the club and as hard as they try to hide it, I've overheard some conversations. Once they find Scott and get what they need from him, no one will ever see him again. The thought of that, the violence, should upset me, but it doesn't. Instead, I feel comfort from knowing that he'll never hurt me or anyone else again.

I don't know how long I'm staring out the window before Noah's body presses against mine. I lean back, allowing his arms to wrap around me as he nuzzles my neck. "I love you, Lucy. She's going to push everything through once the owners accept the offer. It also helps that I'm going to be paying cash."

My head whips around to look at him in shock, especially after the impact of hitting his head with mine. We both reach up, rubbing our heads." First off, ouch. You got a hard head, Noah Adler. But did I hear correctly, cash?"

"Yeah. When I left my old home and came here, I sold my house and all but a few things that I wanted to hold on to. Some mementos of Bianca and Carmen's. Jenner invested it all, then all the money I've made over the last five years here with the MC. You're never goin' to want for anything, baby."

"You spoil me, Noah. But I'm going to keep working. I like it at the diner. JD and Georgie have been nothing but amazing to me. Oh, um, Noah, I have something I need to tell you."

"Please don't tell me you're havin' second thoughts about movin' in together. If you are, I'm still gonna get this place for you."

"No, I'm not having second thoughts at all. There's nothing more I'd rather do than live with you. And honestly, as thankful as I am about not having to go back to the place Scott and I shared, the clubhouse is not somewhere I want to live long term. The things I've seen I'll never be able to cleanse from my mind." Noah laughs loudly, causing our bodies to shake.

"Okay, I agree there. What is it you have to tell me?"

"I think I know where Scott may be. Looking out in the yard at that tire swing reminded me of something."

"Let's go." Taking my hand in his, we pass by Janice, the real estate agent, and wave goodbye. She throws her hand up in response, then flashes us a thumbs up. Guess things are looking good for us and our dream home.

As soon as we get in the car, Jenner's voice comes through the speaker.

"Fuck man, I told you to be patient, that they'd take the offer," Jenner barks out, before giving Noah a chance to say a word.

"Not callin' about that, man. Lucy thinks she knows where Scott is. We're on our way back to the clubhouse."

"Okay, I'll have everyone ready." Then the line disconnects.

"Lucy, where is it?"

"His great-grandmother on his father's side. She died when he was eighteen and left everything to him, including her house. It's being held in a trust until he turns twenty-five. It's been rented out, but currently, it's empty. If he wanted to escape to a place no one would know him, it would be there."

He reaches across me into the glove box and pulls out a pen and paper. "Write the address down for me, please. I'm goin' to leave you at the clubhouse. Just go to the room and lock the door. Stay there until I come back."

I just nod my head. If he's there, then I know this is all going to be over soon. I'll finally be free of Scott Davis.

Preacher

We're standing just inside the wood line of the property, out of sight. Jenner was able to get an aerial view of the property and the perfect place to park our van. We're waiting for night, so we can slip in under the cover of darkness.

Scott's here. We spotted him going out to the back and bringing in some wood.

"How we handlin' this?" Cyrus asks as he cups his hands around his mouth, trying to warm them up.

"Me and you are takin' the front door. Sundance and Gunner are on the back. Snake and Wheels will be on either side of the house in case he makes it past us and Jenner's waiting in the van so we can get the fuck out of here when it's time to go."

Everyone nods. Once the sun goes down, we're moving in.

Two hours later and it's time to get the fucker. We all creep along the wood line, careful not to make noise as we move into position. We have the element of surprise, and we know he's here alone. So, unless he has some kind of superpower, there's no way he's going to get away.

"Wheels, you go to the left of the house and Snake to the right. I'm giving us all four minutes to get in place, so at eight twenty-two we move in. We need the fucker alive so we can find out what he knows, but that doesn't mean you can't make the bastard hurt, especially for what he did to Lucy. Let's go!"

We all move out stealthily across the yard, no longer covered by the trees. My eyes stay focused on my watch once we move onto the porch. I make sure to keep my body pressed firmly against the vinyl siding, tucked safely between the door and the window, so he can't see me if he looks out.

When the time clicks over, I don't wait another moment. Spinning around, I open the screen door and use all the force I have to kick in the front door. Scott jumps from the chair, tripping over the pants pooled around the bottom of his feet, and falls right on his face.

Looking around, I see a woman on the television being railed from behind while sucking on some sixty-year-old man's cock. *Was the dude actually jacking off?*

"No way, man. I ain't getting anywhere near his dick. Look, is the fucker still hard?" Sundance announces loudly as he backs away, one hand in the air, the other holding a Glock pointed right at Scott's head.

"Umm, he's probably gonna be hard for a while. Looks like he took himself a blue pill," Gunner announces with a laugh as he holds up the pill bottle sitting on the table beside Scott.

Scott's still cowering on the floor, his hand down, trying to cover his cock as he gazes at all the guns pointed directly at him. Wait, what's that smell?

"Okay, nope, nope, nope. I'm not touching his ass; he just pissed himself." Sundance makes a face, and I shake my head. Fucker can kill a man a million different ways, but piss and a cock make him squeamish.

"Well, looks like you drew the short straw, Sundance. Get his ass tied up so we can get out of here," Gunner orders as Wheels comes strolling into the house with a rope slung over his shoulder.

It takes them a little longer, neither wanting to touch him. Scott finally realized he was in for a bad night and decided to fight back. He got one lucky hit on Cyrus and got shot in the foot for it. When he dropped to the floor squealing like a pig, Wheels clocked him over the head with the butt of his gun, knocking him out cold.

"Finish tying him up so we can get the fuck out of here. I want to get what I can out of him so I can get back to Lucy," I order, leaving them to it as I turn and head outside, sighing a breath of relief.

After I'm done with him tonight, he'll never hurt anyone else again.

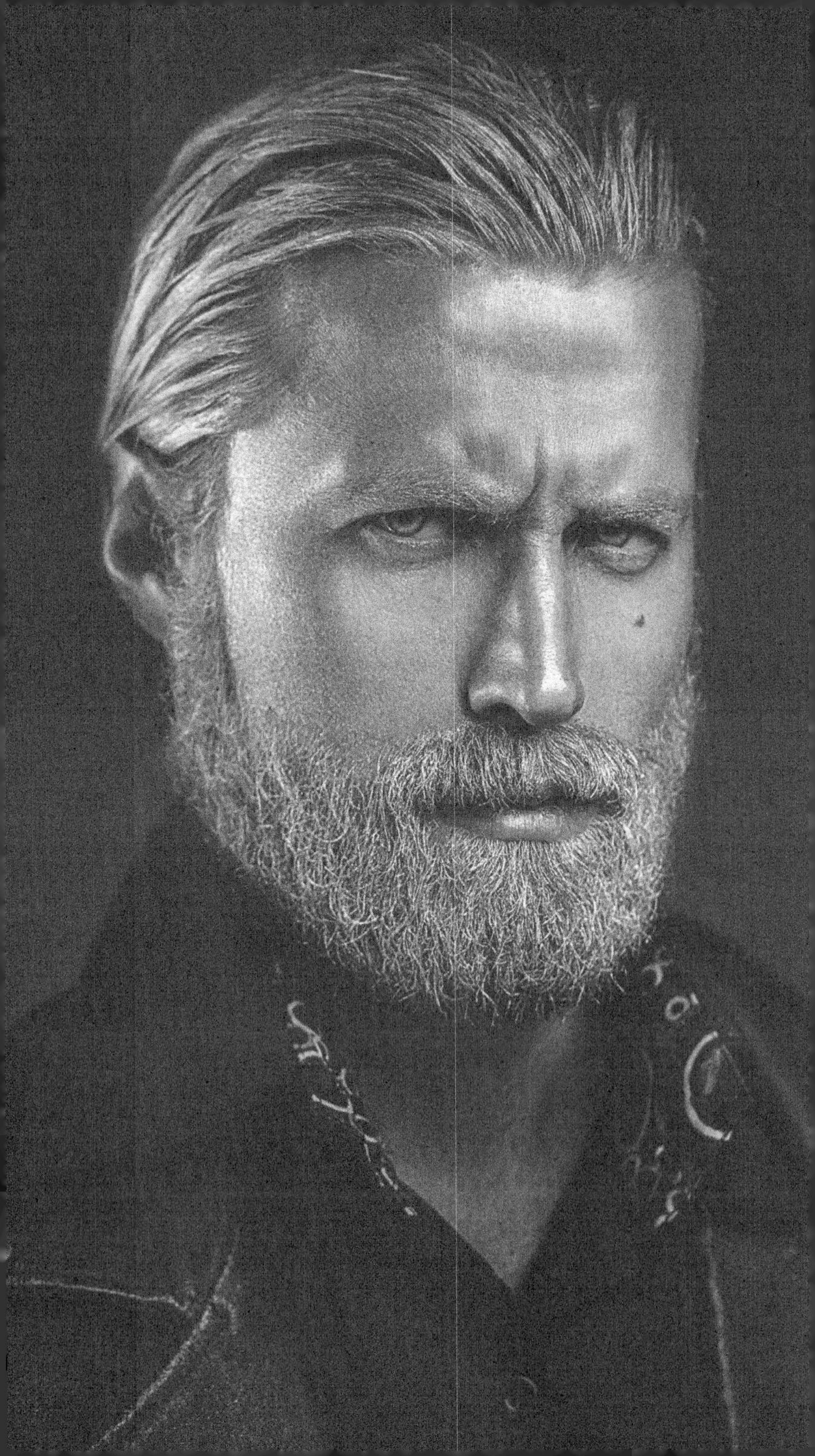

CHAPTER 30

Preacher

I've got the fucker strapped down to my metal table. I want him to hurt, just like he hurt my sweet Lucy. He's still knocked out, but it's time to wake him so I can have some fun before I gut him. There won't be any sympathy like the last one. This is both business and personal.

Sundance steps over to the table, lifting the bucket above Scott's head, and tips it over, dumping the ice-cold water over him. The water crashes down on his face, causing him to jump, but he's only able to go so far.

"What the fucking hell?!" he screams, his eyes bugging out in fear as he catches sight of me and the meat cleaver in my hand.

"Yes. What the fuckin' hell? Seems you have your hands in a lot of places, Scott. But none of them are where they should be," I tell him.

"Fuck you, biker scum!" he spits at me. My fist immediately flies out, busting his fucking nose. A feeling of satisfaction washes over me as blood gushes from it.

"No, I think it's you who's goin' to get fucked. I'm not the one who's gonna die."

"You're seriously gonna kill me over some fat ass bitch, who ain't even that good in bed? My parents told me marrying her was a mistake. I wish I would've listened to them."

"I'd suggest you keep your mouth shut about my ol' lady," I growl through clenched teeth.

"Yours? Last time I checked, she was my wife, dumb-ass," his snide voice snaps back.

"Don't worry, we're takin' care of that and when you're dead, well, it won't really matter, will it? So why don't you tell me about your involvement with James and your friend who didn't show up at the House of Puss?"

He just laughs, a maniacal laugh that could rival one of a cocky villain.

"What's so funny, dick?"

"You and your whole fucking club. You're out of your league and don't even know it. They know all about your pitiful fucking club. The big bad bikers, what a joke. By the time they're done with you, all you'll be is a bedtime story. A fairytale."

"Big words for someone who doesn't have a future."

"Neither do you."

I turn away from him, calming my temper. I'm fucking tired of his mouth and it's time he sees I mean business. Raising the meat cleaver, I spin it around quickly and the sound cuts through the air as I guide it down to my target. His leg. Chopping into it, but not completely through it.

Scott screams out in agony as the corners of my lips turn up in a smile. That felt good.

"You're a fucking psychopath!" he screams.

"Who are you workin' for?" I ask again, harsher this time.

"None of your damn business."

"Okay." I perform the same motion, landing the cleaver in the same spot, almost fully severing his leg. Scott's face goes pale and his screams stop as he passes out.

"What a fuckin' wimp. Both James and the kid took more than he has," Cyrus jokes as he pulls a pack of cigarettes from his pocket, taking one out and lighting it up. Guess his stint at trying to stop failed.

"Really, man, couldn't give it up?" I ask, gesturing toward the cancer stick in his mouth.

"Fuck off. Lots of shit goin' on. I'll quit again next week. Let's wake his ass up."

Stepping over to my worktable, I open the drawer and pull out the sticks made of smelling salts and walk back over to Scott. Placing it under his nose, his head immediately bolts up and his eyes open.

"Come on, man. You can have the bitch. Just let me go." Ahh, now this was what I was expecting from a slimeball like him, begging.

"Oh, you hear that, guys? He really thinks he can tell me who I can have. Fucker, I take what I want. And I took the best thing you'll ever have. Lucy. Now she's mine. What you can give me is the name of who you're workin' for."

"They'd fuckin' kill me if I betrayed them!" he blurts out in panic. Fuck, this moron really is stupid.

"Oh, Scotty boy, do you really think we're gonna let you walk out of here tonight?"

"Preacher, that's cold, man. You already fucked the shithead up. He ain't walkin' nowhere. His one leg is barely hangin' on," Cyrus points out, laughing.

"So true. I should really take care of that." And with one final swing, I cut through the last bit of bone and muscle, amputating his right leg.

Sundance fires up the torch, pulls the severed leg away, and cauterizes the stump. "Preach, man, I think you got a future as a butcher." We all snort at his joke.

"Come on, let me go. *Please.* I'll leave and never come back."

"Oh, let you go? Did you hear that, brothers? He'll leave and never come back," I taunt.

"And the manners. He even said please. Come on, Preacher, you should let him go," Cyrus says, playing into it.

"All you have to do is tell us who you're workin' for, Scott," I remind him, even though I have no intention of letting him leave this room alive.

"Fine, fine. I report directly to Jackson Dupree," Scott finally tells us. The name rings a bell.

"Dupree, I know that name," I think out loud.

"He's on the police force. Short guy with a big potbelly. He pulled Gunner one day on his bike and was a prick until Hernandez showed up," Cyrus reminds me.

"So, what you're saying, Scott, is that Dupree is running all of this? He's over the embezzlement from our club? Why's he doing it?" I lean over, getting right in the fucker's face.

"No, dumbass, that's who I report to. Whoever's running the shit isn't from this fucking podunk town. You think your fucking businesses are the only ones getting money taken from them right under the owners' noses?"

Shit, this goes deeper than just us.

"Okay, who's in charge?"

"I don't know. That's a need-to-know, and I was working my way up the chain. Now come on, man, I did my part. I need to get out of here and have my leg checked since you mutilated it. We're done, come on, man." His voice is growing weaker.

"Sure thing, Scott. We are done." Swinging the cleaver, I come down right on his neck, cutting through his carotid artery, and blood splatters all over me. His eyes go wide and his arms are tied down so he can't even grip his throat in hopes of controlling the bleeding.

"I'm out of here, clean the mess up and dispose of him. I'll let Gunner, Hawke and Jenner know what we found out."

I drop the cleaver to the floor with a clang and head out of the building, snatching a towel off the table as I go to clean my face. Cleaning here isn't even a thought on my mind right now. I want Lucy. To feel her beneath me and assure her the threat is gone, and she's mine now.

💀 💀 💀

Pulling up to the clubhouse after leaving Sundance and Cyrus at the warehouse to clean up, I decide to head to the office first. Gunner and Hawke need to know what we found out, and Jenner needs to check into Officer Dupree. We need to know everything we can, including what time he fucking takes a shit, so we can get to the bottom of this.

It's infuriating; one lead just sends us to someone else. Whoever's in charge of this shit is a genius at keeping their identity hidden. But Jenner is good and the rest of us are determined, so they won't remain a mystery forever.

Stepping inside the clubhouse, I immediately see Gunner, off to the side, one of the club whores hanging off of him, desperately trying to get his attention, but failing. His eyes are focused on someone else across the room. A question for another day, though. Now I need to fill him in so I can go to Lucy.

"Gunner!" I call loudly, getting his attention.

His eyes shoot to mine and I gesture with my head toward Jenner's office. Gunner removes the girl's hands from his arm, pushes off the wall, and heads my way. Just as I expected, Jenner's seated behind his desk, hands flying across the keyboard of his laptop.

Once Gunner steps inside the room behind me, he shuts the door. "Get Hawke on the line."

"Okay, man, figured you'd be busy for hours." He hits a few buttons on his phone before we hear it ringing through the speaker.

"Gunner," Hawke's voice carries through the line.

"Hey, man, we got Scott and a name," I tell him quickly.

"And you're back already? How long did you play with him?" Hawke asks, just like Gunner.

"I played some. But I wanted him dead more than I wanted to have fun. He suffered, though. I got a name we needed. Scott was just another middleman, but he gave us who he reported to. He also said this is bigger than we suspected. We're not the only ones that money is being stolen from." The room's quiet as everyone takes in what was just unloaded on them.

"What's his name?" Gunner asks, breaking the silence in the room.

"Ah, you're going to love this, brother. Remember that dick head cop that pulled you over?"

"Dupree, yeah, I remember. I'd love to rip that fucker's heart right out of his chest."

"Well, that's who Scott was gettin' his orders from," I let him know, crossing my arms over my chest smugly, waiting to see the delight on his face at ending the man.

"He's mine," Gunner's cold voice rings out. I can see the fire burning in his eyes, and I know he's already plotting Dupree's demise.

"Okay, we know who the next person is. It's not who we want, but we'll take it. Lay low for the next few days, especially with the Scott situation bein' taken care of. Jenner, dig up what you can and keep an eye out for anything that pops up. I'll see y'all in four days," Hawke orders before hanging up.

"Okay, I'm heading to my room to see Lucy," I tell them before taking off.

Stepping up to my door, I pull out my keys and open it. The bathroom door is open, and the light is on, casting a glow on Lucy's sleeping form. Her arms are pulled up under her chin as she grips one of my shirts in her hand.

Quietly walking over to the bed, I lean over and kiss her on the forehead. Her eyes flutter open as she gazes up at me.

"You're back?" she asks softly.

"Yeah, baby. It's over. You never have to worry about him again. Go back to sleep, I'm going to shower, then join you."

"Okay," she mumbles as she closes her eyes, drifting back off to sleep.

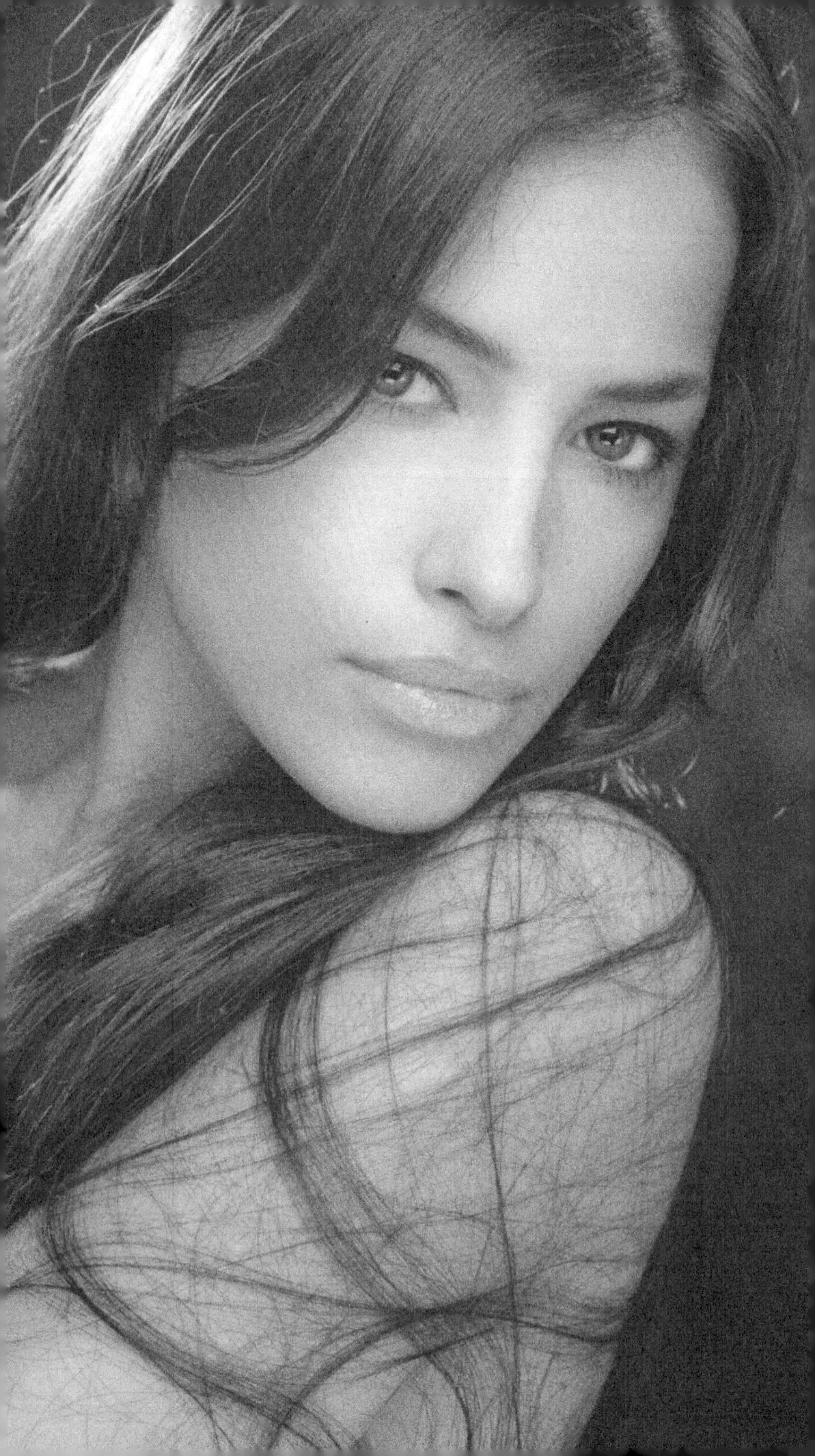

CHAPTER 31
Lucy

One month later

We've just about moved everything into the house. Moving isn't so bad when you have the help of the local MC, mainly the prospects. I didn't have to lift a finger. Instead, I was in charge of making sure they placed all the boxes and furniture in the correct rooms.

Noah asked if there was anything else I wanted from the home I shared with Scott and I didn't even have to think about it. There was absolutely nothing I wanted, but I did return to the house to retrieve the picture of my parents. As much as I hate them for pushing me into this life, and not helping even though they knew how he treated me, they are my family. I don't want to regret not having this picture one day.

Stepping into the house that day, I didn't realize how hard the memories of what happened there would hit me. I survived the hell I was living in, but many women didn't. The realization made me want to help other women like me. Women in abusive relationships who don't know how to escape. Since no one can find Scott and the house is technically mine, I decided to put it to good use. I just needed to talk to Noah and see if the club could help.

"Where do you want this one, babe? It's the last one," Noah's deep husky voice asks from behind me.

"The library." I ordered some books for my shelves; some delicious smutty MC romances and I can't wait to read them. My very own survivors' gift to myself.

"I'm going to put it in there, but then we need to go meet Hamilton. He needs to talk to us." Shit, this can't be good. He's my attorney for the divorce case.

"Where are we meeting him?"

"At the courthouse."

"Why?" My anxiety kicks in, and my stomach twists in knots.

He steps up to me, wrapping his arms around me as he pulls me flush to his body. My heart rate speeds up, as it always does when he's close. Electricity dances along my skin, as heat pools in my core. Just as he presses his lips to mine, kissing me deeply.

His lips leave mine, leaving us both gasping for air. "Do we have time to break in the bed?" Since confessing our love, my body has craved Noah Adler. Breaking in our new bed will truly make this home complete.

He grins and lifts me up, tossing me over his shoulder with a firm swat to my ass, taking off up the steps. I don't mind because I have the greatest view of his ass.

His movements become smoother, and I know we've reached the top of the steps. It doesn't take long before he's tossing me down, my body bouncing on the bed. He gazes down at me like a predator watching his prey.

"Take off your clothes, Lucy." His commanding tone soaks my panties.

I don't even reply, simply lifting my butt from the bed as I shimmy out of my leggings and panties, tossing them on the floor, before sitting up and removing my shirt and bra. I'm left naked in front of him, while he's still dressed.

"Spread your legs. Show me my pussy."

Fuck, this man is going to be the death of me. I do as he says, placing my pussy on display. Showing him the evidence of my arousal. His tongue slides along his bottom lip and fuck if I didn't wish he was licking mine.

"Play with your clit, baby. I want to watch as you make yourself orgasm."

My fingers glide down my stomach, sliding over the raised scar where Scott almost killed me, right down to my heated core. The tips of my fingers slip across my clit, thrumming back and forth as butterflies dance in my stomach, and a moan passes between my lips.

"That's it, baby, let me hear you moan." His voice makes it even more erotic. The deep seductive tone, and the control he has over me, sends me careening over the edge.

My free hand moves to my breasts, tracing circles around one of my pebbled nipples. I arch off the bed as the wave of pleasure washes over me and my orgasm hits.

"God, baby, you're fuckin' hot like that. All worked up for me." His voice makes it through the haze I'm in, my orgasm so intense I'm unable to focus on anything but the pleasure exploding inside my body. I hear him moving, the zipper on his pants, the clang of the metal on his belt as it hits the hardwood floor, just before the bed dips, and I feel his hot breath on my skin.

"We don't have much time, baby. All I want to do is dive in between your thighs and feast on your pussy, but we have somewhere to be. This is goin' to be fast, but I'll make sure you come again."

I can't find my voice yet, so I nod. All I want at this moment is my man buried deep inside me. He takes hold of my legs, one at a time, placing them over his shoulder, then grips his already hard cock, stroking it, before lining up at my hole. In one quick motion, he fills me. Noah thrusts in and out, slowly at first, as I savor every moment. His hips begin to move faster, going deeper and deeper each time. He finds my clit and presses the pad of his thumb down, applying pressure as he slides it back and forth.

"Fuck," I cry at the sensations overwhelming me.

"Shit, baby, the way your pussy's grippin' me. I love it."

"Noah, I'm going to come."

"Go ahead, soak my cock in your sweetness. I'm going to fill you full of my seed and make you pregnant with my baby." Damn if this man's words don't throw me over the edge. I clamp down, holding him in a vice-like grip as stars explode behind my eyelids.

It's not long before I feel his cock twitch, shooting ropes of hot cum deep inside of me. His hips still, and he grunts as his whole body jerks.

He empties himself and falls back on his heels, sliding out of me, my legs still over his shoulder as he grips them tightly. "Lucy, each time with you is like the first."

"Same, baby." Sex with Noah is like nothing I've ever experienced before. He cares about my pleasure, not just his, so different from how Scott is, was. It's still hard to remember that sometimes.

A few moments later, he lowers my legs and moves off the bed. He goes to the bathroom, and I hear the water running for a minute or two, then turns off. He steps back out, a rag in his hand as he comes and cleans me up. Just the touch of the rag on my sensitive skin sends shockwaves through my body, my nerves still on fire.

"Okay, we need to get dressed." He tosses the rag on the floor before picking up his clothes and putting them on.

Standing from the bed, I do the same. Anxiety takes back over about why we need to see Hamilton, and at the courthouse, of all places.

"Lucy, Noah," Hamilton greets us in the hallway in front of courtroom 2A.

"Hey, man, how are you?" Noah asks, both men smiling as if there's nothing wrong.

"I'm good. But the two of you will probably be better after I give you the news." He shifts his briefcase from one hand to the other.

"What news?" I ask, fearing that they've found out what's happened to Scott, and they're going to arrest Noah. But then common-sense seeps in and I know that can't be it. Neither of these two men would be smiling if it was.

"Come with me. Let's step into a private conference room so I can explain everything." Noah takes my hand in his and we follow Hamilton to a room just down the hall from the courtroom.

Once we're inside, he shuts the door and we all sit at the table. He must sense my apprehension because he turns to me with a smile. "Lucy, it's okay. It's nothing bad. I promise you."

"Spill it," Noah blurts, but I almost feel like he knows what it may be from the grin on his face, and the way he's gently squeezing my hand.

"As you know, Scott's missing." He throws up some air quotes that cause me to giggle. "With our connections on the inside, we have been able to push through your divorce. It's official as of today." He slides a folder over to me and I open it, seeing the documents.

"Really, I'm divorced?" I ask, shocked. I was thinking it would take much longer.

"Well, once you sign those papers and I file them. Until then, no." He laughs, and I let go of Noah's hand, pick up the pen, and hurriedly sign them, not even reading it first. I have full faith that if Noah trusts this man, then I can, too.

"Now we'll keep the restraining order in place until he's pronounced dead by his family. But I don't see them doing that. Of course, since Scott was also not here and unable to be reached, all property has been given to you."

"So, I'm officially free after all this goes through. I can change my name, get married, do anything I want?"

"Yes, ma'am."

"I don't know what to say. Thank you so much." Standing from the table, I move around it and hug Hamilton.

Once I've released him, I look back at Noah, who motions for me to come to him. I eagerly obey, stopping in front of where he now stands.

"Lucy Davis, I love you. You're my everything, and my life is so much better now that I have you in it. I want you to be my ol' lady and to marry me." He goes down on one knee, holding out a tiny black box with a diamond ring in it.

"Yes, yes, Noah, I'll marry you." He slides the ring on my finger before stepping over to Hamilton, who opens his briefcase and takes something out. He hands a cut, similar to Noah's to him. Noah holds it up. It has the club's logo on it and on the back, it says, 'Property of Preacher.' My eyebrow raises in question.

"It's an honor, babe. It means you're mine and off limits to anyone else. Think of it as an extra sense of protection."

Taking the cut from him, I put it on.

"I'm always yours, baby. Now let's get out of here and finish what we started this morning," I lean in and whisper.

"Hamilton, thank you, man. Let us know when it's final. I don't want to wait long to marry Lucy."

"I will. It's why I had you meet me here. I'm going to file it now." Hamilton picks up the folder and his briefcase and leaves the room.

"Let's go, future Mrs. Adler." God, just the sound of that is amazing.

"Okay, future husband." He takes my hand in his, moving faster than I've ever seen, as he leads me out of the courthouse and to his bike. Guess he wants to finish what we started this morning just as badly as I do.

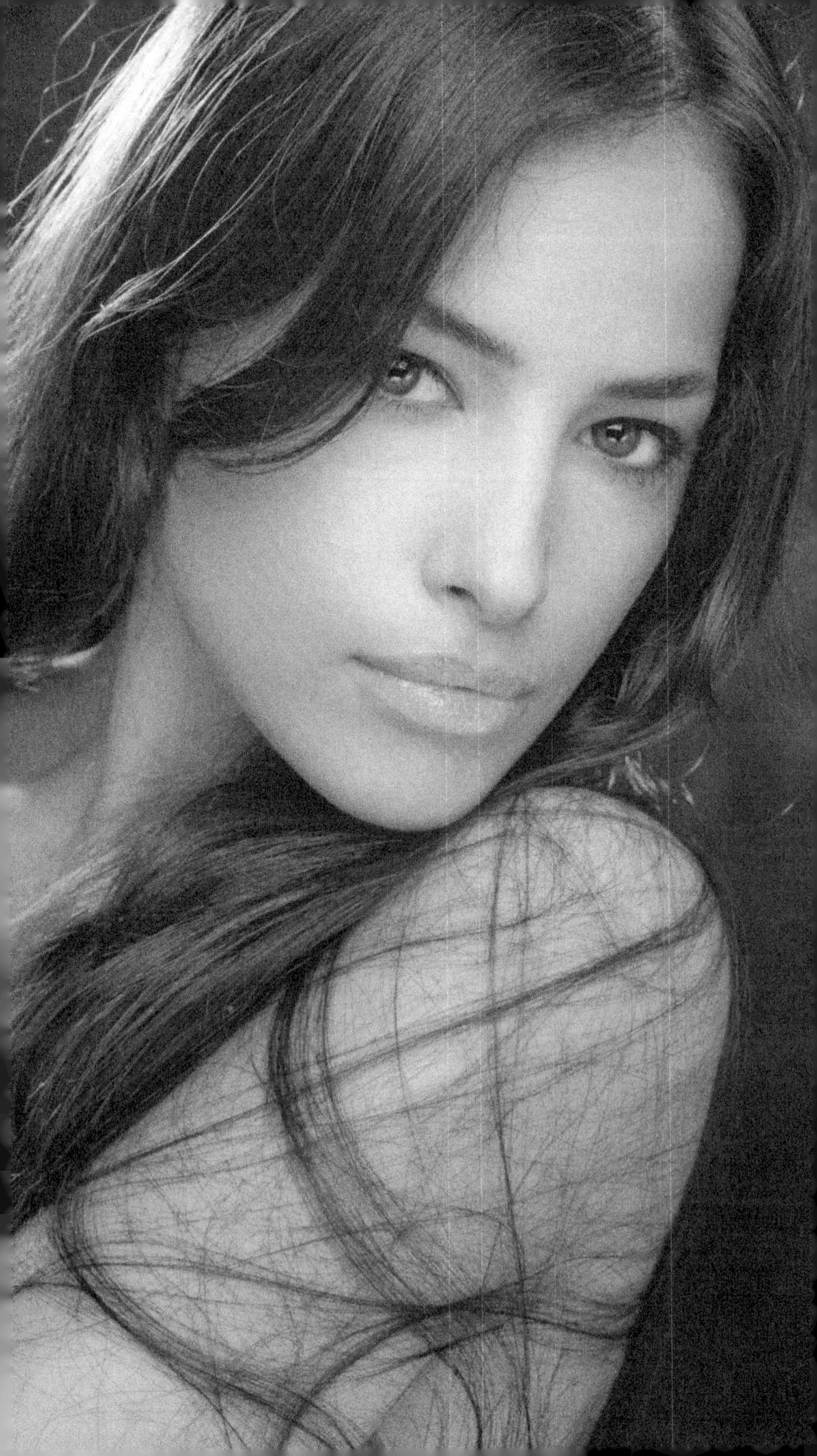

EPILOGUE 1

Lucy

Two months later

"As I stand before you today, I'm taken aback by all the amazing memories here in this church. When Samuel first emailed me telling me of his daughter Mariela having her baby, and her desire to have me baptize her, I had reservations. Not about the baptism, but about coming back here. As many of you know, this house of worship holds a very terrible memory. It's where I lost my wife and daughter, and that caused me to lose my way. I'm no longer a pastor in a church, but I have found my way back to God. I lost it for a long time, but a group of men I consider brothers helped. The biggest change, though, came with my beautiful new wife, Lucy Adler." Noah gestures to me from where he stands at the pulpit.

I always knew he was handsome, but seeing him standing there in a suit and tie has my heart melting. Coming here was hard for him, but spending the day yesterday with Samuel and his family and other members of the congregation has helped him.

There was no judgment for the path his life is on now. Simply happiness for a friend. Noah continues on and then the family steps forward with the baby. Noah takes her from Mariela, cradling her close to him. I see the way he gazes down at her, the namesake of his wife and daughter. Just another way for their memory to live on.

A couple weeks after moving into our home, I found the pictures of Bianca and Carmen that he's kept and hung them above the fireplace, along with our wedding picture. When he came home from the job he was working for the club that night and saw them, he broke down crying. Seeing them there as a part of our lives was the final thing to bring him back. Knowing that I could accept how important they were and still are in his life.

It was that small act that brought his faith in God back, but his life is what it is now. He's a different man, but he knows he can have faith, even with being part of the MC. Noah is, after all, their enforcer. Killing in the name of justice is what he does now, and I can't complain because it saved me.

I'm so lost in my thoughts that I almost miss the end of the service. He holds the baby up, proudly showing her to the congregation before Mariela takes her back in her arms, standing happily beside her husband, Emmanuel.

The congregation stands, moving to congratulate the family, as I gaze lovingly at my husband. He hasn't noticed yet, his eyes fixated on the baby, and I know now is the time to tell him.

Slowly climbing the steps to the altar. I take his hand in mine and pull him to the side.

"I love you, Noah."

"I love you too, Lucy. Are you ready to go? I know you haven't been feeling well lately."

"No, we can stay. I know you wanted to visit with some of the congregation before we head back to Kentucky. But I have something I need to share with you. I've been holding it in for a while, waiting for the right time."

Worry crosses his face, and he steps closer, taking me by the arm. "Baby, what is it?"

I smile, knowing that he's always thinking of me. "Nothing's wrong. I know you've been busy with club business and I understand that. But I need you to make sure you're going to be available in eight months."

He raises a brow, understanding lighting in his eyes. "Really? Are you telling me what I think you are?"

I just nod my head rapidly, a stupidly happy smile on my face as he wraps me up in his arms. "I'm going to be a dad again?" he cries into my shoulder.

"Not again, baby. You've always been a dad. Your daughter has always been in your heart. Now you have a new child to add beside her. Our baby will always know what an amazing big sister they had and about the amazing mother she had. The woman who filled their daddy's heart until he found us."

"God couldn't have given me two more perfect wives to spend my life with. I'm so blessed that you are the last, the one I get to grow old with. Let's go home, Lucy. We got a nursery to decorate and all my brothers need to know they're going to be uncles as we usher in the next generation of the club."

Wrapping his arms around me, he guides me over to the others, offering his apologies for having to leave, but promising to return, wanting to baptize our child in his first church.

The End but the last of Noah and Lucy!

Turn the page for a bonus epilogue!

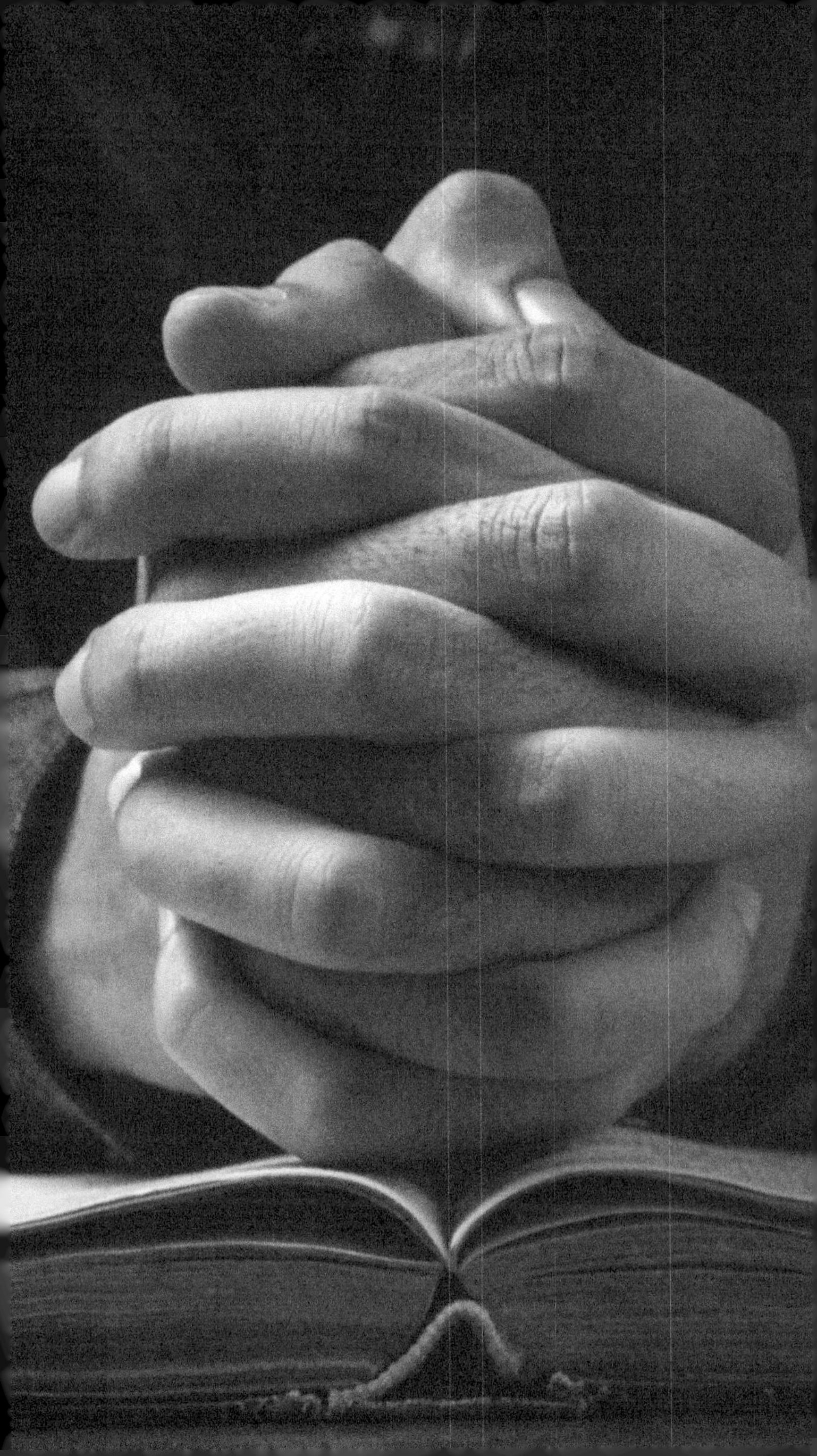

EPILOGUE 2

Preacher

"Hey man, how are you?" I ask, stepping into Hawke's office. I can see Rizzo seated in the chair, her body looking frail. I'm ready to find out what's going on.

"Good, how's Lucy feeling?" Hawke asks, his eyes focused on Rizzo.

"Complainin' about how they lied when they called it morning sickness because she's sick morning, noon, and night."

"Has she been to the doctor?"

"Yeah, we had her first appointment yesterday, and they did some tests. Doctor Williams assured her that it's perfectly normal in the first trimester, but they'd keep an eye on it." Shutting the door behind me, I move across the room, taking a seat in the chair in front of Hawke's desk.

Crossing my arms over my chest, I glare at him, waiting for him to speak. But he doesn't and I grow more pissed off. He's been holding us at arm's length about what's going on. Hell, Rizzo hasn't even told me and we're close. I'm tired of waiting. Something's wrong, because she looks like death.

"That fucker Dupree has been causin' a problem lately," he finally mutters.

"Yeah, I heard some of the prospects complainin' about it," I add.

"Asshole's pullin' them over for anything he can. I've told them to stop wearin' their cuts while they're out. That way, there's nothing to identify them with. I'm hopin' it prompts him to come after one of us. I'm tired of messin' around. I'm callin' a meetin' tonight with the officers. We're gonna vote. Handle it now or wait. But my vote is for now. I need this shit with the club handled sooner rather than later. I..." He stops speaking, and I notice he's staring right at Rizzo, fighting the urge to stand as he raises, then lowers himself back into the chair.

"Stop," she barks, but her voice is weak and shaky as she gets up.

"Where are you goin'?" he asks her sternly.

"To the bathroom. Geez, Hawke, I'm not an invalid. I can pee all by my damn self," she bitches as she walks around the chair, still holding onto it.

She takes a step, releasing the chair. I go to turn back to Hawke, but before I can, she crashes to the floor. We both jump from our chairs, racing toward her. Her eyes are closed, and she's not responding. Hawke pulls his phone from his pocket and calls 911.

Racing to the common area, I holler for Jenner, who's sitting at the bar, letting him know the ambulance is on the way and who it's for. By the time I make it back to the room, she's drifting in and out of consciousness, and the man who's always been strong is crying like a baby.

"It's time, Hawke. What the fuck is wrong with Rizzo?"

Rizzo's story coming 2024!

AFTERWORD

I want to thank you all for reading my first story in the Merciless Few MC World.

I know that second epilogue wasn't quite what you were expecting. My alpha and beta team fell in love with Rizzo, and I knew her story had to come next. Sorry, but I had to leave that little bit on a cliffhanger, but I can't wait to bring you, her story. And for you to find out who she is with!!!!

GIVE NO QUARTER
SHOW NO MERCY

THANK YOU

As always, I want to thank my amazing family, both blood and not. My three boys, my besties and the amazing book community that surrounds me.

I want to send out a special thank you to all the authors who are part of the Merciless Few MC Shared World. I am so honored you invited me to be a part of this amazing world. It has been a blast and I can't wait for all the books to come. Thank you.

To my Alpha and Beta team, thank you for all your help in making this story so amazing. I loved every bit of feedback that you gave me.

To Rizzo. You always send me encouragement and I love it. I hope you like how I added you to the story and the character I created for you. I can't wait to share her story with you.

To my ARC and street teams, thank you for all loving my stories. Some of you have been with me since the beginning. Thanks for spreading my works to everyone.

Shayna, my PA. What would I ever do without you? You know how much I love you, even when I know I drive you crazy. I know I can be a needy bitch.

Lastly, to the readers. Without you, I would be nothing. Thanks for taking a chance on my crazy ass and reading what pops out of my head.

About Bre Rose

Bre Rose writes under a pen name in both the contemporary and paranormal why choose genre primarily, but does have works that are MF. Bre is a native of North Carolina and mother to three amazing sons and two feline fur babies more affectionately known as her hellhounds.

She's always been an avid reader then progressed to becoming an ARC, BETA and ALPHA reader for some of her favorite authors. After some encouragement she decided to tackle writing the stories in her head and is loving every single minute of it. When she isn't reading or writing she enjoys traveling the world and still has some places to mark off her bucket list. She also enjoys spending time with her family and advocating for the differently abled population.

To keep up to date with all upcoming releases and all things Bre then simply join her Facebook reader group

Bre Rose Petal Readers.

Check out all my links to my socials here. https://linktr.ee/breroseauthor

ALSO BY BRE ROSE

Check out my full body of work here
https://books.bookfunnel.com/breroseauthor

Memphis Duet
Finding Memphis (Book 1)
Saving Memphis (Book 2)
Memphis Duet Omnibus
Memphis Spinoffs
Unbreakable
Memphis Beginnings: Earl's Novella
Memphis Christmas: Holiday Novella
Prophecy Series
Shay's Awakening (Book 1)
Shay's Acceptance (Book 2)
Shay's Ascension (Book 3)
Beyond the Pack Series w/ Cassie Lein
Rise of the Alpha
Destroying the Alpha

Claiming My Alpha

<u>Brighton High School Reunion Shared World</u>
Reuniting With Desire

<u>Fairytales with a Twist Shared World</u>
Charleston Curse

<u>Merciless Few MC Shared World</u>
<u>Kentucky Chapter</u>
Sinner Choice
Rizzo's Story
(Coming 2024)

<u>Standalones Stories</u>
Love On the Ice
(Coming October 2023)

<u>Morelli Family Series</u>
Assassin's Seduction (Book 1)
(Coming Jan 2024)

<u>Breaking Hearts Duet</u>
Against All Odd (Book 1)
Fighting the Odds (Book 2)
(Coming soon)

<u>Sports Romance w/ Cassie Lein</u>
All on the Field Kindlevella
(Completed)
All on the Field (ebook)
(Coming 2023)

Made in the USA
Las Vegas, NV
29 January 2025